The Hapsburg Falcon

J.R. Trtek

ISBN: 1434854612

ISBN 13: 9781434854612

Library of Congress Control Number: 2013914783
CreateSpace Independent Publishing Platform
North Charleston, South Carolina

Cover Image: London Rain by F. J. Mortimer, Hulton Archive, Getty Images

To the memory of my grandmother, who was ten when these events occurred.

CHAPTER ONE:

The Uses of Deduction

"There are days when I long to reside elsewhere." So spoke Sherlock Holmes one damp afternoon in late spring.

Standing at the bow window of his sitting room, I turned to contemplate my friend as he replaced a violin string. "Truly?" I asked. "You would consider leaving Baker Street?"

"Rather, I should consider leaving Britain."

"You cannot be serious, Holmes. Surely you exaggerate."

"Do I? Well, pardon me, Watson," he begged with a wan smile. "My luggage is not yet packed, but the remark does bear a germ of truth—and you may blame the old nemesis: inactivity. More than once during your current stay at 221, I've commented upon London crime's loss of vigour. That malaise, I fear, has now spread across the whole of our island."

"Such is your reward for more than twenty years of labour in the field of detection."

"'Reward' is a less than fitting characterization," he replied wistfully, plucking the new string. "Rather, if your generous conclusion is correct, then in hindsight, I should have contained youthful enthusiasm to preserve some challenges for old age."

"But to choose emigration—"

"Ah! But consider the abundance of opportunity that lies abroad. There is such promise beyond our quiet metropolis and placid countryside. Why, this morning's *Daily News* reports the unsolved and rather brutal murder of a Greek art dealer in Paris. Even from the brief, printed account, it appears a most singular case, Watson, ripe with many exceptional features of interest."

Holmes sighed and leaned back in his armchair, his eyes languid as he tuned the Stradivarius. "Were these digs near the Seine rather than the Thames, I daresay we should even now be upon the scent; instead, I sit and restring violins while you anxiously await more bad news from the race-course. If I may ask, how much were you persuaded to place upon this latest of dark horses, as the Americans would term it?"

I stared with wide eyes at my companion as he stood to scrape his bow across the strings. "I fear I do not understand," was my brusque reply.

"Indeed," remarked Holmes, pausing in his stroke. "As it is yet another of Mr. Finney's supposed 'certain winners,' your reticence does not surprise."

"Why would you believe that I—"

"Come, come, Watson. You know my—"

"Yes, Holmes, I know your methods."

"Or rather, Doctor, you know *of* them."

"I have *read* of them, I believe."

"*Touché*," said he, chuckling. With care, Holmes placed his instrument in its case, set both to one side, and, arms crossed, considered me with an amused air.

"Watson, you have passed nearly one hour doing little more than intermittently staring out the window. In all the years we shared this residence, Baker Street itself never fascinated you so, and I very much doubt your most recent absence has spawned some new interest in the local environs. No, yours is the behaviour of one awaiting a visitor—and a very anxious wait it has been too, for all the pacing I've witnessed. Yet despite its presumed importance, this call is to be brief, for otherwise you would have politely informed me of your need to employ the sitting room. But then"—he arched his brows playfully while his lips gave hint of a sly smile—"I fancy you prefer I should not learn of this visit at all."

"Yet how—"

"Then there is the all too prominent pair of shillings you have time and again pulled from your pocket to admire as you stood looking down into the street. That is your usual tip to a message-boy, is it not? Yes, I believe you expect a vital telegram."

"Your mention of horses—"

"—was occasioned by a remark you made two nights ago upon our return from that concert at the St. James's Hall. You asked Mrs. Hudson for a small store of molasses to be set against your account. Why? You are even less fond of it than I, but in those years when you lodged here, you often provided a watered mixture of it to your friend—the untutored would think him a patient—Mr. Finney."

"The man continues in excellent health but refuses to believe it," I said. "The potion gives him no benefit, but neither does it harm him, while soothing his concerns in the bargain."

"Yes, and as I always understood that bargain, Mr. Finney, in lieu of payment, evened his debt by supplying you with race-course information, which was equally efficacious, if more damaging to your pocket and peace of mind."

"According to him, this horse is vastly under-rated!"

"I've no wish to debate handicaps," said my friend, raising one hand. "There are two more beads on my deductive necklace of facts, but your confession makes further elaboration pointless. And so there you stand, Watson, braced to learn the details of this, your most recent equine disaster."

"Such sarcasm is beneath you, Holmes!"

"Do excuse the sharpness of my edge, old fellow," he said with sudden compassion, approaching me at the bow window. "Though I must add that the apparent state of your accounts does give me cause to worry. But halloa," he cried. "Look there! We have a visitor now, though not your anticipated messenger. The subject of conversation, I venture, is unlikely to be alleged thoroughbreds."

I glanced down into Baker Street and saw Inspector Stanley Hopkins leave a hansom and advance briskly toward the door of 221.

"Perhaps there is reason to hope, eh, Watson?" Holmes was suddenly a changed man; his voice fairly sang. "He appears most troubled, does he not? And our friend Hopkins is not an emotional man. We may yet have set upon our table a challenge worthy of the old days!" And quickly unpacking his Stradivarius again, he reeled off bars of Paganini in a raucous, music-hall style.

Moments later, Holmes's landlady, Mrs. Hudson, admitted the inspector into our sitting room. During the past few years, Stanley Hopkins had lost more than a touch of his youth in rough proportion to the number of stone he had gained, but his bearing was erect as ever, the intelligent glint of his eyes undimmed.

"Take the basket-chair if you will, Hopkins," said Holmes. "May I offer you refreshment?"

Hat in hand, the man from Scotland Yard gently shook his head and set his large frame down at once. Holmes curled up in the armchair while I kept my station at the window.

"It is not that we ever fail to enjoy your company for its own sake," Sherlock Holmes continued. "Or that we tire of news concerning Mrs. Hopkins and the child, but I do hope this visit concerns business rather than leisure."

"Yes, it's business," replied Hopkins. "Serious business, I can tell you, sirs, and business of a most delicate sort."

"We are a rapt audience," said Holmes, swinging one leg over the chair's rest. "Raise the curtain, please."

"I have come to request your assistance—and that of Dr. Watson—in determining the whereabouts of the Honourable Robert Hope Maldon."

"Hope Maldon? The family of Lord Monsbury, the cabinet minister?"

"Yes. I refer to his youngest son, in fact."

"Hum. I recall no mention of a disappearance."

"The newspapers have cooperated in hushing up the matter, Mr. Holmes."

"Ah! Of course. Well, Watson, perhaps all the while I should have been blaming censorship for our quiet times. But on with your story," said the detective, again changing pose, this time drawing up both feet to sit with his hands wrapped round his shins.

"An odd story it is," said Hopkins, taking from his buff coat a notebook. "Mr. Hope Maldon, age twenty-four, resides alone in a suite of rooms at Breton Mansions. On the morning of the seventh, more than a week ago, he hailed a cab in front of that block of flats. In his possession were two pieces of luggage."

"Have you any notion as to whether they were both fully packed?" Holmes asked without hesitation.

"In truth, one was nearly empty," said Hopkins crisply, with a hint of pride. "So the driver of the cab replied when I asked him that very question. He distinctly recalled the fact, because a traveller with empty luggage is an oddity."

Holmes smiled. "'Can be' is perhaps a characterization superior to 'is,' but pray, proceed."

"The young man was delivered to St. Glevens Hospital by way of the Camberwell Road. There he commanded his driver to wait at the kerb while he walked a short distance to the south end of the building. At that location, which opens onto a court, Mr. Hope Maldon stood beside a pillar-box[1] for several minutes, as seen by the driver, his luggage remaining within the cab. Have you a question?"

Holmes tilted his head to one side. "I was about to ask the fate of the luggage, but you anticipated my inquiry. Go on."

"Suddenly," Hopkins continued, "the young man took a bright blue kerchief from his pocket and, according to the driver, ostentatiously flourished it before regaining the cab to return to Breton Mansions. Since then——"

"Did the driver more precisely define the nature of this 'flourish'?" inquired Sherlock Holmes.

"I don't get your question, sir."

My friend placed his feet upon the floor and gestured as he spoke. "Did he wave the kerchief, and if so, was it up and down, from side to side, or in circles? In combinations of these, perhaps? Were there pauses? And in what direction did he face? Was the kerchief presented in turn to all points of the compass or to just one?" Holmes then stared silently at our caller for a moment and added, "That, Hopkins, is my question or, rather, my sequence of queries."

The man from Scotland Yard nervously brushed the knees of his soft, tweed trousers. "Truth to tell, Mr. Holmes, I did not think to pursue such details. I have to give you best there, I am afraid."

---

1 A pillar-box is a large cylindrical public mailbox.

The detective shrugged and leaned back in his chair. "Let us call it no matter. What happened next then?"

"Mr. Hope Maldon returned to his flat and has not been seen since that day. Those facts are the sum of all I can relate."

Holmes frowned and made a steeple with his fingers. After a brief silence, he spoke in subdued tones. "Forgive me, Hopkins, but I must confess you disappoint. Such cases of supposed disappearance are quite more commonplace than the public suppose, and a number of possibilities suggest themselves. For example, the boy may have——"

"Sir, there are additional details of relevance."

"Oh? I thought you said you'd no more to give. Well, man, don't bait me. What are these details?"

The inspector put away his notebook and, blushing mildly, replied, "I do not know."

Holmes raised his brows and glanced at me before turning back to our visitor. "At last you *have* baffled me, Hopkins," said he, raising open hands to the air. "How could you not——"

"Mr. Holmes, it is the young man's father, Lord Monsbury himself, and he alone, who possesses that additional information. He spoke to me last evening concerning his son's presumed disappearance, and he requested—I should more properly say commanded—that in this matter the Yard stand aside for you. The earl personally told me there are vital facts he would relate to you and no one else. As I declared a moment ago, my notebook has nothing more for you; the further history must come from Lord Monsbury himself."

"Well!" said Holmes, slapping the armrest. "The case is hardly outré at first glance, but we shall see. In my present state of boredom even small riddles must substitute for grand enigmas. Hopkins, I shall take the lure as if the good doctor here had cast the fly himself. Consider the case accepted—for the time being. And you, Watson? Would you be game for a midday drive, or will you stay to await your caller?"

"I shall go, of course," I said stiffly. "Mrs. Hudson may receive any message that arrives for me."

"Good. As always, I shall very much desire the benefit of your perspective. Indeed, fresh air will benefit the both of us, I daresay. I do propose, however, an examination of the young man's rooms at Breton Mansions before calling upon Lord Monsbury. Is that possible, Hopkins?"

"Of course it is, Mr. Holmes," replied the inspector with a smile. "I expected such a request from you and shall be pleased to be part of the company. We have had the premises under guard for several hours."

"Excellent. Please allow us to change, and if you would kindly whistle a four-wheeler, we shall be down presently."

The inspector descended to the street while Holmes and I retired to our respective rooms. As I came down to re-enter the sitting room, Holmes hailed me from below, where he already stood poised before the door to 221, ready to depart.

"I have your hat and waterproof," he said as I silently counted the seventeen steps to the ground floor. "The light rain has abated but may still return," Holmes added as I took my garments from him. "Oh, and I have, in discreet terms, instructed Mrs. Hudson with respect to your expected caller."

"Thank you, Holmes. I believe, however, that—"

"I included the matter of the two-shilling tip, old fellow," he said pleasantly. "We may even up later."

"Very well," I said, donning my hat and begrudgingly nodding my appreciation.

"I do think Hopkins to be the best of the litter," Holmes remarked while helping me into my waterproof. "The Yard is well served by him, despite his occasional failures of note. I find it difficult to forget the Milligan investment scandal, but Hopkins did learn a valuable lesson from that episode. Mind you, the man still lacks a consistent thoroughness, but he is resourceful in his way."

"He is resourceful enough to invite you into this affair."

"That was the Earl of Monsbury's doing," corrected my friend. "But lead on, Watson. Perhaps fortune smiles and challenging mysteries await us."

Minutes later, we were all riding south. Holmes's fear of renewed precipitation had proved unfounded for the immediate future, and emerging sunlight made even the dun-coloured houses of Baker Street seem radiant.

"I confess, Doctor," Hopkins said as we inhaled the fresh breeze. "Your presence at 221 gave me surprise. You still have your residence and practice in Queen Anne Street, do you not?"

"Yes," was my reply. "However, as my fiancée is away on family business, Holmes graciously invited me to share his hospitality during her absence."

"Oh, I see," said Hopkins as our cab turned into Oxford Street. "Somehow I had the notion you were already wed, sir."

"The wedding is planned for August," I told him. Then, realizing that I had allowed my personal communication with Hopkins to lapse during the past many months, I tactfully added, "Of course, we are only now about to send out invitations. You and your wife will receive one, of course." I made a mental note of the impromptu commitment.

"Ah, Oxford Street," said Holmes, smiling subtly in my direction as his interruption drew the inspector's attention away from my social embarrassment. "I tell you, no other thoroughfare so conveys the pulse of London. It is a shame our ride today will follow but a fraction of its total continuation—in all, a straight-line bisection of the imperial metropolis, gentlemen, from Hanwell to Barking."

"There is a slight kink as it enters the City,[2] I believe," added Hopkins.

"True," said Holmes with a nod. "Nonetheless, one traversal of its full length would provide anyone, native or visitor, with a full understanding of this grand capital." Holmes then expounded on the architectural history of the portion of road along which we travelled.

In time, we glided past the edge of Hyde Park, its moist green shades shining brilliantly. The sight of distant strollers and riders helped ease my pique at Holmes's recent remarks concerning my wagers. Indeed, as I took in the fresh, rain-washed panorama and recalled bathing in the Serpentine during summer, I silently confessed to myself that his comments had been all too accurate and that my anger had been grounded in the defensive airs of a foolish man.

Eventually we passed Victoria Station and then crossed the steel and granite of Vauxhall Bridge. As we came to Kennington Oval, our conversation turned toward the matter at hand for the first time since boarding the four-wheeler.

"In this, as in any case, there are points of focus," Hopkins declared. "A few, I think, may be considered." The inspector briefly regaled us with his own intuitions in the matter without interruption from Holmes. "And, in my own view," he concluded, "Mr. Hope Maldon's behaviour beside the pillar-box is perhaps the most intriguing detail we yet have."

"Oh, it is not quite that," objected my friend. "Something else is of greater interest."

"Oh? And what might that be?"

"Why, that he stood beside the pillar-box at all," declared Sherlock Holmes. "But look, this is Breton Mansions now before us, is it not?"

It was. Passing a man with a hurdy-gurdy, who, with a young, dancing woman in a sailor's uniform, entertained a motley assortment of children and washerwomen, our four-wheeler stopped, and we departed it to survey that new block of flats where the vanished youth had lived. Gazing up at its imposing height, I commented disparagingly upon the building's facade, speaking loudly to make myself heard over the sound of the hurdy-gurdy.

"Myself, I'm no judge of art or architecture," shouted Stanley Hopkins in reply. "I must assume civilization is the better for it." He looked down to the assembled throng at the corner. "That is a catchy tune, though, is it not?"

"I believe it to be 'Hail, Columbia'," noted Sherlock Holmes. "An American march," he added in a kindly tone when confronted by our two blank expressions.

"The German and Italian street bands frequently play Yankee pieces these days," Hopkins noted. "And the other day I saw a listing at a restaurant for a Manhattan cock-tail!"

---

2   The City here refers to the historic heart of London, encompassing only that part inhabited through the Middle Ages and not the present metropolis as a whole.

"Americans everywhere now, it seems," I added, trying to ingratiate myself with Hopkins by supporting what I took to be his point.

The inspector shrugged. "Well, to return to business, Mr. Hope Maldon's rooms are on the first floor, and there is a lift available. Shall I—"

"We should prefer the stair, I think," remarked Holmes as we gained entry to the building. "Dr. Watson and I have avoided all use of lifts since that distasteful incident at the Ventura Hotel." My friend smiled coyly, and I shuddered at the memory of that gruesome murder more than fifteen months past.

"As you will," said the inspector glumly, leading us up the stair.

At the top, we encountered two other representatives of Scotland Yard, to whom Hopkins nodded as we walked past. "This will be the young man's suite," he said with panting breath. "It was sealed late last evening and, to my knowledge, has not since been disturbed in any manner. You are the first to investigate the premises, Mr. Holmes."

"I welcome the opportunity," said my friend as we walked past another police guard and into a dim sitting room. The room's lack of furnishings lent it a sense of spaciousness, which its true dimensions did not warrant. Holmes strode quickly toward one corner of the room, where the floor was littered with broken glass from framed photographs that lay amid the shards, evidently swept from a nearby table. Holmes stopped at once and wrinkled his nose.

"My, this place wants airing. Might the two of you open windows?" he asked, to my astonishment.

"Open the windows?" said Hopkins. "Are you certain that is what—"

"I am most certain," replied the detective, stepping before the table.

"But, Mr. Holmes, there is still a damp chill—"

"Indulge my fancy, Hopkins, please. And, pray, assist him, Watson."

With shared reluctance, we unlatched and opened a pair of windows facing the court below, immediately magnifying the sound of the hurdy-gurdy still playing outside. I turned around to face Holmes, who stood with his hands buried within his coat, his mind deep in thought.

"Ah," he said as if leaving a trance. "That is so much the better." Now humming "Hail, Columbia" in sympathy with the street musician, he removed his waterproof, took off his frock-coat as well, and carefully placed them, along with his topper, upon a nearby chair. He took deep breaths as he started once more to roam about the flat. "The out-of-doors sharpens the mind, surely."

"Even as it numbs the toes," added Hopkins, staring grimly at me as I wrapped my waterproof more tightly round my shoulders, and we both stepped away from the open windows. Giving my friend a suspicious glance, I weakly trod in place to warm my body.

The detective chuckled. "I understand the sacrifice you two are making," said he. "Believe me when I say it is very much appreciated."

Holmes then spent several minutes engaged in that unique form of investigation I had witnessed so many times over the course of the years. He began with the scattered pile of photographs, shattered frames, and debris that lay upon the floor, speaking to himself in disjointed comments about the placement of every shard before pulling each from its position as if performing a delicate surgery. He examined the portraits that had remained untouched upon the table and then proceeded to expand his survey across the entire room. He brushed hair from the shelves of a nearby empty bookcase and kicked the legs of chairs with the toe of one boot. He bent down to the floor to study scuff marks in its wooden planks and ran his fingers through every inch of carpet. Then, swiftly and methodically, he turned over the contents of drawer after drawer in both desk and cabinets. On occasion, he voiced satisfaction at some discovery, but most often his mind appeared to teem with silent thought. At last, when he reached the open windows, he shouted as if for joy.

"Here!" he said. "How could this have escaped the notice of not one but both of you?"

Hopkins and I joined Holmes at the open windows, where my friend pointed to fresh gashes and scratches in the frame and latch of one.

"What was the state of these windows when we entered?" asked Holmes.

"Both were securely latched," said Hopkins. "Dr. Watson and I opened them, as you requested."

"Those marks are undoubtedly recent," I said. "There was an intruder."

"At least one intruder, Watson," said Holmes, leaning out the open window frame. "A second person, however, was in these rooms much later."

"How so?" asked the inspector.

"Look you there," said Holmes, leaning back into the room and pointing down. "Observe the faded yellow shred upon the floor, below this windowsill. I expect that it is the remnant of a daffodil bloom from the court below," the detective continued. "Those flowers, Hopkins, did not begin to open around the town until this very week, well after Maldon was last seen. It would appear a rather agile person scaled the building's ornate facade from the court below and then forced open the window. It was not a bad bit of work, though I think I could have done a better job of entering without damage to the surface."

"I'll pass over that comment, Mr. Holmes," Inspector Hopkins said. "You mentioned two people having been in these rooms, however."

"It is obvious that the first intruder could not have latched the window after leaving the room through it, and I think it most unlikely that the same person who required stealth to enter this building would have boldly walked out through its very front door."

"Such would not be impossible," I noted quietly.

"True, Watson, but I call your attention to the condition of the interior windowsill itself."

"It is well crafted, I suppose," said Hopkins.

"Yes, it is finely milled," replied Sherlock Holmes, running his long fingers over the surface. "And it is damp. Very damp. You may even notice where rain has trickled down onto the wallpaper."

"Thus the window was open for some time before being closed and locked," Hopkins declared. "In particular, it was open during the light rain of the past few days."

Holmes nodded silently. "That does not preclude Watson's conjecture that the intruder might have left through the building's front door, but it still argues for a second individual being present at some later time in order to close and latch the windows."

"Or the same person waiting some time before closing them and then leaving," I suggested, half in jest.

"Yes, Watson," Holmes replied coyly as he closed both windows. "Someone who, unlike you, enjoys the out-of-doors."

"Perhaps it was you then, dear fellow."

"I am sure, having lodged at 221 these past several days, that you will corroborate my alibi, Watson."

"And who might have been that second person?" asked the inspector with slight impatience, seemingly not amused by our repartee.

"I cannot say," said Holmes with renewed seriousness, walking across the room to fetch his frock-coat. "Indeed, at present we do not know how many plausible answers there may be to that question. Concerning the first to enter, meanwhile, I fear there are few conclusions to be drawn at all, other than that the person who broke into these rooms was an expert climber and a middling cracksman."

"What of the photographs?" asked Hopkins.

Holmes donned his coat in a somewhat awkward manner, glancing at me with an odd expression. "Yes, that is the only other violence done here. The pictures that were thrown upon the floor have at least one common element—this person, whom I take to be our vanished Mr. Robert Hope Maldon." Holmes picked up one photograph from the floor and pointed to a man in the image, a wide-eyed, thin youth with a moustache.

"That's him," confirmed Stanley Hopkins.

"All the portraits thrown to the floor include him," Holmes repeated. "And none of those left upon the table do, save perhaps this tinted one, which I take to be the man as an infant in the arms of his mother. My, the colourist has given her such bright blue eyes! We may, perhaps, infer that our intruder was not a Hope Maldon family member or intimate with their history."

"Are there other points of interest here?" Hopkins asked.

"A few," said Holmes, crossing his arms. "Let us, however, remain with this collection of photographs, both those on the floor and still on the table," he said.

"Family scenes, some of them," observed the inspector.

"Yes," replied Holmes, looking in my direction as if to coax a response.

"But nowhere is there a likeness of the father, Lord Monsbury," I said.

"Very good, Watson. Lady Monsbury is some years deceased, is she not? And those must be siblings or cousins or whatnot, I gather. Yet the earl himself is everywhere absent. What does that suggest?"

"Estrangement."

Holmes nodded. "Now turn your attention to all these bookshelves."

"They are largely empty," I said.

My friend raised his brows.

"Largely empty of *books*," said Hopkins. "But they contain several bookends. The books that were there are now gone. Perhaps the young man took them with him?"

"That is unlikely, especially since half his luggage contained nothing, you said. It is far more probable that he sold the volumes. And there..." continued Holmes. "What do you make of that section of wall?" he asked, pointing toward a blank area near the two windows.

"That space on the wall..." said Hopkins as if meditating. "I see within it a rectangle, which appears less faded from the sunlight, as if—"

"A painting once hung there," I completed.

"And it is gone now," suggested Hopkins, "because—"

"Mr. Hope Maldon sold it, and perhaps other furnishings, for needed money," I said, taking my turn in providing a conclusion.

"Excellent, both of you," said Holmes. "The only additional comment is that gambling debts may be to blame for the young man's lack of funds."

Hopkins and I both turned inquisitive looks on our companion.

"I did have an advantage over the pair of you in deducing the fate of books and *objets d'art*. Scattered notes and letters in the young man's desk suggest he has a fondness for cards and that he does not succeed at that vice."

"What of possible evidence in the court below?" I asked. "You've already alluded to daffodils."

"Have you examined that area?" Holmes said to the inspector.

"We have and discovered nothing," Hopkins answered. "But perhaps it would be best if you added your talents there as well."

"I shall be glad to try," Holmes replied, reaching for his topper and waterproof. "I fear, however, that the continuing rain, though light, has likely destroyed any evidence either of us might have found. Still, I shall take a look before we pay our call at Lord Monsbury's."

Aside from the barely distinguishable mark of a footstep, which my friend declared to be of no value, Holmes's survey proved fruitless as predicted. We then left through the arched court entrance and regained the street to find that the hurdy-gurdy had vanished, and its audience dispersed. I began to whistle for another four-wheeler when Stanley Hopkins stopped me with a light touch upon the forearm.

"You'll be needing transportation for only two, gentlemen," he said.

"Are you not joining us?" asked Holmes.

"No," the inspector said. "The earl made it very clear to me that he would talk to you alone concerning the information he possesses. I believe I can put my own time to better use at the Yard rather than waiting upon you at Lennox Square."

"Very well. Will you then ring us up or call at Baker Street later today?"

"I can come round, if it will suit."

"It will. The doctor and I should certainly be back at our digs by four o'clock, I fancy. Call upon us then, please."

We bade farewell to the inspector and then whistled for a hansom to take us on the next leg of our journey, to Lennox Square and the home of Lord Monsbury.

"You will allow yourself to be retained in this case then?" I idly asked once we were in the cab.

"But of course, Watson. My perception of the affair has changed significantly over the course of the hour, and I now should not trade this matter for any other. Indeed, I should refuse even the sphinx as a prospective client."

"That is resolution."

"Yes, but there is the matter of the woman involved, you see."

"Woman? What woman?"

Holmes chuckled. "What woman, indeed! Why, the one in the photograph."

"What photograph?"

"The one you have not yet set eyes upon," my friend replied. "I took it from the table and hid it in my coat pocket while you and Hopkins so graciously turned your backs in order to open windows for me."

"I assumed that was a deception at the time, but, of course, I did not ask you to justify the request in Hopkins's presence."

"As always, Watson, you are as discreet as you are perceptive. And do forgive me, old fellow," said he, while grasping my arm. "I could not be certain how this picture might affect even you, and I thought it best that Hopkins not witness your reaction to it."

"My reaction? To a mere photograph?"

"Yes. Perhaps you should view it now," he replied, producing a small, framed picture from his pocket. "Behold the woman in question."

Behold the woman. How apt those words were, for, in truth, it was *the* woman, as Holmes had so often termed her.

I stared at the likeness with disbelief. "But she is dead!"

"Evidently not," Holmes said, watching shop fronts pass us by. "Evidently not."

"Alive," I said. "She is alive. But, Holmes, how could she have survived? How could that fact have escaped you for so many years? And how has she fared in all this time? All this time, Holmes, and yet—"

"My dear Doctor, a picture is nominally worth a thousand words. You have raised the value of this image to a million speculations. We should not waste time in useless conjecture; the coming interview at Lennox Square commands our attention now, Watson. Watson?"

"She is alive." I believe I must have uttered it yet again as the cab sped north toward the river and I gazed upon the face of Irene Adler.

CHAPTER TWO:

A Pillar of State

As our distance from Breton Mansions grew, so did the strength of my composure and, in turn, my curiosity about Holmes's calm acceptance of Irene Adler's apparent resurrection. As we rounded Kennington Park, I could not resist the temptation to plumb his thoughts.

"If she survived that Swiss avalanche," I offered, "perhaps her husband still lives as well."

"One then wonders what Godfrey Norton will make of the Honourable Robert Hope Maldon."

"I do not understand."

"You are a once and future husband, Watson," my friend replied. "Tell me, what husband desires a rival?"

"Do you imply that—"

"Of course I do. The relation between the woman and Hope Maldon is more than casual, if you will take the trouble to glance at the inscription on that photograph you have been clutching so fervently these several minutes."

I took a moment to read the expression of endearment written across the bottom of the picture and then looked again at my friend. "But can you not help feeling exhilaration at the thought that she is, after all, still alive?" I asked.

"Some might say that life in itself should be a cause for exhilaration," he said drolly as our cab veered round a large wagon, whose horses had decided to move no farther.

"Do you recall our last sight of her?"

Holmes shrugged and stared out the hansom window.

"She was dressed as a young man," I said. "I remember distinctly, because it became a scene in my story."

"Yes," Holmes said disdainfully, "as a portion of frivolous narrative coda most irrelevant to the particulars of that case."

"She had the cheek to wish you a good evening, Holmes," I said as if to taunt. "You did not penetrate her disguise even then, did you?"

"Look, Watson," said Holmes. "The building that housed Morse Hudson's shop is being razed. How many Napoleon statues were there in all—four or five?"

"Six," I said, "and they were busts." I knew as I answered that I gave him information he already possessed, despite his feigned ignorance. Yet if Holmes at that moment intended to deny me his inner thoughts concerning Miss Adler, the vividness of my own recollections of her more than compensated.

In the episode my editors titled "A Scandal in Bohemia," Sherlock Holmes had acted to remove a threat of blackmail against the hereditary king of that country. The presumed villain was Irene Adler, and her weapon was another photograph, a compromising scene of the monarch and adventuress together. Employing a brilliant stratagem, in which I humbly assisted, Holmes located the damning evidence, but Miss Adler saw through his scheme and denied us its possession. In her goodness, however, she vowed never to use the picture, allowing the king to safely conclude his own political marriage while she wed the lawyer Godfrey Norton in a ceremony at which Holmes himself served as witness, disguised as an unemployed horse groom.

No other woman had so completely outwitted him, a fact which my friend had often appeared to savour with an odd pleasure in the years that followed. There was no doubt that he admired her as the best of her sex, and he had never since spoken any but kind words on her behalf. It should be understood most emphatically that his attitude was not grounded in romantic love, for such passions were alien to Holmes's nature. Yet her portrait—taken as payment from the Bohemian king—had graced his mantelpiece ever since, beside a jewelled snuff-box, also given to my friend by the grateful monarch.

And here, in my hands, I held yet another picture. It showed the face of a now older woman, whose smile seemed posed and not the expression of youthful optimism she'd once had. But time and changing fortune were immaterial to me; in my own eyes, at that moment she was still very much, as my friend had so often termed her, *the* woman.

"We have arrived."

Holmes's words interrupted my reverie. Glancing out the window of our hansom, I saw that far more time had elapsed than I had sensed, for unnoticed by me, the cab had crossed Westminster Bridge, passed through Trafalgar Square, and delivered us to our destination—Lennox Square. Holmes paid the driver, and within seconds, we were standing at the entrance to the imposing London home of the fifth Earl of Monsbury. Moments later, after ringing, we offered our cards to a pale, elderly servant.

Holmes leaned upon the area railing as we waited outside. "It is necessary to proceed delicately here, Watson," he said.

"Because we believe the father and son do not get on well?"

"Yes." My friend stepped away from the railing toward the front steps. "We noted the absence of any paternal memento in the young man's rooms, and consider in addition this: why else would the son move from this magnificent house to live in the dismal quarters we just visited?"

The servant returned to lead us inside, where we gave up our coats and hats, passed through a hall lined with a procession of family portraits in oils, and gained admittance to the study of Parliament's renowned eminence grise. The earl was a tall, dour man who greeted us with stiff formality.

"I told the Yard you were the one I wanted," he said to Holmes in a stirring sotto voce. "And you're the secretary, aren't you?" he asked of me. "Supposed to have been a medical man at one time, I believe. War hero in Natal as well, I was led to understand."

"This, indeed, is Dr. John H. Watson," said my friend. "A man famed as my accomplished partner in detection, a distinguished veteran of the late *Afghan* war, and a struggling biographer for almost two decades. What you wish to relate to me shall be for his ears also."

The old man nodded while surveying me with a cocked eye, an action which increased my embarrassment at Holmes's exaggeration. "Yes," the earl went on. "That inspector from the Yard—Hopkins it was—he said you might insist on that if your man was along. Well, do you know where Robert is? Take chairs, gentlemen. Please forgive me, but could you do with a drink also? No? Very well. I apologize, for my mind is occupied with the Estimates[3] these days—but do you know where he's gone to?"

"At this moment, I fear I do not," Holmes replied, leaning back in his chair as I took to mine.

Our host nearly dropped into his own chair and sighed. "That is hardly what I expected to hear. Your reputation for efficiency seems not in accord with the reality."

"Lord Monsbury," said Holmes, "I said I did not know your son's whereabouts; I did not say I could not discover it. My own investigation is not quite two hours old, and as for my reputation"—he gave me a look of mock reproach—"well, my prestige among the readers of sensational literature notwithstanding, I am only mortal."

The cabinet minister lowered his head. "I apologize for my presumption, sir. I thought you had been engaged in the matter since yesterday."

"Inspector Hopkins came round to us only this morning with news of the disappearance and your request for my services. That misunderstanding aside, the inspector also said you yourself possessed additional facts vital to the case, which you wish revealed only to us."

---

3 Estimates are parliamentary budget requests.

"Indeed," said the old man, transfixing me again with the severe gaze of his intense blue eyes. "The information is most confidential." He paused, as if reluctant to go on. "Of course, Mr. Holmes, your reputation for discretion is well-known in high circles, both here and on the Continent." He paused yet again, as if in deep thought. "Five continents, I am given to understand. I trust *that* has not been exaggerated."

Holmes raised his chin almost imperceptibly. "Rest assured it has not."

The earl clasped his hands together. "Robert, you see, has taken with him certain corporate shares from this house. In point of fact, he has stolen them; that's what he's done."

Holmes appeared unmoved by the disclosure. "Is that all?"

"Is it not enough?" pleaded the father. "They were entrusted to my care last year by a colleague in Parliament. Think of the effect upon *my* reputation, gentlemen, if I cannot produce them on demand. Those shares must be found at once, and they will be found in Robert's possession!"

Holmes remained impassive. Quietly, he said, "Do you believe your son took these shares to pay his gambling debts?"

"Ah, so you do know something after all!"

"I've examined his rooms, and his desk held notes and letters which suggest he may no longer fully control his financial destiny," replied Holmes.

"Well then," said the cabinet minister. "Since you've already divined the boy's character, there's no need to mince words with you. Robert's a wastrel. He's never understood the concept of proper behaviour, never followed my wishes from the day he was brought into this world. Worried his poor mother right into the next one, he did."

Lord Monsbury's veined hands clenched each other ever more tightly. "He has no sense of responsibility or honour, sir. We share a family name, the two of us, but nothing else, and I must confess I can find in myself no honest affection for the boy. Condemn me if you will for my sentiments, but there they are, and there they stand. I require only one thing," he said, pounding the arm of his great wooden chair. "And that is the return of those shares."

Sherlock Holmes brushed his coat sleeve, and for several seconds, there was an uncomfortable silence among us. At length, the detective spoke.

"May I ask where these shares were kept?"

"They were in a wall safe behind that picture there, between the busts of Tacitus and Petrarch."

"Have you any idea how your son might have had an opportunity to take them or even to have known of their existence? From what you have said, I should not think he would be welcome in this house."

"He is not. The boy comes round every three months to obtain his allowance and visit his former rooms, as his mother asked upon her death-bed. It is an obligation I undertake in memory of her."

"He receives this allowance from you personally?"

"Of course not, Mr. Holmes. I'll not speak to him. Stephenson, my secretary, gives it him. I make certain I am not at home when Robert calls."

"And yet he knew of the shares?"

"Obviously he did. He took them when he received his last allowance, did he not?"

"Tell me, Lord Monsbury, have there been recent changes in your household staff?"

"None of a major nature in over two years, sir. I pride myself on this house's efficiency and stability—and on the honesty of those who work here."

"When did your son last pay his quarterly visit?"

"It will have been three weeks come Friday."

"And when did you realize the shares were gone?"

"Two days ago, Mr. Holmes. If you mean to fix whether they were in this house between Robert's visit and then, I cannot say. The last time I confirmed possession of them was a month ago."

"Can you then be confident your son is, indeed, the thief? Perhaps another—"

"It was Robert," maintained the old man. "I know it was Robert. I say it was Robert, and it is Robert I engage you to find."

"Please pardon me, Lord Monsbury. I mean no effrontery but seek only to clearly establish my precise charge from you—whether it is to find your son or the missing shares. If it is the latter, then I shall not presume your son to be the thief; indeed, I shall not presume the shares were necessarily stolen at all. On the other hand, if your son is to be the quarry, then I shall endeavour to locate him directly, with the shares of secondary concern. Now, with those choices before you," said the detective, his arms outstretched in a subtle supplication, "am I to cast my net for your shares or your son?"

The old man's face flushed with anger as he said, "I desire you to find the latter, sir."

"Very well," replied Holmes, rising to his feet. With more than a bit of embarrassment, I followed the lead of my friend.

"Find him," the earl repeated, glaring at Holmes, his creased neck pulling up from his stiff white collar. "Find him, and you will find those shares at the same time; I tell you! Discussion of your commission is, of course, unnecessary," he said with a palsied wave of one hand. "You may name your price, Mr. Holmes."

"My fees, Lord Monsbury, are on a fixed scale. I do not vary them, save when I remit them altogether, which I shall not do in this instance. Trust that your bill will come due in time. I wish to ask only one thing of you at the moment. Is your secretary in the house?"

"Stephenson? Yes, of course. You wish to see him?"

"I wish to have him see us out, if he might."

"Of course. I shall ring him," said the old man, rising from behind his massive desk. "You understand, of course, that Stephenson is unaware that the shares are missing. I leave myself to the mercy of your discretion, sirs."

"That trust will not be betrayed," replied my friend. "I assume, however, that the disappearance of your son may be mentioned in the man's presence."

"It was he who first called my attention to Robert's vanishing," Lord Monsbury replied as the study door was opened by a thin, young man, whose prodigious head of blond-red hair contributed in no small amount to his total height. The earl introduced him to us as Diarmund Stephenson, his secretary.

"Mr. Holmes wishes your escort from this house," the cabinet minister continued. "You shall soon call with definitive news in this matter, I do hope," he told the detective.

"I fear I cannot assure you as to that point," replied Sherlock Holmes as we left the study. "Detection is more akin to cricket than rugby; we do not play by the clock."

With that, we left our client to himself and were led past the family gallery and down the stair by Mr. Stephenson, who chatted constantly about the disappearance of young Hope Maldon.

"That is the reason for your coming here, isn't it?" he asked anxiously. "I caught what I supposed to be an allusion as I entered the study. If I may say, Mr. Holmes, Robert's vanishing is most shocking and disturbing. Believe me when I say my own concern for him must rival that of his father."

"That I do not doubt," replied Holmes as we reached the ground floor. "You are well acquainted with the son then? Indeed, the earl indicated that it was you who first learned of the young man's disappearance."

"Well, yes, I did inform Lord Monsbury that Robert was missing from his rooms."

"One can conclude then that your relation with the earl's son is not limited to the transfer of his allowance," declared Holmes. "His last visit for that purpose was three weeks past."

The young secretary gave a start. "Yes, I get your point, sir. Well, in truth, Robert signs for his allowance, and by my oversight, he failed to do so on the occasion of his last distribution. I sought him at his rooms but to no avail. It was then that I reported his absence to my employer."

"Hum. My impression is that the two of them are not on the best of terms."

"The earl and Robert? Yes, that, unfortunately, is true," replied Stephenson, watching the approaching servant as we reached the house entrance. "It's not hard for an outsider to tell that, is it? Tragic—the misunderstandings, I mean."

Holmes cocked his head while accepting his coat from the servant. "What misunderstandings?"

"Robert has always believed that he has been wrongfully judged—with respect to his character, you see."

"Tell me again, Mr. Stephenson," Holmes said, taking his topper in hand, "and this time, most truthfully; how close are you to Mr. Hope Maldon, to whom you repeatedly refer by his given name?"

"Allow me to be very circumspect here, Mr. Holmes. In my capacity, I must be. You understand."

"Of course."

Stephenson watched as the servant handed me both my coat and hat, and then he dismissed the man and began to hesitantly explain. "In truth, we have, for some time, met socially. Soon after coming into the earl's employ, having first met Robert when he called for his allowance, I chanced upon him one day at a wine lodge in the Strand, and we fell into a most enjoyable conversation. Discovering much in common, we thereafter dined together regularly, and upon occasion I joined him at the music hall or for a game of cards. All this has been without the knowledge of the earl, of course. You will not inform him of these things I tell you?"

"Be assured of my discretion," said Holmes.

"Then please accept my apology for misstating matters only a moment ago. The story of Robert not signing for his allowance was somewhat a lie. Well, perhaps more an omission of sorts. Almost two weeks ago, after his return from a tour of America, we had an appointment to meet at the St. Pancras Hotel, but Robert never appeared. I called later at his rooms, but he was not in. I left messages numerous times, but they all remained unanswered. It was then that I began to fear for his safety. In fact, whenever Robert received his allowance, he never signed for the money. He refused to do so out of pique, I suppose. Afterward, I would always initial for him. In this last instance, I had neglected to and so used that blank space as my pretext for calling Robert's absence to the earl's attention."

"Mr. Stephenson, are you aware of any problems Mr. Hope Maldon may have in his private life?"

The secretary paused. "Yes," he said, "and from the sound of your voice, I'd say you're aware of them as well, sir. The gambling, I mean."

Holmes nodded. "Tell me, would you expect your friend to act rashly upon his problems?"

"To steal or embezzle, you mean? I should like to think that Robert would never consider such extreme possibilities."

"Thank you then," said Holmes, boldly opening the house door himself. "Should you learn of anything relevant, I trust you will inform me?"

"Of course," said the secretary, accepting Holmes's card. "Please excuse my repetition, sir, but I do fear for Robert's safety. An absence of this sort is very much out of character with him."

"Try to replace fear with uncertainty, if you can," said Holmes. "That will not provide comfort, but it may allow you moments of relative peace."

We both strode past Stephenson and bade him farewell. Stepping once more out into the street, I hailed a cab for the return to 221.

"The mighty present a different picture in private life," I observed as we boarded a hansom. "That was not the Lord Monsbury whose speeches one reads in the *Times*."

"Indeed, it was not. Cabby," called out Holmes, "to St. Glevens Hospital!"

"Not Baker Street?" I asked.

"Not directly, old fellow," said my companion as our vehicle turned round. "St. Glevens is not far removed from our way home, and I strongly wish to examine the scene."

"I thought it odd we were not longer at Lennox Square," I said.

"I wished to leave that place," Holmes replied simply. "An unhappy house is difficult to endure, even for those who are merely visitors. Moreover, the earl was a most unhelpful witness. Did you notice that it only was at the end of the conversation, and then merely in passing, that he revealed that his secretary had informed him that his son was missing? And what did you conclude concerning Diarmund Stephenson, by the way?"

"Rather an earnest young man," was all I could muster.

"He is that," replied Holmes. "And perhaps a bit more."

"Where does our hunt for the shares begin then?"

"Please recall that the father asked for his son, and thus, the shares are to be of secondary concern."

"But those shares could mean the man's career!"

Holmes made no comment and merely tilted his topper over his eyes as the cabman drove on. Minutes later, we arrived before St. Glevens Hospital.

"A familiar sight to you, I believe," Holmes said as he stepped out onto the pavement.

"Yes," I replied, following my friend from the cab. "Blanding was a resident here some years ago. My, the place does not appear much changed since that time."

The driver waited as Holmes directed, and we walked along the kerb to the south end where, as Hopkins had described, a red pillar-box stood at the entrance to a wide court, in which several nurses in heavy coats were taking the air.

"You said Hope Maldon's mere standing beside this letter-box is of importance," I remarked.

"Indeed," said my friend as he walked round it. "Now, Watson, we know the lad displayed a kerchief in the air from this point. What does that suggest?"

"A signal."

"Well, yes, of course. But answer me this, my young Plato: why stand precisely here? What is gained by coming to this box to give a signal?"

After a moment's silence, I admitted I did not know.

"Why, quite possibly to *read* a message to which one may then respond," said Holmes, putting his face next to the metal surface. "I'll wager my shag to your Beaune that it may still be here. Let me see...No—those scratches are quite weathered, and these are the marks of a petty vandal."

Holmes covered successive inches of the painted box, and after half-a-turn round it, he discovered what he sought.

"I believe this may be it, Watson!"

He motioned me to look, and as I stood and peered past the end of his long forefinger, I could discern the pattern roughly etched there: "WLOO 3P."

Holmes studied my face expectantly.

"Waterloo Station," I ventured.

"Excellent, Watson. This may have directed our young Hope Maldon to catch a train at three o'clock in the afternoon from Waterloo. That would, of course, be the boat-train."

"He is on the Continent then?"

"He at least intended to be. Recall, Watson, that Waterloo Station is but a short distance from Breton Mansions, to which he returned. He thus had but a few minutes' walk from his block of flats to the station, where he would have boarded the train. That no one noticed him among other travellers during that short stroll is quite unremarkable."

"But why all this elaboration?" I asked. "To convey this message, why did his informant not come to his rooms or send a messenger or simply ring him up?"

"I fancy the informant did not call at Breton Mansion for fear of being seen or intercepted by someone else. That same fate could have awaited a hired messenger. And she did not ring him up for the obvious reason that Hope Maldon's flat is not furnished with a telephone, as you should have noticed."

"Pardon the oversight. I have noticed, however, that you refer to this other person by the feminine pronoun. You believe it was Irene Adler?"

"No," said Holmes. "I merely believe it likely to have been her. A man might have been inclined to kneel in order to place this message in a less visible section of the pillar-box. The position of these marks at just below eye level is not definitive, but it is consistent a woman being the furtive etcher."

"And do you surmise that Miss Adler may have watched from a hospital window as Hope Maldon signalled his receipt of the message?

"Perhaps," replied Holmes with an impish smile as we strode back toward the kerb.

"I believe only a small number of windows held a clear view of the pillar-box, unobstructed by trees."

"Five," replied my friend.

"And so now into St. Glevens itself?" I asked.

"Not at present. Recall that Hopkins will call later for us at 221, and I wish to use the intervening time to sort what facts we have collected. Tomorrow I shall perhaps send Shinwell Johnson to further investigate this site and make inquiries within. His talents will be more than equal to the task that remains here."

We regained our cab and travelled in silence back to Baker Street. There we alighted and then walked—Holmes lagging somewhat behind—under a now-threatening sky toward the fanlight of number 221. Before either of us reached the door, however, it opened to reveal Mrs. Hudson, and even I could discern from her expression that something was amiss.

"What is the matter?" asked Holmes, stopping before the landlady. "Pray, tell me calmly."

"A woman is waiting upstairs," said Mrs. Hudson, leading us into the house. "She's one in dire straits, she is. I always can tell who's the neediest that come to you, can't I, Mr. Holmes? Let me tell you, sir; she is one of the worst I've seen in all these years, with a look in her poor eyes to melt anyone's heart."

"Oh, truly?" said Holmes, removing his hat and waterproof. "Watson, this must be the storm following the calm. *Apré ennui, dèluge.* You said she was upstairs, Mrs. Hudson. Are you possibly referring to the maid's quarters?"

"No, sir. She's in the sitting room of 221B. I could not refuse the poor lady, sir! She asked—"

"Quite all right," said Holmes calmly, though I could detect alarm at this violation of his sanctum. "Well, Watson, it has been some time since we have called upon someone in our own sitting room rather than the other way round. Let us go up immediately then and meet this female in distress."

We ascended the stair, Holmes leading and even taking two risers at once. Reaching the closed sitting room door, my friend paused for what seemed an unusually long time.

"Well?" I asked. "Do you wish *me* to knock instead?"

"Knock?" said Holmes. "Of course not. Recall again that it is *our* sitting room." He abruptly opened the door, and from beyond I heard a faint, feminine gasp and caught flashes of colour.

And then I gazed upon her face for the second time that day. It was not a flat image this time, no mere likeness etched in silver compound and bounded by a tin frame. This was life itself. She stood before Holmes's armchair, hands across a pale blue bodice. Then one arm rose, and a set of trembling fingers pushed back a tress of greying hair to set it among companions of shining auburn and gold. The strands immediately returned to their disobedient position, and I felt they should fall no other way.

"Greetings, Mrs. Norton," said Holmes as if he had last seen her but yesterday. "Have you been waiting long?"

"No."

My mind hung upon the voicing of that one syllable for what seemed an eternity.

"I trust you will forgive this invasion," she continued. Her large grey eyes seemed to cast their own glow back and forth between myself and Holmes.

"Might we not all sit?" I timidly suggested, noting great weariness in her voice and the extreme pallor of her skin. "Did Mrs. Hudson offer you any refreshment when you arrived, madam?"

Irene Adler looked to Sherlock Holmes, who motioned toward chairs.

"No, she did not, Dr. Watson," said the woman, glancing at me as she took the sofa. "But I require none. You *are* Dr. Watson, are you not?"

"At your service," I replied, embarrassed as my voice broke as if I were but a growing boy.

"We have never before been introduced. Still, I know of you, having read many of your several stories. Then, too," she added, addressing my friend, "*We* have never been properly introduced either, have we, Mr. Holmes? When we first met, you posed as a priest—"

"A nonconformist clergyman," corrected Holmes. "I have never assumed the guise of a priest. But tell me, why have you chosen to rise from the dead so suddenly and then call upon us here at this particular time?"

Irene Adler smiled. "So direct," she said, her eyes now pleading, her pale skin suddenly blushing. She clasped her hands, which seemed oddly large and ungainly, and stared away toward the bow window, presenting to us her fine profile.

"We had no idea you were even alive, Miss Adler," I said, uncertain how to proceed. "Whatever your—"

"Tell me, Mrs. Norton," Holmes interrupted, "do *you* know where the Honourable Robert Hope Maldon is?"

Our guest's head turned sharply toward us again, her eyes grew even larger, and one hand rose to her mouth to stifle any sound. Then, silently, her form slumped against the sofa back.

"She has fainted, Holmes!"

"Well, I believe brandy is your universal prescription, is it not?" the detective said in an idle tone. "Find some, please, while I fetch a glass."

CHAPTER THREE:

The Woman's Story

We gently settled a limp Irene Adler across the sofa, and then I rapidly prepared brandy and water in a glass provided by Holmes. Rushing back to our guest, I placed the drink upon a table nearby and then knelt down beside her to examine both the woman's eyes and pulse.

"She is not in jeopardy," I said. "She is regaining her senses even now."

Holmes seemed to ignore my observations. Indeed, he had stepped over to examine an unfamiliar set of luggage, which I, for the first time, noticed upon the bearskin rug. The detective lifted each piece in turn then made as if to open one.

"Holmes! It is not—"

"Please attend to your duties, Watson, and I shall see to mine."

Then Irene Adler began to visibly stir, causing my friend to retreat to the mantelpiece, upon which he leaned.

"Do forgive me," said a weak, feminine voice. Irene Adler's eyes opened full toward me, and I immediately rose and stepped back from the sofa.

"I must apologize for such a spectacle," she continued, sitting up to address us both. "I embarrass myself."

"No, it is I who must be excused," Holmes replied with a hint of contrition. "I fear my earnestness can sometimes become a callous thing. Dr. Watson has provided you brandy and water in that glass." Holmes pointed toward the drink.

She smiled, nodded at me, and then took the glass in her trembling hands to sip slowly. "Your sudden mention of Robert was most unexpected," she said after a moment's pause.

"Do not attempt to rise suddenly," I said. "You should remain—"

The bell rang below. Someone was calling at 221. Irene Adler's eyes became wide.

"It is much too soon for Hopkins," said Holmes, watching our visitor intently. "Surely he would not be so early!" The detective strode quickly from mantel to window, and Irene Adler shot to her feet.

"Please!" I urged her. "You must not—"

"The house door is already open. Mrs. Norton, my own room is past that door," the detective continued. "If you will—No, wait," said he, still peering down into Baker Street. His face relaxed, and he calmly declared, "Remain; there is no need to fear."

I took a step toward him, but he halted me with a sharp motion of the hand. "The caller has left. Truly," he added, speaking to the woman. "There is no need for alarm."

Miss Adler sat down again, and seconds later, I heard a familiar, stately tread upon the stair, followed by a knock at the sitting room door.

"Enter," said Holmes.

"Is the lady better?" Mrs. Hudson asked, and Irene Adler smiled and expressed appreciation to her. "Oh, good. Such a dear one," the older woman declared. "And here's a message that's come for the doctor."

I took a telegram from her, and Holmes stepped to my side. "The bad news from Finney, I gather. Three to five he charges you for it. But tell me," he abruptly asked Miss Adler, turning to face her, "could you stand an offer of food?"

The woman paused, glass again in hand, seemingly uncertain how to answer.

"Mrs. Hudson," Holmes said, "are there still cold cuts to be had?"

"Oh, yes. I'll bring them up straightaway," the landlady said even as she went hurrying down the stair.

"Thank you, Mr. Holmes," said the woman. "You are most kind."

"Mere hospitality, Mrs. Norton."

"Miss Adler," she corrected. "I wish to be called Miss Adler again."

"Your husband...?"

"Though *my* death in Switzerland was falsely reported, his was not."

"Accept our sincere condolences then," said Holmes, once more approaching the mantelpiece.

"It has been several years," our guest replied. "My pain has softened, but I appreciate the sentiment."

"Pray, tell me," continued Holmes. "Why have you never come forward to correct the reports of your death? Do you still, after all this time, fear retaliation from the king of Bohemia?"

The woman sipped from the glass once more, looked down, and nodded.

"Yes," the detective said. "And I believe you have every right to fear him. Do you believe it was he who arranged your husband's death and barely failed to see to yours?"

"Holmes," I said sharply, "how can you—"

"Dr. Watson, do not trouble yourself," Miss Adler said. "Remember that we are speaking of things past." She stared firmly at the detective. "Long past, indeed. They are events which are as textbook history now." Her eyes returned to me. "We can, all of us, freely discuss Godfrey's fate dispassionately, as Mr. Holmes understands even without such assurances by his widow."

The detective turned away, sensing, no doubt, the subtle edge to her remark. He grasped his cherrywood pipe from off the mantelpiece and gave a deferential gesture to Miss Adler. "We noted your 'death' at the time," he said. "Watson duly recorded it in one of his early romances, though obliquely as I recall. Well, you needn't fear. The king does believe you to be deceased; indeed, he was so pleased at that morbid news, now proved so joyfully inaccurate, that he sent this as a gift." Holmes picked up the jewelled snuff-box and held it out to her.

"Such a huge amethyst," Irene Adler said, admiring it as my friend held the box before her. "He was always so very grateful, if uncompromisingly ruthless." She put down her glass and accepted the box from Holmes. "You do not use it?" she asked after opening the lid to find it empty.

"It serves a purely decorative purpose."

"A most expensive ornament then," she observed.

Holmes smiled as she handed it back to him.

"I notice as well an old portrait of myself there beside it."

"It is the one you left for the king of Bohemia in place of the other, more controversial one."

"Yet you now have it."

"Yes," replied Holmes. "It is the other memento of that 'scandal' that I—and the doctor retain."

This remark, uttered in a tone of mock horror, coaxed from our visitor a wan smile, which quickly vanished.

Holmes then took to his armchair. "Watson, pray, do not remain the only one standing. We have much ground to cover before Hopkins arrives."

I obeyed my friend's request, setting my still-unopened telegram upon his deal-topped chemistry table before finding relief in the basket-chair.

"Mrs.—Miss Adler," continued Holmes. "Have you the strength to answer questions?"

"Will they be your style of question?"

Holmes paused for a moment, seemingly taken aback. "Yes," he finally replied, turning the cherrywood pipe over and over in his hands. "Yes, I suppose that is an apt description. Are you willing then to supply the style of answer I should prefer?"

"I believe so," she said, taking the brandy and water in hand. "The substance will go beyond textbook history, though, will it not?"

"It will."

"Very well. Go on, sir."

Holmes leaned back, holding the cherrywood pipe stiffly in one hand. "You wish to be addressed once more by the surname Adler. Is it your expectation to very shortly relinquish that appellation a second time?"

The woman nodded. "Robert and I have not yet fixed a date, of course, but…yes, it is our intention to wed."

"I see. If I may continue to be so bold, what is his father's opinion of the match?"

"The earl does not know."

"Of the marriage only?"

"Of the marriage… and of me as well."

"The union will be presented as a *fait accompli?*"

"Yes." The woman looked down. "We felt—rather, Robert felt the difference in our ages, if nothing else, would present his family with an objection."

"Hum," said Holmes. He inhaled quickly. "Perhaps it would. Forgive me for repeating my very first question to you, but do you now know where your fiancé is?"

"Why, no," our guest said fervently. "It was—is my hope that you might find him for me."

"That is why you jumped back across the Styx and into Baker Street after many years of silence?"

"It is."

Holmes placed the cherrywood pipe in his lap and clasped his hands together. "I must tell you, Miss Adler, that I am already in the employ of your young man's father and charged by him to find your fiancé."

"Can you not find him for both of us?"

"Two separate clients, one common objective?"

"Yes. Do the ethics of detection permit that?"

Just then our landlady returned with a plate of meats. Holmes rose, took the platter, and set it upon our table.

"I've plenty more when it's needed," Mrs. Hudson told us.

"Thank you," Miss Adler said.

"Your efforts, as always, are appreciated," Holmes said as he ushered the landlady from the sitting room. "Miss Adler, allow me to halt my questioning for the moment. In its place"—he spread wide his arms—"we offer food and hot coffee in a few minutes, once my spirit-lamp is fired up."

We three sat round the table and enjoyed our small, impromptu meal. As we ate, Holmes related to our guest the events of the day, including Hopkins's visit, our visit to Breton Mansions, and his hiding of the portrait, as well as our interview with Lord Monsbury. Omitted, however, was any mention of the missing shares and our trip to St. Glevens. I took Holmes's frequent glances in my direction as silent instruction to make no additions or corrections, and so, following the practice of two decades, I merely chewed quietly upon my ham and beef, all the while studying intermittently, when chance gave me the opportunity, the face and figure of our guest.

"The doctor and I have kept from the police any evidence of your existence, let alone association with the case," Holmes assured her. "Watson himself has placed under his own personal guard the photograph we found at Breton Mansions; have you not, old fellow?"

"Why, yes," I said, producing from my coat pocket the small, framed portrait I had been absent-mindedly carrying about with me. Awkwardly, I set it upon the table.

Irene Adler took up the portrait. "I gave it to Robert only days after we had first met. What motivated you to seize it and keep it hidden?"

Holmes leaned back in his chair. "Perhaps it was concern that the news would get back to Bohemia. Perhaps it was whim or intuition. Whatever the reason, the fact is that I have considered your request for help," he said. "And I must tell you that while my ethics, as you term them, require that I honour my obligation to the Lord Monsbury, my sense of justice also requires that I act upon your behalf as well."

"These parallel obligations will not hinder you in the search for Robert? They will not conflict?"

"In my youth I was an adept juggler, even accepting donations for my performances," Holmes said, glancing in my direction to enjoy the look on my face at the admission of this fact, previously unknown to me. "And while I have not practiced the art in years, one never forgets the sense of it, literally or metaphorically."

"I cannot adequately express my appreciation to you," the woman said.

"No matter. Allow me to remind both of you that a representative of Scotland Yard will call within the quarter hour, however, and he must not learn you are here, Miss Adler. As you may have surmised, our house is between maids, and I think it best if you and your luggage retire to the vacant room upstairs until Inspector Hopkins is gone. We shall then have time to hear your own account of the matter in greater detail."

We dealt rapidly with the last of our meats, and then Holmes and I escorted the woman upstairs with her luggage.

"Watson," said Holmes as we reached the second floor. "Acquaint Miss Adler with her new surroundings. I must quickly go down and instruct Mrs. Hudson. Miss Adler, I am certain you realize the need for silence when the inspector is here."

"Of course," said the woman.

My friend bounded down to the ground floor, and I was left alone with our guest.

"This was my room when I resided here," I stammered while opening a door opposite my present, temporary quarters in 221. "A maid would be quartered here now, if one were currently employed in this house. The room itself is very plain these days, I fear."

The woman smiled. "Doctor," she said in a soothing voice, "do not think less of me if I tell you I have familiarity with environs far worse than this cosy, little area."

"No one could think of you in any but the highest terms, madam," I said impulsively, perhaps blushing at my declaration.

Her mood suddenly changed to one of mild despair. "And as plain as it is, it is still a step up in life for me. Dr. Watson, I must confess to you that these bags and their contents are all my worldly possessions." She looked away and, finding the room's only chair, sat down and exerted all her efforts to keep from weeping.

"Miss Adler, please," I murmured as I stood at the doorway, not knowing what condolence to offer.

"Do not tell him I carry my whole estate with me," she said, meeting my eye with sudden firmness.

"Of course," was all I could think to say as I transferred her luggage from the landing into the room.

The house bell rang, and I looked to Miss Adler. "Not a word," she reminded me sharply.

"I promise," was the solemn, whispered oath I gave. She nodded and then offered her hand, which I briefly clasped as a seal of our agreement. Then, with the faintest of smiles, she watched as I withdrew from the room.

Having entered 221, Stanley Hopkins lumbered up the stair in the company of Holmes. The two of them greeted me from below and entered the sitting room. Nervously, I looked back at Miss Adler's door, now closed, before walking across the landing to my own room, where I read the latest number of the *Lancet* for near unto half an hour.

At length, after I had quit my medical reading and then exhausted all items of interest in the day's *Telegraph*, Hopkins departed, and when the house door closed below, both Miss Adler and I discovered the other peeping out into the hall. Together, we descended the stair in the deepening gloom of early evening to find Holmes stretched out upon the sofa, clay pipe in hand, an ethereal lacework of smoke floating over him. He smiled as we entered.

"Did Hopkins bring more news?" I inquired.

"Mrs. Hudson has graciously agreed to postpone supper," he said while turning to a sitting position in one agile motion. "We must get on with your story, Miss Adler."

I ignored this rebuff to my question and stepped behind the woman, pointing at Holmes's pipe with raised brows as his eyes met mine.

"Do you mind?" he asked her, holding the smoking clay aloft.

"Why, no," she replied. "Of course I do not."

Holmes looked back at me with a satisfied grin and then clenched the pipe between his teeth. When we were all seated, he leaned back in the sofa and said, "Pray, continue to tell us your side of things, Miss Adler."

"Where shall I resume?"

"Let us start from the death of Godfrey Norton."

"As you wish," said the woman. "Godfrey's estate was not inconsiderable, but I, of course, could not claim it without revealing I had survived the avalanche. Fortunately, my husband had brought with him a large sum of notes, with which I was able to buy my passage back to America. I lived in New York for some years under another name and then employed that alias when I returned to England."

"What motivated that?" asked Holmes. "The trip here, I mean."

"A simple wish to come back. Is that an answer you can understand?"

"Yes, it is. Go on."

"It was on the ship that brought me back to this country that I met Robert, who was himself returning from a journey to America. We grew attached to one another during the voyage, and by the time the Atlantic had been crossed, I had agreed to marry him. It may seem impulsive and rash to you, given our circumstances, but we are devoted to each other."

"Were you aware that his reckless spirit extends beyond love to the realm of gambling?" Holmes asked.

"Yes," the woman replied with mild embarrassment. "Indeed, I tried to turn him away from cards."

"But success eluded you?"

Irene Adler looked down. "It did. His gambling, Mr. Holmes, is akin to an addiction."

"Gambling *is* an addiction, Miss Adler," Holmes responded. "Comparable, perhaps, to the lure of those narcotics from which I myself was saved by one who was, and remains, my dearest friend."

I looked at Holmes, whose gaze was fixed upon our guest, and felt the full emotion of comradeship well up in my eyes.

"Robert kept gambling, despite my efforts to dissuade him," Miss Adler continued. "Money was the one great threat hanging over our impending union. I have almost none of my own, Mr. Holmes, and Robert seems to squander what little that comes to him."

"Is the name Diarmund Stephenson known to you?"

"That is Robert's father's secretary. The name is familiar but not the person. I have never met the man, but Robert has talked of him often enough. He must possess a kind soul, for I've understood he has been very warm toward Robert when my dear has called at Lennox Square." The woman looked at Holmes warily. "To visit that house must be a terrible experience for him."

Holmes blew a cloud of smoke. "Allow me to return to the subject of your late husband. You said his estate was not insignificant and that he had carried a large sum of notes with him to Switzerland."

"Yes."

"Did you know at the time that his wealth was accumulated, for the most part, from criminal dealings?"

33

I stiffened at my friend's revelation. It was knowledge he had never shared with me, and Miss Adler herself became visibly shaken.

"If you did not know, I apologize for the revelation," said the detective. "My investigations subsequent to the affair involving the king of Bohemia uncovered the fact that Godfrey Norton was not the most ethical of solicitors."

"I learned that too, in time," the woman admitted after a moment's silence. She looked down at the floor, her face seemingly tranquil, but I sensed agitation in her grey eyes. "I knew of his other side, but you must believe me when I say that I was not aware of it until well after we were wed."

"Yet once aware, you did not hesitate to profit from his continued crimes and then use them to advantage after the tragedy in Switzerland."

"What other choice had I? My own money amounted to so very little, and I needed much more, both to leave Europe and maintain the appearance of my death. Godfrey's money, no matter what its source, paid my passage back to America and kept me safe."

Holmes shrugged. "And so you found yourself, years later, once more in London and in love but still with meagre income."

"Yes, but Robert told me he had a plan that would make a fortune for us."

"What was the nature of this plan?"

"Robert never confided that in me. He said merely that our future would be assured for all the days that might come."

Holmes leaned back with raised brows and bit down upon his pipe. After a moment, he withdrew it from his mouth, setting it aside. "Did he ever say that this plan would require an initial investment?" my friend inquired.

"Perhaps," said the woman with hesitation. "To be honest, Mr. Holmes, I do not recall."

"Was there any talk of others joining in this scheme, whatever it was?"

Irene Adler looked over at our bearskin rug. "Sometimes he hinted at such possibilities, but I remember nothing definite in that regard. Certainly, he never mentioned allies by name."

"Was there mention of potential adversaries?"

"No."

Holmes stood up and approached the mantelpiece, his back to us. He asked, "He never made any allusion that might allow you to guess even the general nature of this enterprise?"

"Never," Miss Adler said. "He spoke of it often enough but always in roundabout ways."

"And you accepted that?"

"If you mean to suggest I was too trusting and naïve, I will not argue the point."

Holmes kept his back to us. "I have difficulty associating that particular fault with you, Miss Adler."

"I am a woman in love. Have you also a difficulty associating me with that particular emotion?"

Holmes shrugged and turned round. "And your young man proceeded with his plan on or about the seventh of this month?"

"Yes, I travelled with him to Paris on the boat-train from Waterloo, as Robert had arranged."

"The trip was without incident?"

"Yes."

"And was your fiancé able to successfully conclude his business there?"

Irene Adler sighed, and her eyes filled with tears she could no longer hold back. "I do not know, Mr. Holmes. Robert went out within an hour of our arrival at the hotel, and…And I have not seen him since!" She reached toward me and clutched at my sleeve. "Not since then, Dr. Watson! I have seen him!" She wept uncontrollably now, covering her face with her other hand as she sobbed.

I placed my free hand upon hers, and looked plaintively at Holmes. He made an expression of mild annoyance and strode back to his pipe.

"Holmes," I said, with an air of warning.

"Miss Adler," the detective continued in a soothing actor's voice while aiming a silent look of reproach toward me. "I am certain you suffer terribly at this moment. I do not pretend to ken its depth. But if this pain is to be only momentary and give way to the happy future you wish for and, by all accounts, deserve, then you must help me complete this interview presently. Can you do this for yourself?"

The woman uncovered her face, turned a brave, crimson-eyed smile toward me, and gently lifted her other hand from my grasp. "I can," said she, facing Sherlock Holmes. "I can, not so much for my own as for Robert's sake."

Holmes once more put down his pipe and stared intently at her. "From whom are you running?"

"What?"

"You said Mr. Hope Maldon mentioned no potential adversaries, yet clearly a portion of your agitation derives from fear. Fear of what or whom? You are distraught from loss of your fiancé, who is missing. Why would he be missing? What agency could have whisked him away from you? I tell you directly that in this affair, you are acting in the manner of the hunted fox. Might I know the identity of at least the hound, if not its master?"

"I cannot say."

"Cannot or will not?"

"I cannot," declared the woman. She breathed deeply, ran her fingers through her grey-and-auburn hair, and then buried her face in her hands again. Then, regaining her composure, she resumed. "Yes, it is true that Robert mentioned enemies—I should have answered you truthfully a moment ago. Please forgive the lie. To live safely all these years has required that I live with lies, you see. Robert was very afraid as well as secretive. He did not reveal the details of his business, and neither did he share the source of his fear. He did make clear to me, however, that one or more persons would oppose him and that they might follow us. He also told me there could be danger. All this he revealed only as our train left London."

"These persons he spoke of, could they have been agents of his father?"

"Perhaps, although, as I have said, he had led me to understand that his father knew nothing of me, let alone the enterprise in Paris," she declared, looking into my eyes. "I apologize for my ignorance. I know it gives you no assistance, but that was Robert's way. He told me he wanted to spare me the anxiety that full knowledge of his plans would cause."

"Did your state of ignorance not give rise to anxiety nonetheless?"

"Yes, but Robert was as a stone wall in these matters."

"I see. When your fiancé was overdue at the hotel in Paris, what did you do?"

"I waited a full day before returning to London, where I kept waiting."

"At his rooms in Breton Mansions?"

"No, I hadn't a key. I fear I must admit to staying at a hospital south of the river," she said with some embarrassment. "I had spent some days there prior to our leaving for the Continent. Twice after my return, I wired the hotel in Paris for Robert but received no answer."

"Was there no one in London you felt you could contact?"

"I know no one, Mr. Holmes, except you—and now, Dr. Watson."

"Did you consider approaching Diarmund Stephenson?"

"No. I feared he might involve Robert's father."

"There was no one else at all?"

Irene Adler sighed. "Robert had mentioned on occasion that he had a solicitor of his own, independent of his father's representatives, a man named Crabbe—Lucius Crabbe. I thought of approaching him but hesitated, again fearing that Robert's father might be alerted. Finally, in desperation, I gathered up my courage to seek you as my only alternative."

"After such a long time," Holmes said. "Well, that exhausts my curiosity for the moment; let us consider the working day to be at an end. I believe Mrs. Hudson will have a full supper prepared soon, and we must, in our turn, prepare for *it*," he declared as if we were to picnic.

I stared after my friend as he abruptly vanished into his private quarters. "Miss Adler," I said quietly, "you must understand that he is—"

"I understand perfectly, Doctor," she interjected, again taking my arm. "He is unique, matchless, nonpareil—the best at what he does, is he not?"

"Precisely."

She smiled. "And Mr. Holmes is so because he seeks to do the best for all concerned. Now, as he has so correctly suggested, let us prepare for what will be, I am sure, a wonderful evening meal."

Our supper was quiet and uneventful. Holmes led a conversation that completely ignored all mention of the case before us. Brushing aside my repeated requests for more information about his youthful attempts as a juggler, the detective nimbly guided us through topics as diverse as the nature of luminiferous aether, Hindoo philosophy, and the life cycle of the cicada. Afterward, Miss Adler retired at once to her room for the night, while I indulged in one last pipe of Arcadia, and Holmes occupied himself with pasting articles into yet another volume of his commonplace book.

"I am uncertain where to place this account of that art dealer's murder in Paris, Watson."

"You juggled for money, Holmes?" I asked.

My friend, still holding up a newspaper cutting, smiled discontentedly. "Yes, old fellow, but it was a short-lived enterprise with no consequences to my current state."

I raised my brows and merely continued to puff.

"It was in my college days," sighed my friend, "if you must know. And it was a most trivial aspect of that experience. My old friend Trevor could corroborate its negligible importance, were he still alive."

"No matter," I finally said. "It merely seems odd that, having shared these walls with you for the better part of twenty years, I should never have heard you make mention of it."

"Whatever the length of time, Watson, some minutiae is always loath to emerge from the shadows of the past. You, for example, have never volunteered to me information concerning your loss of a toe."

I gave a start.

"This is how we began our day, I believe," my friend continued with a smile. "Is it too late in the evening to recount my reasoning?"

"I rather think so," I told him. "Now, you were asking for advice in filing, were you not?"

"Yes," he replied, again holding the cutting aloft. "This piece about the murder of the art dealer in Paris. Where might I place it, do you think?"

"Allow me to suggest that 'Murders, Continental' be used," I said.

"I long ago defined my files more precisely than that, Doctor." He sighed. "'Murders, Parisian' and 'Murders, Art' are the choices available."

"'Murders, Art?'"

"It would begin a new category, which strikes me as an excellent step. And so 'Murders, Art' it is, and this article becomes its first entry."

I put down my pipe. "Tell me, Holmes, did you ever believe that—"

"No, Watson," said he. "I did not believe when I woke this morning that we would find ourselves housed under the same roof with Irene Adler." He looked up from his work. "Nor, I must say, did I ever expect that you would forget to open your telegram from Finney."

I looked quickly over to the chemistry table in the corner, where, after the excitement of the day, my message still lay undisturbed.

CHAPTER FOUR:

One Step Behind

My exhaustion from the events of that day must have been far greater than I appreciated at the time, for the following morning I woke much later than my usual custom. After bathing and dressing hurriedly, I came down to the sitting room, where I found Holmes in consultation with Shinwell Johnson.

"Greetings to you, Doctor," said the bluff former criminal, rising to offer me a hearty handshake. Now an agent several years in Holmes's employ, he was dressed in clean if rumpled plaids, and as he self-consciously brushed the makings of a beard, his black eyes flashed with amusement. "There's been no time for grooming in my life, as you can see, Dr. Watson."

"Indeed not," said Holmes, chuckling. The detective lay upon the sofa, cloaked in his mouse-coloured dressing-gown. As had been so true throughout our two decades together, it was impossible for me to discern if he had slept at all the previous night. "Johnson here has been occupied in gathering up loose ends remaining from the Preston forgery case, and I have now assigned him to the Hope Maldon affair." He turned toward the agent. "You are clear concerning your instructions?"

"That I am, Mr. Holmes, and I reckon I'd best be about them."

"Good," said my companion with a faint smile, rising to see Johnson to the sitting room door. "I would appreciate receiving your report by this afternoon, if possible. Ring us up first, if you will."

"Aye," said the agent, who then mumbled an anxious farewell and promptly left the house.

"There are so many possibilities," said Sherlock Holmes when we were alone. He returned to the sofa and set his head upon the cushion, fixing a melancholy stare at the faded ceiling. "We must cast the net, Watson. We must cast it as wide as..."

"Possible?"

"If you wish. As for myself, I was seeking a simile but in vain," Holmes replied. "Your ending, however, is quick and apt, and, therefore, perhaps the more desirable." He again rose to his feet and approached the hearth.

"Has Miss Adler——" I halted as, on the floor above us, a door opened.

Holmes crossed his arms as he stared into the fire. "No, Watson," he said softly. "I have not heard her stir until this very moment."

Seconds later, the woman came through the open sitting room door. "Such a wonderful morning," were her first words. "But then, I always find hope in the day's beginning."

A night's sleep had worked minor magic upon Irene Adler's face and demeanour. The lines of strain were softened, the woman's smile no longer a mere pose, and her hair was swept up in a buoyant, if slightly inelegant, fashion atop her head. With a manner as airy as the simple white blouse and grey skirt she wore, Miss Adler expressed her desire to sit by the fire, and Holmes, with suave ostentation, offered her the pick of the room. After a moment's thought, she settled into his armchair.

The detective distractedly gathered the folds of his gown before, yet again, returning to the sofa. "We shall move your chair closer to the hearth if you wish," he offered. The detective glanced toward the fogged bow window. "Perhaps we will soon have the last frost of the season," he commented idly.

"I am quite comfortable where I am, thank you," the woman declared. She glanced at the glowing coals and then asked, "Have you yet formed a plan with respect to Robert?"

"Plans, actually," was my friend's reply. "For we may have need of more than one." He gestured me toward the basket-chair, and as I sat down, he quietly told Miss Adler, "I should inform you that your fiancé was seen in the town two evenings ago."

Our guest turned round sharply, and I cocked my head with interest at this sudden announcement.

"Here?" Irene Adler said. "In London?"

"Yes. At the office of the solicitor you mentioned, Lucius Crabbe."

"When did you learn of this?" I asked. "Was it Shinwell——"

"No," Holmes answered abruptly.

"Then——"

"No, it was not Stanley Hopkins, either." My friend rose and strode to the bow window to peer down into the street. "I merely rang up the office of the solicitor this morning and asked if Hope Maldon had lately been round. It was that simple, truly. As I have told you in recent months, Watson, the telephone may, in years to come, have a profound effect upon the art of detection. I speak with respect to efficiency, of course, but also of—"

"And what report had the solicitor of Robert?" Miss Adler asked.

"At this moment I know nothing other than that he appeared there briefly," said Holmes with an air of benign detachment. "Mr. Crabbe struck me as, well, a bit incoherent, if you must know. You see, on the other hand, one disadvantage of investigation via telephone is the lack of physical presence, with an accompanying impairment of intuition. I fear I could not guide the solicitor into any informative direction at all during our brief conversation. There may be little to be gotten from the incident, except that your fiancé was alive and on this side of the Channel two nights ago."

"That alone should be cause for rejoicing," I said to soften Holmes's tone. "And are you then going to call upon this Mr. Lucius Crabbe?" I asked him.

"Of course. The story must be got straight in person. I hope you shall add your company, Watson. Would a generous sample of ham, eggs, toast, and a smattering of marmalade sustain you for the next few hours? And you, Miss Adler," my companion went on. "Do you care to join us, both in breakfast and travel?"

"I gladly accept the former, but I think it best to stay here," she answered. "My nerves at present could not possibly sustain—"

"Of course," I said comfortingly. "We shall, I am sure, bring you glad tidings."

"Allow me to ring Mrs. Hudson," continued the detective. "Fortunately, this house is between cooks also, and so we shall enjoy one of Mrs. Hudson's breakfasts, as in the old days."

After a hearty morning meal, Holmes and I left Miss Adler at Baker Street and took a cab to the Tottenham Court Road, upon which hunched the sombre offices of Lucius Crabbe. We were escorted to the solicitor's inner sanctum by a young skeleton of a clerk, who awkwardly kept offering to take our coats.

"No, thank you," said Holmes one final time as we entered Crabbe's study. "We shall be pleased to keep them. Solicitor Crabbe, I am the Sherlock Holmes who spoke to you via telephone earlier today," he said as the clerk closed the door behind us. "We wish to interview you concerning—"

"Young Hope Maldon, yes. I remember our talk, you see," the man replied, offering us chairs with one veined claw of a hand. The seats he indicated were filled with jumbles of paper, but after a delicate relocation of the piles, among still other heaps of pages, Holmes and I were able to lift the weight from our boots. Crabbe himself was a stooped, near-sighted man of perhaps seventy, with black hair utterly devoid of grey, for artificial reasons, which were all too obvious.

"Noxious Scot invention," Crabbe said, clenching his fist at the telephone across the room while gently lowering himself into a chair. "My sons insist on keeping it, you know. Don't like it going off so, however, and inside your own rooms as well. But it's going to be their office someday, isn't it?" Crabbe said, gazing about. He stopped and looked off into space. "Yet I suppose they'll fight over it as well, eh? Who's going to be king of the hill and all that, don't you know?"

"Mr. Crabbe?"

"Eh? What?"

"Solicitor," continued Sherlock Holmes. "Let us return to Mr. Robert Hope Maldon. You are retained by him, I understand."

"Yes…Oh, yes. His father's in the cabinet, you know. A few say he'll make premier, but I can't see it myself. Used to think the boy's business would be a feather in our cap, but what good has he been to the firm, eh? None at all, really."

"If you recall, sir," my friend went on. "You said to me this morning that young Hope Maldon had been to this office two days ago."

"Oh, yes. Left his card, left his card. His card, where is his—"

"Could you describe—"

"His card? Oh, yes! It is rather on the lesser side, you know…Here!" Crabbe shouted, pulling from his vast deposits of legal papers the personal card of Robert Hope Maldon.

"Thank you," said Holmes, taking it from Crabbe. With mild disappointment, he handed it to me. "Could you tell me about Mr. Hope Maldon's appearance here?"

"Yes, he was here. At least, that's what they told me."

"They?"

"The Henrys."

"The Henrys?"

"Yes. The Henrys were the ones who told me, sir."

"And who might these Henrys be?" inquired my friend.

"Two clerks: young Henry and old Henry." The solicitor smiled and shook one finger as if to scold. "Not related, though, I can assure you."

"It was they who spoke to Robert Hope Maldon?" asked Holmes. "Not you?"

"Indeed, yes, they did. Never saw the runt myself. No, I tell you; I did not. I had left long before he arrived, you see."

"Well then," said Sherlock Holmes. "May we see these two clerks, both with the name of Henry?"

"Certainly, gentlemen," said Crabbe. "It was young Henry himself that led you here. Mr. Henry!" he called out to the closed door. "They can tell which one it's for by my tone of voice, you see," he confided. "Got them trained that way."

The door was opened by the young clerk who had escorted us to Mr. Crabbe's sanctum.

"Come here, please, Mr. Henry! These gentlemen wish to speak to you, as well as the other Mr. Henry. Take them out, and talk all you want to them. That all? Good day then, I say."

We left the midnight-haired solicitor to his papers and mutterings and returned to the anteroom, where Holmes explained our purpose to the younger Henry.

"It will be no difficulty to tell you all I know," the clerk said. "For there's precious little in that pile. Mr. Henry!" he called, and from yet another room appeared a second clerk, an older but far more vigorous individual, whose head bore a halo of bright blond hair encircling a florid, shiny scalp.

"These gentlemen are seeking information about the Hope Maldon fellow's visit here the other night," the young clerk advised.

"I am James Henry," the older man declared. "What is it you wish to know?"

"Well—might I call you James Henry, rather than Mr. Henry?" asked Holmes.

"Of course, sir. That style is usually the easiest for those not acquainted with our offices here."

"And I am William," volunteered the younger of the two. "William Henry."

"Fine," said Holmes. "Now, James Henry, both you and William Henry saw and spoke to Mr. Hope Maldon two nights ago?"

"Yes, we did," replied James. "He knocked upon the door—the two of us were working late that day, the solicitor having already gone home early as usual—and he gave me his card. 'Get your employer,' he said rather gruffly. It was painfully hard to make out his exact words; the man was so deathly hoarse."

"He did not appear well?"

"Can't really say how he appeared, I suppose, only how he sounded," the elder Henry replied. "He remained in the street and never entered the office to give us a good look at him, and he was all muffled up. But as to sound, well, his voice was but a few shouts from the grave, if you were to ask me."

"He was coughing all the time," young William Henry added. "Coughing as if to lose his insides."

"That he was," James Henry agreed. "Well, sir, since Solicitor Crabbe was not in, there was nothing for us to do but ask Mr. Hope Maldon if he wished to leave a message. That he declined to do, saying he needed to speak to Mr. Crabbe in person, and then he left."

"With no further conversation?"

"Not a word, sir," affirmed the older Henry.

"Hum. Tell me, did Hope Maldon carry anything with him, such as a valise or luggage of any kind?"

"No, sir," William answered at once. "He was unencumbered," said the youth, with pride in his vocabulary. "Unencumbered, that's what he was."

"He did not, for instance, make use of a cane perhaps?"

"Nothing at all. His hands were empty, save for the card, I suppose."

"I see," Holmes said as James Henry nodded in agreement. "Tell me, were his hands gloved?"

"Yes," said the younger Henry. "Nice new gloves they were, all tan and shiny."

"Might I ask what the visitor did with his empty hands?"

The younger clerk shrugged. "Didn't do anything with them except keep holding them together, like this," he said, wringing his own pair together slowly.

"Yes, that's all he did," agreed James Henry. "I remember watching it, because of those shiny, new gloves."

"And he never stepped into the offices here at all?"

"No," answered James Henry. "He stayed outside, as I've already told you, and then he left."

A few more questions were posed; then my friend thanked both for their time, and without further inquiry, we left the solicitor's premises and regained the street, where Holmes whistled for a cab.

"To Baker Street, please!" my friend said as we boarded.

In time we again found 221, where Mrs. Hudson informed us that Miss Adler had retired to her room almost immediately after our departure, and she directed Holmes to a card lying upon a table in the vestibule.

"A very portly young gentleman came to see you, Mr. Holmes. As you were out, he left that."

"Thank you, Mrs. Hudson," said Holmes, taking the card.

"Robert Hope Maldon?" I asked facetiously.

"I fear not, Watson. A person named Jasper Girthwood," he said, reading the card before handing it to me with a twinkle in his eye. "He is not one of your friend Finney's associates, is he?" he asked as we stood at the foot of the stair.

"I have never heard the name before," I replied, returning the card and following behind him in our ascent toward the sitting room.

"Nor have I," said my friend, holding the card up to the light. "Observe the notation scribbled upon the back. 'I must consult on a matter of urgency.' Our casebook seems fairly brimming now, Watson," he added, placing the card in his coat pocket.

"What of your current business, the Hope Maldon affair?" I inquired as we entered the sitting room. "What *is* your strategy?"

"Grasp for a solution," Holmes said, "and then hang onto it."

"If I ask for your tactics instead, will you be more forthcoming?" I asked, reaching for my pipe and Arcadia mixture.

Holmes smiled. "Sorry, old fellow. You weaned me from the needle, but I fear impishness is incurable." He threw himself down into the armchair and made a steeple with his fingers. "You see, our problem is not yet well defined. Were it so, both strategy and tactics would be more clearly cut. Instead, we must keep casting the net, as I told you earlier. Cast the net, and see what form takes shape beneath it. Then I shall have my definitions *and* my stratagem."

Holmes looked past me suddenly. I turned round and saw in the doorway Irene Adler, once more, to my eyes, transformed.

"What news?" she asked. Now all colour was once more drained from her face, and her motion across the room to the basket-chair was both nervous and hesitant. I stood looking at my full pipe for a moment, then walked to the mantelpiece, where I set down both pipe and my vestas.

"Please, Doctor, do not abstain on my account," Miss Adler told me.

I turned and shyly looked at the woman with a questioning glance.

Her eyes narrowed, as if observing me observe her. "Please do as you would in my absence," she continued, attempting a smile. She turned to Holmes, who had taken to his armchair. "I have worried all morning about Robert. I have been speculating, gentlemen, on what news of him you might bring from Mr. Crabbe. If I have lost some of the gaiety I had this morning, that is the reason," she said, once more looking at me, nodding as if to give me permission to light my Arcadia.

I slowly took a vesta and did so.

"Well, our news is perhaps neither good nor bad, merely indifferent," said Holmes, who then related the meagre results of our interview at the solicitor's.

"You pursued no inquiries other than that one?" the woman asked.

"At present, I have no other targets of inquiry," replied Holmes, crossing his arms. "Though I have operatives in the field even now, and I will myself be going out shortly once more."

"Oh?" I said. "What is our destination to be?"

"On this occasion, Watson, I fear I must leave you behind," said Holmes as he sprang to his feet. "There are matters I must pursue alone."

"As Sherlock Holmes?" I asked.

My friend only shrugged. "Miss Adler," said he. "Forgive me when I agree that you do look unwell. Perhaps you should retire to your room again for the balance of the day. May I ask if our hospitality has been adequate?"

"Why, of course. It has been far more than merely adequate. I could not ask for better accommodations, and Mrs. Hudson is the best, most cheerful of companions."

"As I mentioned a moment ago, the doctor will, for the moment, be remaining here at Baker Street, if that gives your mind additional ease," Holmes continued.

"Yes," said our guest. "I would most appreciate that. And I also appreciate your concern, Mr. Holmes."

The detective smiled. "Watson," he said. "Please accompany Miss Adler up to her quarters. Then come back down to the sitting room; I shall give you instructions before leaving. And do tell Mrs. Hudson to follow the usual procedures in my absence," he added as he entered his own room.

Laying my pipe upon the mantel, I offered the woman my arm and led her up the stair.

"Will Mr. Holmes go out about the town in disguise, as you sometimes related in your stories?" she asked as we ascended.

"Perhaps," I replied as we gained the top of the stair. "He does so now far less frequently than in the old days. There were instances, back fifteen years ago or more, when he would become as many as five people in the course of a single afternoon. I wondered then who the real man was."

Miss Adler smiled faintly. "I sensed he did not wish me to see him in another guise," she said, peering down over the railing. "Strange that he should feel so. I saw him in one such pose once. Well, thank you, Doctor," the woman said as she entered the maid's quarters.

"It was twice," I said, before she closed the door.

Miss Adler gave me a questioning look.

"You saw him twice in disguise."

"As the clergyman," she said haltingly. "As the clergyman and...?"

"He was the horse groom at your wedding, the unemployed groom who acted as witness to the ceremony itself."

Irene Adler stared at me as if seeking to reshape my features. Then a glint of understanding swept across her face, and she burst into uninhibited laughter, of a kind that, I confess, I found somewhat unbecoming.

"Thank you," she told me at last in an exhausted voice. "I did not know, you see. I did not know," she repeated. "It has given me some small joy," the woman said before closing her door. Muffled laughter followed me a short way down the stair and then was gone as I reached the first floor and the sitting room entrance. There I paused, thinking her confession of ignorance odd, for some reason I did not yet grasp. I then heard Holmes call from the sitting room, and I entered.

"Well?" said the detective, standing before me, completely transformed in appearance.

"The navvy[4]," I said.

"Yes, Watson. It been awhile since he come out, ain't it?" my friend replied, assuming his new character.

Just as quickly, he again became Holmes. "I shall return to the vicinity of Solicitor Crabbe's," said he, adjusting the leather straps round his trouser legs, "then try an engagement at Breton Mansions. It may be a forlorn hope, but perhaps in this guise, I shall be able to pick up some few scraps."

"I shall hope for the best."

---

4   A navvy is a laborer, especially one employed in construction or excavation projects. The term was coined in the 18th century to apply to those working on navigation canals.

"I fear we shall need it," said my friend. "Watson, in addition to attending to our guest, I require you here should Johnson have anything to report. You will await the telephone?"

"Of course. Have you other instructions?"

"No," Holmes answered while knotting his red polka-dot kerchief. "If that fellow Girthwood calls again, receive him. I rather fancy the thought of two meals on our plate at once. I'll see me self out now, sor," he said in the person of the workman as he stuck his thumbs in his heavy leather belt and left with a shuffling gait.

Alone in the sitting room of 221B, I moved the basket-chair nearer the bow window and took up a recently purchased volume of sea stories. The book resting in my lap, I glanced across the room at the short shelf of my own work, which Holmes grudgingly allowed to remain on display. I watched their embossed spines glitter in the now rapidly varying sunlight, then turned to the book immediately before me for comfort, and in its pages, I lost all track of time until I heard the telephone.

It was Shinwell Johnson, who informed me that he would come round later in the afternoon. I told the agent of Holmes's absence and of my uncertainty about the time of his return, whereupon Johnson agreed to ring up again before coming to 221.

It was then, as I stood in the middle of our sitting room, debating the relative merits of my book versus those of my Beaune and Arcadia combined, that I heard another chime, this time the house bell.

I stepped to the bow window, but gazing through the fogged pane, I could see nothing beyond the usual street bustle. Then the house door closed, and I observed, lumbering away amid the crowd, the wide backside of a man cloaked in an Astrakhan coat. This huge, bear-like apparition vanished into the masses, and I turned as I heard the tread of Mrs. Hudson upon the stair.

"It was that Girthwood individual again," said the landlady, offering me another of his cards upon a tray. I took it from her. "I told him you were here, but he refused to talk to anyone, save Mr. Holmes himself."

"Thank you, Mrs. Hudson."

"Mr. Holmes asked that I make certain Miss Adler is—oh," she said, turning round. "Here's the dear one herself. Might I get anything for you, Miss?"

Irene Adler stood in the entrance to our sitting room, to my eye, looking calm if apprehensive. "I feel I want for nothing," she said.

"Might I prepare a small midday dinner for the two of you?" suggested Mrs. Hudson.

Miss Adler and I looked at each other, and in a manner I found most pleasing, we silently agreed between ourselves to accept the offer. "It would be welcome," I said aloud, and Mrs. Hudson hobbled past our guest and down the stair to ready the meal.

"Might we talk?" asked Irene Adler, taking a hesitant step toward the middle of the sitting room. "I feel all this rest has done me well, but I must confess to a degree of boredom."

"I have heard that complaint much in recent days," I replied, relating Holmes's dissatisfaction with his own professional idleness. The information amused her somewhat, and I invited her to join me at the table to await Mrs. Hudson's preparations.

"The telephone rang," Miss Adler abruptly said.

"It was Shinwell Johnson," I replied, finally setting down Mr. Girthwood's personal card. "He is an operative of the agency; Holmes referred to him at least once yesterday, if you recall."

"Yes, of course. Mr. Holmes leads a vast organization these days then?"

"Oh, it is hardly vast, though its scope is far larger now than it was in the beginning, when the organization was comprised of just Holmes."

"And you."

"Yes, I enlisted early, I suppose. And in those days, there were also the Irregulars."

"Irregulars?"

"A group of small boys employed by Holmes to act as look-outs and information gatherers." I smiled at the memory. "More than once, however, they came close to danger, and Holmes decided it was the better course to not put the lads at risk."

"And so what did this agent, Mr. Johnson, convey? News of Robert?"

"I do not know what information he has gleaned. Holmes wished to hear directly from Johnson himself, and as our friend was absent, I requested Johnson ring back later."

"Of course. And that card you set upon the table. Was that from a caller? For the house bell rang, did it not?"

"Yes, it was that Mr. Girthwood, who came by yesterday. He apparently has some matter, urgent in his own eyes, for investigation, but I can assure you that Sherlock Holmes is intent on giving his full energies to solving your problem before all others."

"The card that man left yesterday had a message on the back. Is this one similarly marked?"

"Truth to tell, I had not noticed," I replied, reaching for the card. "Jasper Girthwood," I read aloud. Turning over the card, I then continued. "'Must talk on a matter of import to us both, G.' He assumes some intimacy, I think, signing in that style. I cannot recall having met the fellow before."

"Might I see it?" asked Irene Adler.

Handing her the card as Mrs. Hudson entered with our meal, I rose to assist the landlady in setting the table but was herded back to my seat by a person intent upon providing through her own efforts alone.

"Did you see this Mr. Girthwood yourself?" Miss Adler asked as Mrs. Hudson left and we began eating. "Did you talk to him?"

"I caught a glimpse of him," I remarked while offering her the plate of toast. "A rather wide fellow, from what I could see. He was walking away down Baker Street, and all that was visible to me was a great Astrakhan with a bowler perched atop it."

Miss Adler smiled nervously and accepted a piece of toast. "But you did not speak to him?"

"No, I did not. Mrs. Hudson is the only one from the household who's had that pleasure. Chutney?"

"Yes, if you please. Doctor, what do you recall of Afghanistan?" the woman asked, steering our conversation abruptly into a new direction. I responded with reticence at first, hardly believing my guest could find much interest in an old army doctor's reminisces, but in the end, I could not resist her entreaties, and soon I was vigorously recounting my experiences in the East. When Mrs. Hudson finally reappeared to collect our culinary detritus, I was regaling my companion with memories in a manner that brought back my younger days spent caressing a glass at the Criterion.

"You are a font of wonderful stories," Miss Adler said. "Your life has evidently been rich."

"I do not know that I can judge any life, let alone my own," I responded. "Even now," I continued—in a tone I now recognize as self-pitying—"in the twilight of my time, I feel incapable of such an assessment."

"You men shrink at old age, yet seem so ready to consign yourselves to it," she told me. "I say no twilight for you, Doctor; it is still midday. But, Mrs. Hudson, allow me to assist you," the woman said, standing up and reaching for my plate. As I glanced at her own, I noticed Miss Adler had idly scrawled some symbol in the chutney.

"No, Miss," begged the landlady. "Allow me."

"No, I insist."

"It is unseemly," argued Mrs. Hudson. "I cannot allow you to—"

"Allow it this once," pleaded Miss Adler. "I cannot pay you rent at present—"

"Whoever spoke of rent? Did you speak of rent, Dr. Watson, with the quarter day coming in just a week? Shame!"

"He did not say a word. Still, I cannot pay you rent, no matter who suggests it, and so you must allow me this one contribution of my labour."

"But you are Mr. Holmes's guest! It is unheard of!"

"You must allow a guest her whims," insisted Miss Adler, who set my plate upon hers, gathered up other remains from the table, and waited for Mrs. Hudson to take the rest. "Dr. Watson, with your permission, I should like to accompany Mrs. Hudson to assist her in her duties."

"Why, of course, I suppose," I said, looking at the older woman for guidance in the face of Miss Adler's impropriety.

"Well, thank you, dear," said Mrs. Hudson at last. "It is still rather shocking, but if you insist, I will allow it this once. Doctor?"

"Of course, of course. I have my reading to finish. Is there perhaps anything I might do?" I then asked. "If mores are to shift in such a cataclysmic fashion, perhaps I should participate in the revolution as well."

"I think it's safest if you just read," Mrs. Hudson told me.

"Yes, to your books, Doctor," Miss Adler lightly commanded me. "We two will do our duties and perhaps have a wonderful chat as well, eh, Mrs. Hudson?"

The older woman laughed, and then both descended the stair, dinnerware in hand. Feeling the fullness of my meal, I slowly made my way once more to the chair in which I had left my volume of sea stories, and, sitting down, I rubbed my fingers over the fresh spine of the book and recalled the personal satisfaction I had felt on first exercising that option upon my own works.

I cast a sleepy smile out the window then sat up with a bit of a start as I suddenly realized what had gnawed at the edges of my mind earlier. Irene Adler had not been aware of Holmes's presence at her wedding until I had told her. In other words, I now understood, as drowsiness enveloped me again, that despite her praise the previous day for my stories, she had certainly not read the one tale of mine in which she herself had played a significant role.

"Well," I believe I uttered in mild disappointment as I lay the unopened book in my lap and promptly fell asleep.

CHAPTER FIVE:

Anxiety in the Air

It was late that afternoon when Sherlock Holmes returned to Baker Street. I had long since awakened from my unplanned nap and was in the midst of answering correspondence, an activity meant to take my mind away from pondering the likelihood that Irene Adler had, no doubt, found me asleep upon returning from assisting Mrs. Hudson. Our guest, I assumed, had once more taken to her quarters on the second floor.

"You were out for some time," I said, quickly putting aside an unfinished letter. "What were the results of your excursion?"

"Viewed in relation to the objective of finding Robert Hope Maldon, the harvest might seem meagre," my friend replied as he reached for his Persian slipper of shag. "There is, however, an intriguing morsel I shall relate to you in a moment." He lit his clay pipe and loosened his kerchief. "I say, has there been any word from Shinwell Johnson?"

"He rang earlier this afternoon and promised to do so again. I offered to relay any news, but he indicated that you wanted to hear his report directly."

"Yes. Thank you, old fellow. It is no reflection on yourself, as you understand."

"Of course," I said. "Truly, Holmes, there is no need to even allude to a justification."

"Quite so. Forgive me, Watson." Still in the guise of the navvy, he leaned against the mantelpiece, his eyes distant. "Having you back in these digs, even on a temporary basis, has rewound my mental clock, old fellow. At times I seem to act as if we were both twenty years younger and still new to one another. Well, is there any other Baker Street news of significance?"

"Mr. Jasper Girthwood called again," I added. "He left another card, with yet another message."

"Really," Homes responded, striding to the table as I pointed to it. "Hum. Once again he claims an urgent matter, I see, but this time one of interest to the both of us?"

The detective set the card back upon the table then took to the sofa. "There is only one matter of interest to me at the moment," he continued, "and that is the Hope Maldon affair. Tell me, what has been the status of our guest?"

"I take her to be in her room. But...ah...I now wish to relate a morsel of my own, before hearing the one that you promised."

Holmes stopped his action of stretching out upon the sofa. "You have been granted an insight into Miss Adler?"

"I believe so."

"Pray, Watson," my friend said quietly, while eyeing the closed sitting room door. "Relate it to me now, if you will."

"We dined earlier," I began. "And then she assisted Mrs. Hudson in clearing the table."

"Indeed." Holmes was now fully draped along the full length of our sofa. "And Mrs. Hudson permitted such a thing? That is a scandal in Baker Street, indeed."

"She truly had no choice. Our guest was most insistent."

"Tell me," said Holmes, setting aside his unfinished pipe and covering his eyes with one hand. "Was this prior to or following Jasper Girthwood's call?"

"Following," I said. "Our meal arrived after he—"

"Did you yourself speak to him?"

"No, only Mrs. Hudson again, though I did catch sight of the man."

"After which Miss Adler exhibited a strong desire to assist our landlady."

"Yes, I believe she meant to probe Mrs. Hudson's reaction to him in order to obtain her own insights into the man."

"Excellent, Watson, though I think Miss Adler's concern is directed at the man's strategy rather than his character, with which I suspect she is already familiar. I shall question Mrs. Hudson later. Until I instruct otherwise, Watson, breathe not a word of this to Miss Adler." Holmes uncovered his eyes but left them closed. "Now then, Doctor, there is more?"

"A corroborative item—I observed Miss Adler's plate at the conclusion of our meal, and I believe she idly, without thinking, made what appeared to be a letter *J* in the remains of her chutney."

Holmes opened his eyes and smiled. "You are devilishly observant, Watson," he said with a wry tone. "*J* for Jasper Girthwood. Note that she wrote the initial of his given name. Yes, it tends to confirm the presumption of familiarity."

"After her voluntary chores were completed," I continued—omitting mention of my nap—"Miss Adler evidently retired to her room, where she has been these past two hours."

"Hum," muttered the detective, staring at the ceiling. "You said you chanced to observe Girthwood—from the bow window, I take it? Describe the man, please."

I related to Holmes the massive vision I had beheld in Baker Street. Upon hearing my description, Holmes's face widened into a sly smile. "Well, the first few shapes are taking form beneath the net, Watson."

"What? How so?"

"My journey in the guise of the workman yielded nothing as to the actual whereabouts of young Hope Maldon, but I did discover that in recent days, inquiries have been made about Breton Mansions, concerning both him and a woman who must be our Miss Adler, in each case by a man who matches your description of Jasper Girthwood."

"Most interesting."

Holmes smiled again. "Ah, but as I replied to Hopkins yesterday, there is something even more interesting."

"And that is…?"

"That he should call here to ask for me," was my friend's response, and then he rose to his feet and walked into his private room to change clothes. Shortly, he emerged as Sherlock Holmes and took to his commonplace book while awaiting Shinwell Johnson's message. I, meanwhile, had resumed work on my remaining correspondence.

Within the hour, Irene Adler came down again. Her manner was more subdued than it had been during our meal and her subsequent helping with chores, yet not as sullen as it had been the afternoon before. Holmes acknowledged her presence with a nod and then returned to his commonplace book. I rose and offered her a chair near myself and whatever conversation I might provide.

"You are well rested, Doctor?" she asked with a coy smile.

"Uh, yes," I replied, glancing at Holmes and then back at her. "I am refreshed."

"Good." The woman stared about the sitting room. "On a day such as this, I incline toward reading as refreshment for myself."

"The library here is a large if disorganized, one," I quietly said by way of apology.

"It may appear disorganized to the casual observer," Holmes said with mock disapproval. Looking up from his commonplace book with a slight squint, he smiled. "My eyesight may be deteriorating, Watson, but my hearing is as sharp as ever. Miss Adler, I do admit that there may be little here to satisfy the taste of the majority of the reading public. If you find nothing, perhaps I can go to our news-agent. There is also a bookseller down the street."

"What would *you* recommend from your own library, sir?" our guest asked Sherlock Holmes.

My friend widened his eyes, shifted his glance to me, and tipped his head as if I should be reading his mind. "The doctor knows."

"Are you certain?" I asked. "I should think something else might—"

"If anyone under this roof might appreciate it other than me, it would be Miss Adler," was all Holmes said, returning to his work.

"Very well." I sighed then stepped to the shelves and pulled down a well-worn volume. "You might examine this. Some in this house consider it the most remarkable book ever penned. Others are not quite as certain of that judgment," said I, reluctantly handing her the book.

"*The Martyrdom of Man*," the woman read aloud. "Winwood Reade, I do not believe I have heard of him. Thank you," she said, taking to a chair by the fire and turning the pages with slow deliberation. I stared at Holmes all the way back to my writing-desk, but he kept his head buried in a pile of clippings.

Very soon thereafter, our telephone rang. Holmes answered its call and, speaking in a low voice with his back turned to us, conversed for several minutes. At the conclusion of the interview, my friend set down the telephone and strode to the hearth, where he asked Miss Adler's initial reaction to Mr. Reade's book.

"Interesting is the word I would apply," she said.

"I might suggest, Miss Adler, that you refrain from skipping any passage. One must start from the very beginning and read each succeeding paragraph. Although Reade's conclusion is an awe-inspiring one, the effect cannot truly be appreciated if you do not make the entire journey continuously from start to finish."

"Was that Shinwell Johnson who rang?" I asked.

"Yes, Watson, it was."

"And did—"

"I shall recount his results in time, Doctor."

I had turned back to my final letter of correspondence when Holmes, still standing, faced the woman and casually remarked, "Oh, if I may ask, Miss Adler, is there any communication you wish me to relate to Mr. Girthwood when he comes round again?"

The woman's eyes opened wide, and as she closed the book in her lap, she regarded Holmes with an expression of surprise. "Mr. Girthwood, did you say? I don't believe—"

"Jasper Girthwood," responded the detective. "The man who has twice left me his card. Jasper Girthwood, whom I must assume, at this point, is the man you and your fiancé have tried to elude. The time is ripe, is it not, to spread out everything upon the table? Keep in mind, Miss Adler, that though in the employ of the cabinet minister, I have taken it upon myself to act on an informal plane to protect your own interests. My intentions in that regard are thoroughly sincere. If I am to protect you in these waters, however, I must know how deep the bottom is."

Irene Adler pressed her palm against the book's cover and slowly caressed its surface. "Yes," she said at last. "You must. Of course you must."

Holmes motioned me to join them, but I had already risen from my writing-desk. Striding across our sitting room, I took to the basket-chair, while my friend now leaned upon the mantelpiece. "Your darker moments in the past twenty-four hours have been inspired by the appearance of Mr. Girthwood in the wings," he said.

"Yes."

"You must have realized I would soon connect the two of you. Why did you not say anything yesterday about him? You knew he had called."

Irene Adler bowed her head before the fire. "I did not know what to do."

Holmes rolled his eyes. "I must say that I find it difficult to believe you are ever at a loss as to what to do, madam."

"You may believe or not believe as you choose, Mr. Holmes!" The woman turned, with an expression of pure anger, to my friend. Wrinkles seized up around her narrowed grey eyes, which then brimmed with tears. "The only flawed belief, perhaps, was mine in thinking I could obtain understanding and help from the likes of you!"

The pair of them glared at each other for what seemed like minutes, each unflinching. "Miss Adler," I quietly implored at last. "And, Holmes, really! Miss Adler, you must forgive this—"

"Please do not speak of forgiving," Holmes told me quietly. Then, to our guest, he said, "Let us, however, if we can, mention forgetting. Watson knows well how my personal imp runs uncontrolled at times. Often we are influenced not so much by what we know is true but rather by what we think is possible. Given my inability to draw definitive conclusions at this time with respect to your fiancé, I fear I have fallen prey to the latter. If you will—if you can, Miss Adler—please forget my remark."

"You are so good at apologies that are not apologies," she said. "You must be well practiced."

Holmes merely shrugged his shoulders.

"I accept your terms nonetheless," she replied at last. "And in contrast," she added, turning toward me, "let me acknowledge and express my appreciation for your genuine concern and compassion, Doctor. I know I shall always be able to rely upon *your* goodwill, come what may." Then, to Holmes, she said tersely, "Your fresh start begins now, sir. Do not waste it."

"I would, of course, appreciate your telling me what you know of Jasper Girthwood," he replied. "Advise me, if you will, on how I must deal with him in representing your interests."

"I have met Mr. Girthwood some few times," said our guest, seeming to choose her words most carefully. "I know him to be an American businessman; *what* business I do not know—save that whatever its nature, it must be quite illegal."

Holmes reached for his cherrywood pipe and toyed with it. "Are you aware of the existence of criminal organizations, Miss Adler?"

"International societies, you mean?"

"Yes. My reference, Watson"—he turned toward me suddenly—"is to the new crime, of which Professor Moriarty was a forerunner: vast monoliths of evil that seek to engulf the world we know. Tell me, Miss Adler, have you gained any impression of whether Girthwood acts alone or on behalf of others and, if the latter, whether they might be members of such organizations?"

"I cannot say, except to note that he was always most sure of himself and seemed to act solely on behalf of his own personal interests rather than those of others."

"Hum, tell me, in exactly what circumstances have you dealt with him?"

"He first approached me claiming to have been an associate of my late husband. Godfrey had never spoken of the man, nor alluded to any individual who might have been him, and I could tell Mr. Girthwood nothing."

"Did his accosting you have any purpose beyond that of mere introduction?"

"Yes. He spoke of some financial dealing that had transpired in the past between himself and Godfrey," said the woman, staring into the fire. "It was a matter that, according to him, ended with Godfrey taking an unfair portion of the profit. I, of course, could be of no use in the matter. Godfrey confided in me then no more than Robert has these past weeks. At the time of my initial response, Mr. Girthwood appeared to accept my claims and let the affair drop."

Holmes merely nodded, prompting the woman to continue her story.

"That was years ago in America. Then we met again, this time when Robert introduced him to me aboard the ship bringing us all to England."

"Girthwood knew your fiancé as well?" asked Holmes.

"They had become acquainted during the voyage, it seemed. I've no doubt that Mr. Girthwood intentionally ingratiated himself with Robert in order to better approach me again."

"I see. Have you any knowledge as to Girthwood's initial purpose in coming to England, other than to contact you again?"

"No, but I am certain of one thing, Mr. Holmes. His travelling on the same ship cannot have been mere coincidence."

"An opinion we share," said the detective. "Did you discuss this with your fiancé?"

"No, indeed—Girthwood acted as if we had never met before, and I pretended the same. I, therefore, never alluded to my earlier meeting with him."

"Why?" asked the detective.

Irene Adler looked at me pleadingly and then at Holmes. "Consider my position, if you can." She, at last, set the book aside, clasped her hands, and then looked down at them. "I saw life with Robert as a new beginning of its own and Girthwood as an incidental reminder of my previous life with Godfrey. To put it simply, as you might wish but refrain from saying aloud, Mr. Holmes, I did not want my future husband to know all of my past life."

"I would—"

"Robert was my new beginning," the woman repeated, this time speaking more to me than to my friend. "I saw a last chance for true happiness and could not bear the thought of losing it. Can you understand?"

Silently, I nodded.

Holmes leaned even more heavily upon the mantel. "Very well. Your fiancé then did not know of your acquaintance with Mr. Girthwood. Are you aware of any subsequent entanglements between the two men?"

"Girthwood was involved in the scheme I told you of yesterday," Miss Adler said. "My understanding was that—whatever the substance of the plan—Girthwood was, in fact, the one who proposed it to Robert."

"That certainly casts a much-different light on this entire matter. I can only urge total honesty from you in the future, Miss Adler."

"I know. Truly, I am sorry. You must comprehend my fear."

"I have a complete comprehension of fear," said Sherlock Holmes, "and an understanding of how to face it. Now, are you absolutely certain that you at no time gleaned any information at all concerning the substance of the plan to be executed in Paris?"

"I gained nothing from any of their discussions, Mr. Holmes. When I was in the company of both men, our talk was little more than forced conversation on the weather or places of interest about the town. It was later, when Robert and Girthwood were closeted together, that they formulated their scheme."

"And your only knowledge of Girthwood has come from these two instances?" Holmes asked, walking back to the sofa to take a seat there. "Earlier, when he approached you with respect to your late husband's estate and, more recently, in the company of your present fiancé?"

Miss Adler seemed to pause as if to think carefully then said, "Those are the only times I have talked at length with the man. On occasion I would see him on the street. Quite often, to tell the truth."

"As if he were following you?"

"Yes," said Irene Adler. "He did follow me."

Holmes made a steeple with his fingers, rubbing the tips slowly together. "What opinions did you subsequently voice to your fiancé concerning Mr. Girthwood?"

"I told Robert that I did not care for the man's company. After some time, I informed him that Mr. Girthwood was following me."

"And what was your fiancé's response?"

Miss Adler looked across the room toward the bow window and frowned. "Robert said my fears were absolutely groundless and asserted that Girthwood was actually protecting us. He said that I should feel more secure when that awful man was following me."

"Did your fiancé ever discuss Girthwood's personal history?"

Miss Adler shook her head. "Other than describing him as a financier, no."

Holmes rested his head upon the sofa back, stared at the ceiling for a moment, and then asked, "I now return to my original question. When Mr. Girthwood calls again, as surely he must, what am I to say to him?"

"You ask my opinion?" our guest replied.

The detective looked at her and smiled wanly. "It is you whom I serve, Miss Adler, as I have tried to stress from the beginning. So, should I admit that you are a guest here at 221?"

"No."

"Then I shall not. Might I tell him you were a guest at 221 but that you have left and I have no knowledge of your current whereabouts? Or should I refuse to admit to your very existence, asserting instead my belief that your remains are still buried under Alpine snow?"

Irene Adler gazed for the longest of times at my friend. "Would it be within your powers of persuasion to convince him I have already returned to America?"

"If the man is possessed of the dogged craftiness I currently assign him, then I rather doubt it," said Holmes. "I took up this case only yesterday, and the weekly liner for New York does not sail until tomorrow. The timing is not right."

"But surely you might convince him I passed through Baker Street last week?"

"He has already made inquiries at Breton Mansions."

At the detective's comment, Miss Adler's complexion paled noticeably.

"I suspect he knows you have been in London during the current week," Holmes said. "How, might I ask, would he come to connect you with 221?"

Irene Adler looked directly at my friend. "I could not resist telling Robert that you and I were acquainted. Your fame is such that I am certain that he in turn mentioned the fact to Mr. Girthwood."

Holmes idly nodded. "In any case, the supposed trip back to America is not a plausible gambit."

"Do you think Mr. Girthwood may have already found Robert himself?" the woman asked cautiously.

"I rather doubt it," Holmes told her with a distracted air.

"You must be the one who finds Robert first."

"If I may suggest," Holmes went on, oblivious to Miss Adler's fervent wish, "a policy of feigned ignorance is still our best choice. Let us assume Girthwood knows you have come here, as I think he must. We shall make it seem you arrived yesterday, presented your case, and left, destination unknown, after I rejected your plea for help."

"And if he does not accept that story?" I asked.

"We shall see," said my companion, smiling.

He was beginning to ask Miss Adler more questions concerning her recent trip to Paris when our telephone rang. Before I could even rise from my chair, Holmes was at the table.

"Halloa, this is Sherlock Holmes," said he. "Yes, I do apologize for that inconvenience. No, I expect to be in for the rest of the day, in fact."

I looked over at Miss Adler, who watched my friend intently, the fingers of her left hand gently caressing the throat of her blouse.

"Yes, but of course you understand that I never discuss any sensitive matter by telephone... If you wish, I have no objection. Of course... That time would suit, yes...Yes, I look forward to it, yes," Holmes continued. He smiled at both Miss Adler and me. "I understand perfectly, yes...Thank you...Good-bye, Mr. Girthwood."

Irene Adler's fingers no longer stroked but rather gripped her blouse. "He is coming here again?"

"He said he would arrive at half-past four," answered Holmes, looking at the clock. "That does not allow enough time to extract as much additional information from you at this sitting as I should prefer, Miss Adler, but it is more than enough for us to prepare 221 for his invasion. Watson, please go down to the ground floor and gather all of Miss Adler's belongings which may be there. Ask Mrs. Hudson; she will know. Oh, and do warn her that supper may be postponed again. Employ the standard apologies, if you will, and instruct her to pretend our guest left yesterday. And you, Miss Adler, have you personal cards or stationery of any kind?"

"I have some few sheets of writing paper, if that is sufficient."

"Good. There is a note, perhaps two, that I wish to dictate to you. Watson," my friend said sharply. "Downstairs, if you please."

I hurried down the stair and, utilizing Mrs. Hudson's mental inventory, collected Miss Adler's coat, hat, and umbrella from the vestibule and brought them back up to the sitting room.

"Put them all in the maid's room for the moment," Holmes said. Then, looking beyond me, he asked, "I assume the doctor may enter your room to do so?"

"Why, yes," said the woman, who sat over my writing-desk with lavender-coloured papers in hand.

"Then upstairs with the lot, Watson," ordered Holmes with a flick of his hand.

I performed my duty, laying the articles gently upon the bed, and after I had descended to the sitting room, I found Miss Adler completing a note as Holmes dictated it to her.

"—sorry that you must refuse my fervent plea," Holmes was saying. "Either the years have changed your character or they have transformed my memory of it. Now I must go seek the help of another who is, I am confident, more understanding. Then please sign your name, Miss Adler, maintaining that same sense of anger of which I spoke earlier...Good, now fold it once there—Stop, excellent, now hand it me. Thank you," said my friend. "Here should be about right," he said, slipping it onto the mantelpiece, the jewelled snuff-box from the king of Bohemia holding it in place. "And the envelope, if you please," he added, coming back to her to receive it. He then held it above the coals until it lit. The detective shook out the flames and set the smoking envelope upon the hearth.

"May I assist in any way?" I asked.

"If I were preparing the room for myself in place of Mr. Girthwood, I should look to hairs upon the antimacassars," replied my friend. "Their present number might suggest a stay longer than several minutes. Hum. Gather up the antimacassars, if you will, old fellow; then take them out and shake each thoroughly."

"Very well," I said glumly. "Perhaps *I* should have the maid's quarters instead," I dryly suggested as I gathered the coverings.

"No, Watson," said Holmes with a distracted air as he surveyed the room. "That will not be necessary, I think. Mr. Girthwood will not be going beyond the first floor."

I descended the stair in a state of mild irritation, only to chance upon Mrs. Hudson, who seized the antimacassars from me after I explained Holmes's request. Our landlady took the pieces to the back yard, where she took advantage of another short spell of dry weather to thoroughly beat them.

"I believe that is more than is necessary, Mrs. Hudson," I said as I stood in the burgeoning shade of her plane tree, looking at the few daffodils that lined the stone walk. "It is only stray hairs that worry him."

"Talk of a person being worried!" snapped Mrs. Hudson. "It's not been often that I'm allowed to keep that room tidy, as you well know, Doctor," the landlady said, swatting each antimacassar with a ferocity that gave me some alarm. "When the spring-clean comes round, Mr. Holmes always declares that floor beyond my touch! As if bullet holes in the walls weren't enough! I do thank you, though, for helping put a stop to him sticking that knife in the mantel. It was a most destructive way of tacking up correspondence!"

"I was glad to be of assistance in the matter."

"I purchased one of those pumping pneumatic cleaners," she continued, "thinking I could treat the carpets on the first floor that way. No need to haul them out here for the beating. But, no, Mr. Holmes simply will not have his quarters disturbed!"

I listened patiently to a few more minutes of Mrs. Hudson's travail then took the cleaned antimacassars from her and bounded up to the sitting room, where I found Holmes and Miss Adler standing in quiet conversation.

"Watson, I think we have but a few more minor details to see to," said Holmes. "Then we must wait."

"And pray," added Irene Adler.

CHAPTER SIX:

A Most Corpulent Fellow

Holmes stood at our bow window, arms crossed, surveying the street even more intently than had I the day before. All traces of Miss Adler's presence were absent from the sitting room, save those the detective had left for a purpose. Despite his earlier assertion that Jasper Girthwood would ascend no higher than the first floor, Holmes had, in the end, decided to evict Miss Adler from the maid's quarters, fearful that any unplanned movement by our guest might be heard in the sitting room below. And so our guest and her baggage were housed in the lumber room at the rear of the topmost floor of 221—lodgings I thought heartless to subject her to, but an arrangement which both Miss Adler and Holmes agreed was the most desirable.

I glanced at the clock and saw that it read nearly half past.

"Holmes," I said, "would you rather that I not—"

"No," he said from the window, his back remaining toward me. "I require your presence, Watson, but I must request that you speak only when spoken to, and even then, make no reference whatsoever to Miss Adler."

"Of course."

"Thank you. You have always steadied me in times such as these, old fellow, more than I have ever troubled to express. Ha! That would be the man, if your description is only half accurate!"

I bolted from my chair and stood beside Holmes, who pointed across Baker Street. There I saw, standing out quite distinctly from the usual crowd, a huge, young gentleman dressed in an Astrakhan coat, cane in one hand, with the same incongruous bowler perched upon his head. He resembled nothing so much as an eccentric bull walrus recently elevated to the Lords. Glancing left as he stepped off the kerb, the man strode slowly and with great effort across the street, aiming directly for the door of 221.

"Mr. Girthwood, I presume," said I.

"In the flesh," replied Holmes. "And most superlatively so."

We heard the bell ring, and when at last our caller had ascended the stair, taking much longer to make that climb than even Stanley Hopkins, Holmes's comment proved more than valid. The individual whom Mrs. Hudson escorted into the sitting room seemed to me more immense than even Mycroft Holmes, my friend's elder brother and vital cog in the machine of the British state. Pouches of fat drooped from Jasper Girthwood's chin and jowls. His hat, once removed, revealed dark curls of hair that wrapped forward on his skull, exuding the smell of lime cream.

"Well, sir, we meet at last!" the man said heartily, stepping forward to grasp Holmes's hand. Our guest removed his greatcoat and tossed it upon the dining table, much to our landlady's consternation. Holmes silently shooed her out as Girthwood slapped his hat and cane down upon the coat.

"Please seat yourself, Mr. Girthwood," advised Holmes. "Allow me to present Dr. John Watson, my associate."

Our caller grunted at me with a smile, his jowls vibrating. "I take it then, sirs," he said, "that I'm to do business with the both of you."

"That is correct," answered my friend. "Dr. Watson is well versed in the Hope Maldon affair."

"Ha! You don't hesitate before jumping, do you, Mr. Holmes? I prefer that quality in those with whom I deal. Gad, sir, give me a leaper to a looker any day, if a bargain's to be struck before evening!"

"Please be seated," repeated my friend.

"In a moment, sir, in a moment," answered Girthwood, warming himself before the coals. "Ah, that is so much better. It's a damp chill I most heartily dislike. Any chill, for that matter. There's the great paradox, you see," Girthwood said, clapping then clasping his hands together. "A man must be careful not to mix business and comfort yet still refuse to do business while in discomfort. Yes, discomfort is the great distracter. Now then, may I?" said the man, gesturing to the sofa, which appeared the only furnishing in the room capable of holding his bulk.

"Please," said Holmes, taking to his armchair while I claimed the basket-chair. "Pray tell us, Mr. Girthwood, what is your stake in the whereabouts of the Honourable Robert Hope Maldon?"

"You seek advantage in the very first sentence, sir. By gad, you're the man for me!"

Holmes merely smiled.

"Yes, the man for me," repeated Girthwood. He then suddenly narrowed his eyes, leaned forward, and said, "And what if I should undertake to hire you, sir? You are in the detection trade, correct? I might be a client. Then should I not be the one to call the tune? Allow me to at once make that very offer. Do you accept, sir?"

"Mr. Girthwood," replied Holmes, who at first reached for his clay pipe then discarded it in favour of the cherrywood. "The card you left earlier this day said you wish to consult me in 'a matter of import to us both.' Since the only professional matter of importance I have at present is the disappearance of Robert Hope Maldon, I assume that is the matter to which you refer."

"Of course it is, sir. Could there ever have been any doubt as to that? A man who states the obvious in one case should be trusted to see the self-evident in the next."

"If you were to, as you say, 'hire' me," Holmes continued. "I should still require information concerning the circumstances of that employment. Thus, Mr. Girthwood, I repeat, what is your stake in the young man's whereabouts?"

"By gad, sir, you are a firm one. No weaving in and out for the likes of you. That is the spirit. Life must be a challenge, eh? Met head on, I tell you." He pulled from his coat a large cigar as Holmes lit his cherrywood pipe. "It is a Corona del Ritz," Girthwood said as he noticed my friend's interest in the cigar. "I daresay you'll find none to better it in this entire city! Would you accept one with my compliments?"

"I thank you, no," replied Sherlock Holmes. "But in a few minutes, I should very much appreciate a sample of its ash."

Girthwood stared at my friend, dumbfounded, and then broke into a hearty laugh. "Ha! By gad, sir, you are a find! A veritable treasure! More and more I know I have come to the right address." He fingered his cigar with delight. "The man for me, indeed, sir!"

"Now then," Holmes said, "you were about to explain your stake in finding Robert Hope Maldon. Has it something to do with your interest in fine gems? Has that brought you here from America, for what I gather is the first time? Is that the nature of your dealings with Hope Maldon?"

Girthwood's rapid intake of breath gave me a start. For the first time, he appeared ill at ease. "How did you come by that set of hypotheses, sir?"

"An impetuous stab, Mr. Girthwood."

"An insufficient answer for my needs," said our guest warily. "I require some explanation. To whom have you spoken?"

"None but yourself."

"Then make yourself clear."

"It is simplicity, I must admit."

"Good. Simple reasons are always the best," answered our visitor.

"Though all faces possess asymmetry in some degree," began Holmes. "That quality in yours is most pronounced about the eyes. Your right eye is heavily lined, as if in response to squinting or holding a loupe. That might suggest astronomical work or a study of microscopic cultures, both of which I reject for various reasons, which I care not to explain. It can also, however, suggest jewellery work or watch-making. Yet, if I may say, your hands have neither the steadiness nor the grace I associate with those professions. Thus, I consider instead the possibility that you have frequent need to evaluate gems. Your tie-pin, by itself, suggests that you at least appreciate them."

Girthwood nodded, admiring his own scarab pin. "A fine stab, I'll give you that," he said guardedly. "If a stab it is."

"As for your recent arrival from America," continued Holmes. "Your accent clearly places that as your place of origin—the mid-Atlantic States, I should think. I surmise you are relatively unacquainted with London, inasmuch as you, a moment ago, referred to 'the city' when we would call it 'the town', and during your approach to 221—we were watching at the window, you see—you glanced left before stepping into the street. While London traffic is still rather chaotic and some drivers still insist on choosing either side, we here would be most likely to first turn our eyes to the right to catch sight of any approaching vehicles before leaving the kerb."

Girthwood's trepidation receded, and he gave a friendly, if cautious, smile. "A logician of the first water! As I walked here, I kept telling myself that I was coming to the right man, and, by gad, I have. You reassure me, sir. But let me say, Mr. Holmes, that if *my* hands were filled with truths, deductive or otherwise, I should be very careful when and how I might open them."

Holmes remained impassive. Girthwood glanced at me but seemed not to notice my presence.

"But, yes, you want to know why I am concerned with Robert Hope Maldon. Well, he is a relatively new business associate of mine, for that, indeed, is what he is. Not that the two of us are partners in a—you would call it a limited, wouldn't you? Well, sir, the point is that our arrangement is what you might also call somewhat flexible, involving, well, forms of barter, shall we say?"

"Unlawful forms?" asked my friend, setting down his pipe.

Girthwood's smile vanished and then reappeared in an even less sincere form. "We must tread very carefully here, the two of us, Mr. Holmes. Discretion forces me to merely repeat that Maldon and I have done business in the form of barter. Now it is your turn to try again."

"What else will you tell me?" asked Holmes, as if our guest were an untrained puppy. He looked down at his pipe but did not touch it.

"I'll tell you that the man has something of mine, something, which by right of the previous arrangement I alluded to, should have long ago passed into my hands. Instead, Mr. Hope Maldon has kept the object for himself alone." Girthwood smiled. "Perhaps you already know what that object is?"

Holmes absently crossed his arms. He looked across to me and then stared at the ceiling. "I fear I do not. Perhaps you will tell me."

After a moment of agitated thought, Girthwood extended his cigar over a tray. "There, sir. There are the ashes you requested."

Holmes nodded appreciatively.

"Your presumed inability to answer my question reveals a great deal to me, sir."

"Mr. Girthwood, you expect me to know more than I do?"

"Yes, and now I must weigh your answers most carefully."

Holmes smiled. "That is the trick, is it not? Is my ignorance real or feigned? Are my answers woven from imagination or reality?"

"To throw me off the scent, yes," said Girthwood, laughing. "Cat and mouse, sir. Yes, I could tell the moment I stepped into this room. It's cat and mouse with you all the way, isn't it?"

"It is that only if you insist that it be so."

"By gad, I'll venture that it is the only way to deal with the likes of you, isn't it?" Girthwood shook with laughter, so much so that he was forced to set down his cigar. "Am I correct, sir?" the man asked of me.

Before I could respond, Girthwood asked Holmes, "Well then, what of *her?*"

"Her?"

"Oh, come now, sir! Squeak, squeak! Meow! By gad, what a joy!"

Holmes reached for his pipe, stared at Girthwood for a moment, and then said, "You realize that she came here."

"Yes, of course I do."

"But you do not realize she left almost immediately?"

"Indeed I do not, Mr. Holmes." The man looked down while fingering his lapels. "You see, I believe my men would have noticed."

"Unless your men were themselves noticed," replied Holmes. "Noticed by their presence or absence."

Both men smiled at one another.

"You are a prodigious bluffer, sir," said Girthwood at last.

Holmes said nothing.

"*My* men didn't see a thing, sir," Girthwood said.

"Do you believe *I* should wish it any other way?"

Girthwood ceased to smile. "If she is not here, then where did she go?"

"I know not," replied Holmes. The detective toyed with his pipe. "Allow me, Mr. Girthwood, to give you the sum of my knowledge."

"A partial sum?"

"The sum total," Holmes said. "I was engaged yesterday by a client, whom I cannot identify, save to say that he is male."

"Oh, really?" exclaimed Girthwood.

"The client wishes me to locate Robert Hope Maldon."

"I'll bet he does," said Girthwood contemptuously. "With what care do you choose your clients, sir?"

"Some may consider my choices careless," answered Holmes. "But they remain my choices nonetheless."

"I won't argue that philosophy, sir. If I'm going to sleep in a bed, I'll be the one who makes it."

"I have since then conducted initial investigations in two or three selected places about town," Holmes went on. "My findings may, perhaps, prove useful, but they have as yet yielded no hint of the young man's whereabouts."

"Your investigations have much in common with mine then," our visitor said.

"Yesterday Dr. Watson and I were visited by a woman also wishing to locate Mr. Hope Maldon. She believed I might help her, but I informed her that I was already bound to another client for that purpose."

"And she left?"

"Yes, although she did send round a letter in her own hand that evening."

"You still have that letter?"

"I believe Watson placed it somewhere. Watson?"

"The mantel, I think," was my response. "I recall you asked me to place it there."

"Yes, of course," said Holmes. "Allow me to——"

"Oh, I wouldn't think of it, sir!" said Girthwood, who, with great effort, rose. "The mantel, you say?"

"It should be there amid the clutter, if the doctor says it is. Rose-colored paper, was it not, Watson?"

"Lavender, Holmes."

"Ah, yes, lavender. You may——"

"Perhaps this one," said Girthwood, already poking among the artifacts strewn along the width of the mantel. "My God!" exclaimed the man, casting eyes upon the king of Bohemia's snuff-box. He picked up the gift, turning it end over end. Then, self-consciously and with some embarrassment drawing out a loupe from his pocket, he examined the jewels more closely. "Gad, sir! Do you realize the value of the piece you have here?"

"I believe I do," Holmes told him.

"Have you no deposit box?"

"Dr. Watson employs a firm in Charing Cross. Why do you ask?"

"The fireplace is no place for a work like this!" said Girthwood, examining the amethyst. He widened his eye, allowing the loupe to drop suddenly into the outstretched mat of his hand. "Do you have insurance?"

"You mean a policy of some sort?" asked Holmes with an innocent air. "Why, no. Can you suggest an agent?"

"Well put, sir," said Girthwood, returning the loupe to his coat pocket. "Mince no words, I say, or your enemies will make mince-meat of you."

"Are we now enemies, Mr. Girthwood?"

"I sincerely hope not," said our guest, returning the box gently to the mantel and taking up the letter Holmes had dictated earlier in the day. "Yes," Girthwood said as he began reading the note. "Ha, yes!" He finished reading and placed the sheet back beside the snuff-box then seemed to notice the half-burned envelope in the hearth. "Tell me," he said, "have you any expectation of hearing from this woman again?"

"I cannot say. I must certainly consider it possible, if not extremely probable."

"Does your intuition as a 'private-consulting detective' tell you anything?"

"It tells me she will not return," Holmes said. "I believe my initial refusal angered her mightily, and I have found that women's scorn is characterized by great inertia."

"You've hit the mark there, sir. Well, I shall leave you gentlemen now," Girthwood declared, stepping over to his cigar to extinguish it. "You may have what is left of the Corona del Ritz, sir, as a token of my goodwill. Perhaps our business will continue, perhaps not." He strode to the table to collect his hat, cane, and coat; Holmes made no effort to rise and assist him. "Allow me to leave a message, which I suggest you convey to your male client and to any female visitors you may have in the days to come: the *rara avis* is mine. Can you remember that?"

"But of course."

"Good," said the man, his face flushed. "It seems we can make no more meaningful progress today, sir. Any additional exchange of information would most decidedly not be in my favour. Perhaps a time will come, Mr. Holmes, when the opportunity for further negotiations will arise."

Holmes nodded from his chair.

"I shall show myself out. Good-day to the pair of you!" So saying, he left the room and descended toward the street.

"Cheeky fellow," I whispered while listening to the stairs suffer under his weight.

"But possibly dangerous," said Holmes, who rose and walked to his table to collect a celluloid envelope, into which he emptied ash from Girthwood's cigar. "His coy manner is a veneer, Watson. Scratch it, and you will find pure malevolence underneath. Trust to it, for I know his sort." He strode quickly to the window and looked down into Baker Street.

"There is now the implication that 221 is being watched," I said quietly.

"Perhaps, though I think not yet," said Holmes, taking the pipe from his mouth and pointing it down three times. "He does not signal to anyone in the street. In addition, when I was out as the workman today, I spent thirty minutes just outside 221 to determine if any such surveillance was under way." He turned from the window. "I detected none. It would not surprise me, however, if Girthwood were to now engage someone to watch this house, though the fact that the man is new to London will, no doubt, work to our advantage."

"Shall I fetch Miss Adler now?" I inquired.

"By all means, do so. The wait must have been a most uncomfortable one for her. Indeed," said he, "allow me to join you. Together, we shall re-establish her in the maid's quarters."

We both ascended the stair to the lumber room, where we assured Miss Adler that Jasper Girthwood had left, and then returned the woman to her room. Once restored to the room opposite mine, our guest accompanied us down to the sitting room, where Holmes briefly recounted the substance of his interview with Mr. Girthwood.

"Do you think he sincerely believes I left to seek aid elsewhere?" Miss Adler inquired.

"I rather doubt the man does anything sincerely," Holmes replied. "In the present case, I expect him to still harbour doubts. One additional item must be mentioned, Miss Adler. He did ask that I convey to you, should I have the opportunity, the fact that the *rara avis* is his by rights, and he expects it back."

"I've no rare bird, Mr. Holmes," said Irene Adler at once.

"Have you any idea to what artifact he might have been referring?"

"None at all. As I have told you, the details of what transpired between Mr. Girthwood and Robert are unknown to me."

"We may not know," said Holmes, taking the basket-chair, "but I think we may surmise."

"Surmise what?" I asked from the hearth.

"All evidence would suggest that the scheme Miss Adler's fiancé and Mr. Girthwood undertook centred round obtaining some *objet d'art*. However, there appears to have been a falling out. My supposition, Miss Adler, is that your fiancé undertook to obtain the artifact alone. He might well have decided there was no need to share its value with Mr. Girthwood and, thus, proceeded to Paris with only you. Is that possible, do you think?"

"I suppose I could imagine him so desperate as to take that course," replied the woman.

"Please pardon the effrontery of my next question. Do you think your fiancé capable of leaving Paris with no intention of sharing its value with *you*?"

"I do not," was Irene Adler's cold response.

"Mr. Girthwood asserted the object, whatever it is, to be his," I quickly added. "Could it be that Hope Maldon stole it from him?"

"No, Watson, I believe the original scheme involved both men and that, together, they sought to obtain some object from a third party. I think it probable that Girthwood was the one who located and identified the object in the first place and then lured Hope Maldon into providing the funds necessary for the execution of the plan. If that is so, then we know more about our rotund nemesis."

"And what is that?" I inquired, noticing that Miss Adler took great interest in my friend's assertion.

"That he himself lacks funds and is thus unconnected with any vast criminal organization. In short, his recent displays aside, Mr. Girthwood may be the real 'prodigious bluffer' among us all."

"We should then discount him?"

"For our own safety and that of Miss Adler, I believe we should not. The lowlife of London will often work on speculation, Watson, if the potential stakes are great enough. Mr. Girthwood may well be capable of eventually surrounding himself with an improvised group of his own."

"And so what is our next step?"

"First we shall inform Mrs. Hudson that the path is now clear for supper," said he. "I had earlier, by telephone, set Shinwell Johnson upon the trail of one or two additional lines of inquiry, and he may ring us yet again. Until then, Miss Adler may return to the wonders of Mr. Reade's book, you may continue your correspondence, and I have yet to examine the day's newspapers."

And so we each engaged in our individual pastimes while our landlady prepared the evening meal. It was then during supper, as Holmes was expounding on the relationship of chestnut trees to the American character, that we heard the house bell ring yet again.

Holmes set down his knife and fork and patted his napkin to his lips. "Allow me to see for myself," he said, rising from the table. As he approached the open door to our sitting room, the detective was confronted by Mrs. Hudson, carrying an envelope.

"It's for the dear," she said. "I told the messenger who delivered it that she had left yesterday, as you'd instructed," Mrs. Hudson went on. "But I took the liberty of saying we could see that she received it, expecting you'd want to see the contents."

"Good," said Holmes, taking the envelope from her and carrying it to Irene Adler. "Please stay, Mrs. Hudson. It is a calculated risk that Girthwood did not send it as a ruse, but by accepting this, we may gain more than we give away. Miss Adler, if you please?" he said.

Our guest opened the envelope and removed from it a card. Then, with an intake of breath, she let go of the paper, allowing it to drop onto the table.

"Robert!" she said with a shocked excitement that frightened me in its violence. "This must be from Robert!" she exclaimed in disbelief.

"May I?" asked Holmes, who, with the woman's permission, took the card in hand. "It is blank on one side," he said, turning it over. "And on the back is but one word—cut from a newspaper and pasted onto the paper—'Soon.'"

"From Robert!" exclaimed Miss Adler again.

"Should we perhaps determine the origin of this?" I offered.

"A good point, Watson," replied Holmes, who turned to our landlady. "Mrs. Hudson, did you think—"

"To ask the messenger whence he came," she completed. "Of course, Mr. Holmes. It was from the Langham Hotel."

"Why should your fiancé send you such a message?" asked the detective. "If he knows you are here, why does he not use the telephone?"

"I cannot say," she replied. "As you recall, I have made mention of the fact that I was acquainted with you, though I did not explain the circumstances." In a wavering voice, she added, "It seems as if mysteries are growing faster than our understanding of them."

"All will come right," I said in consolation. "You have a rock of support here in Baker Street, Miss Adler."

"Please allow me to return to the issues at hand," said Holmes with mild irritation. "Miss Adler, it appears that you must stay and hope your fiancé comes to you."

"But what of Mr. Girthwood? If my Robert attempts to come here, does he not stand in danger of being intercepted? "

"Yes," said Holmes. "Watson, I believe matters are piled high with complexity, so much so that we may have to engage the full resources of this agency."

"Not only Johnson, but Pike and Hollins as well?"

"Yes, and Upshaw, Mercer, and Stannard in addition. One way or other, Miss Adler, this fortress will be secured."

"Are you certain?" the woman asked.

"We can but try to make it so," replied Sherlock Holmes.

CHAPTER SEVEN:

Two Visitors

The second full day of Irene Adler's presence under our roof dawned quietly. I descended to the sitting room to find that, once more, Holmes had been the first of our party to be about and Miss Adler would be the last. My friend greeted me from the carpet, where he lay surveying the agony columns from a much-rumpled copy of the *Daily Gazette*. This accustomed position did not surprise me, though I was taken aback by his being dressed for the street rather than draped in one of his dressing-gowns.

"If you will allow, Watson, I shall ring for your breakfast presently. This day's work may prove demanding, and we must be off the mark without delay."

"Numerous destinations lie ahead?" I inquired.

"For me, perhaps," the detective replied. "But the demands, I fear, may, in the end, fall disproportionately upon you."

After a moment silently spent in my own exercise of deduction, I said, with an air of mild disappointment, "I am to remain here to guard Miss Adler."

"Yes, and you understand I should entrust that duty to no one else?"

I smiled modestly.

"In this matter, I do not jest, Watson. Shinwell Johnson and his peers have proven a great boon to this agency, but some tasks are beyond their ken."

"Perhaps that is the burden you bear for having no peer in this realm."

"I've no need for ingratiating comments, Doctor. Save that phrase for your narrative of this case, in the event, heaven forbid, that it is ever written."

"The case must write itself first, unless you already have an ending."

"One way or another, there will be an end to it," Holmes muttered. "Though the substance of that final curtain, I currently know not." With effort, he rose to his feet and, sighing, gathered up the remains of the newspaper. "Your own copy of the *Chronicle* is there, intact, upon the table, old fellow. But to continue my previous thread, I shall be out the balance of this morning, and while, as I remarked last evening, I think it unlikely that our Mr. Girthwood has yet mustered forces with which to assault 221, we cannot be absolutely certain."

"Is there no other address at which Miss Adler might be more secure? Should we not take Stanley Hopkins into our confidence?"

"Neither suggestion appeals," my friend replied. "Baker Street is the nexus of our operation, a centre we can ill afford to do without, and to place our guest elsewhere would divide our forces. Moreover, if the message of last evening is to be believed, young Mr. Hope Maldon will arrive here soon. On the other hand, giving greater play to the Yard would compromise Miss Adler's need to remain deceased in the public eye in general and in that of the king of Bohemia in particular. No, this shall be our one and only fortress, and our own troops shall be the only forces involved. And you, Watson, must be their commander in my place while I reconnoitre."

"Your dress suggests to me that your departure is imminent."

"You've assumed my attributes already. Good!" said he. "I expect to return by mid-day, but do not be alarmed if I do not. Pray, Watson, admit no one above the ground floor. If Girthwood should call, you are home but ill; do not receive him. If it is Hopkins, attend to him downstairs if you must. As you can, maintain a casual watch upon the street. Trust that you will not be left completely alone. Earlier this morning, I gave much the same directives to Mrs. Hudson, and I instructed Shinwell Johnson to post two of our men outside."

"I shall recognize them?"

"They are Upshaw and Mercer; both are already on duty outside."

"Ah, good. Holmes, should I consider keeping my service revolver at the ready?" I asked as I reached for my newspaper.

My friend took his coat and hat and then paused for a moment of thought. "Place it unloaded where it may be brandished," he said, "but no more. I truly believe Girthwood is not yet a physical threat to us, but we must not be complacent."

"I understand."

"As you always do," he said, taking my free hand to bid me good-bye. "I shall return, I hope, within a few hours."

With that remark, Sherlock Holmes descended the stair, left 221, and strode out into Baker Street. Looking from the bow window, I saw him nod imperceptibly to Upshaw, one of the junior agents, who leaned against a shop window, consuming a biscuit. The young man slowly rotated his gaze upward, and our eyes met. I held up my folded copy of the *Chronicle*, and he touched his free hand to the brim of his cap. Then, casually, I strode to my small trunk, opened it, and uncovered my pistol.

"Your breakfast, Doctor," said Mrs. Hudson from the open sitting room door. "Here's curried fowl, eggs, and ham."

"Thank you," I replied, quickly covering the weapon that had travelled with me round the world. I turned to meet our landlady.

"Have you any changes in the orders Mr. Holmes gave?" she asked.

"None," I answered. "Thank you, Mrs. Hudson."

It was only when she had reached the bottom of the stair that I removed my unloaded pistol and cached it in my writing desk. As I began my breakfast, I heard Miss Adler coming down. We said our greetings, and then, with the woman's permission, I rang Mrs. Hudson for a second plate. Within minutes, Irene Adler and I were each enjoying hearty servings of fowl and eggs.

"Doctor," said Miss Adler suddenly. "Is this house being watched? I have caught sight of a stranger lounging outside in the back."

I put down my cup. "Yes," I told her. "We are guarded by Holmes's men, and rest assured that everything is being done to protect you. In particular, I shall remain here with you at all times."

"And Mrs. Hudson?"

"And Mrs. Hudson, too, of course. What that woman has done in the service of the agency may astonish you. Might I relate some of that history at some point?"

"After breakfast, I would be delighted to hear your stories, as I have enjoyed reading them."

"Yes," I said, putting my napkin to my mouth. "You paid me that compliment earlier, as I recall. Wish you more fruit?"

At almost the moment our meal was completed, Mrs. Hudson stepped in to take away the remains. As I rose to give our landlady full play of the table, I heard the house bell ring.

"I shall run down and see who it is!" cried Mrs. Hudson, who set our empty plates back upon the table and took to the stair at once. I, meanwhile, strode to the bow window and looked down. A man stood there before our door, which opened, prompting him to remove his hat. The full head of hair thus revealed allowed me to recognize him at once, and bidding Miss Adler to remain quietly in the sitting room, I hurried down and assumed control of the situation.

"Mr. Watson!" said Diarmund Stephenson from the open doorway. "Dr. Watson, I mean," he added, dipping his head and putting fingers to his mouth. "Dr. Watson, yes. May I step in?" he asked, looking back and forth between myself and the landlady.

"Yes, of course. This is Mr. Stephenson," I said to Mrs. Hudson, "secretary to our current client. I shall receive him there in the waiting room, if it will suit. Oh, and, Mrs. Hudson, please go on with that other chore you spoke of. My plate can wait to be cleared upstairs," I said, so that Stephenson might not accidentally observe evidence that two people had breakfasted above.

"Yes," replied Mrs. Hudson, seemingly understanding the reason behind my request. She retired to the kitchen area, while I led Stephenson into the waiting room.

"How may I help you?"

"Is Mr. Holmes about?" the young man asked, taking to a chair.

"He is out at present. I expect him to return later in the day." I gathered the ends of my coat and sat down in an identical chair opposite him.

"I see. Well, then I am uncertain as to how to proceed. I had wished to speak to Sherlock Holmes, you see."

"Does it concern Mr. Hope Maldon?"

"It does."

"Mr. Stephenson, please trust me when I say that were Sherlock Holmes present, he would tell you to treat me as his full partner," I said boastfully, though my intent was to pry information from Stephenson rather than proclaim my own self-importance. Leaning back, I made a steeple with my fingers. "What you came to tell him, you may relate to me instead."

"Well, of course I trust your word, sir," the secretary said, coming forward in his chair to sit earnestly on its edge. "We all know Robert's missing. That's why you and Dr.—I mean, Mr. Holmes were there the other day. Lord Monsbury wishes to find Robert, does he not?"

"Go on," I urged, ignoring the question with purpose.

"Well, I believe there's more to this than the mere disappearance of a person, Dr. Watson. I believe that some property of the minister is gone as well. Were the two of you aware of that?"

"Why do you suspect this?" I asked, again wishing to reveal nothing to my visitor.

"I am truly reluctant to say. It would place me in a very bad light, I fear."

"How so?"

"I shall seem the very model of impropriety, Dr. Watson, but I suppose I must spill out the entire truth before you. The fact is that, from time to time, I check upon certain possessions of the earl."

"Please explain."

"Lord Monsbury's house holds a number of valuables, as one would expect. A number of these are kept in a wall safe in his study."

"You know where that safe is located?"

"Yes, and I know where a spare key to it is hidden in the library."

I paused to form my next remark. "And you periodically check the contents of the safe. That seems most irregular. Can you tell me why you do this?"

"For a bit of larcenous fun in the beginning, I suppose," the young man said. He pushed back his rambling head of hair. "I rather enjoyed pulling out all the important papers and jewels and such, holding them, and then putting them back."

"But you never removed any of these items."

"Not permanently, no. Indeed, after awhile, I convinced myself that I was doing right by the earl in taking my inventory of the safe every few weeks."

"Of course. But you said something was missing?"

"They are corporate shares, Dr. Watson. They first came into the safe some time ago. I know not from whom the earl obtained them; however, after you and Mr. Holmes paid your visit two days ago, I had the opportunity, while Lord Monsbury was away, to again perform a survey of the assets stored in the safe. The shares were gone, sir!"

I writhed slightly in my chair, reaching for a comment that was on the tip of my tongue. "They were gone, you say," were, however, the words that tumbled out.

"Gone, yes! Suddenly, just like that! Everything else was still there: the jewels of his late wife, various deeds, and other contracts." He paused for one moment and then, in a hushed tone, added, "The Victoria Cross awarded his late brother."

"But why should the shares be considered missing?" I asked, grasping what I wished to say. "Perhaps Lord Monsbury removed them himself. To be absent is one thing, to be missing quite another."

Stephenson looked down and blushed. "Perhaps. I cannot help but think, however, that if the shares truly are missing, Lord Monsbury might well cast his suspicions upon poor Robert."

"You are truly concerned for the young man's welfare."

"I am, Dr. Watson. I told you at Lennox Square that I have seen Robert socially without the knowledge of his father. Let me now add that Robert has confided a great deal to me. He is now as a younger brother to me," he declared with a wistful smile. "I have, I suppose, gone behind Lord Monsbury's back in this, but to me even imagined blood is thicker than employment."

"What is the nature of these confidences?"

"They are personal," said the young man. "I refer to them only to underscore my genuine affection for Robert. We have spent several afternoons of comradeship at the Criterion and other—"

"The Criterion?"

"Yes. You are familiar with the place?"

"It has a place in my heart as well as my palate," I said. "Mr. Stephenson, I regret that I cannot reveal to you any of the confidential details to which Sherlock Holmes and I have been privy during the short course of this investigation. I will note your concerns to my friend, and I am certain he will gladly offer all that he can to ease your anxiety."

"Any such assurance I gladly accept. May I, however, ask but one more question? Does Lord Monsbury know the shares are gone from his safe? Has he mentioned them to Mr. Holmes?"

"If I knew the answer, I would not say," I replied.

"And do you know?"

"I cannot say yes or no even to that," I replied. "Surely you understand my position."

"Oh, I do," Stephenson said earnestly, rising to his feet. "Please forgive my presumption. Mark it down to concern for Robert, if you will."

"I shall," I said, standing also. "I think it speaks well of you and your character." After brief parting pleasantries, which included comparisons of the Criterion, I showed him the door, bade him farewell, and ascended the stair.

"Who was the visitor?" Irene Adler asked as I entered the sitting room.

"It was Diarmund Stephenson," I answered. "The secretary to your young man's father."

"Ah, yes," Miss Adler said. "Robert has mentioned him to me many times, describing him as a dear friend. Did he refer to me in any way?"

"No. Would you have expected him to do so?"

"I cannot say. Robert claimed to have never revealed his relation to me to anyone else, but that is not to say he did not."

Just then I heard the house door open and close.

"It is so early," I said. "Could that be Holmes?"

It was. I quickly began down the stair to provide him with the details of Stephenson's visit, but my friend halted me midway and forced an upward retreat before his relentless tread.

"Quickly to work, Watson!" he said, his hat and coat not yet removed. "Yet another caller approaches!"

"Who?" I asked as he shepherded me back into the sitting room.

"Miss Adler, please retire promptly to your quarters and bolt the door."

"Is it Mr. Girthwood?" I asked.

"No, I believe it to be his emissary."

"What is his appearance?" the woman asked, with sudden alarm.

"I do not know his name, but I am acquainted with his like," replied Holmes. "Trust me when I say all will be well. Upstairs, please."

With some trepidation, our guest quickly ascended the stair to the maid's room. As I heard the bolt slide shut, the house bell rang below. From the stair, we could see Mrs. Hudson approach the door. Our landlady looked up to see Holmes nod vigorously. The detective then, again, herded me back into the sitting room and closed the door.

"I gave her instructions as I entered. You will recall that when Shinwell Johnson last rang us up Mister Girthwood had yet to call here."

"Yes, I suppose," I said out of courtesy, my mind unable to sort out the last two days' chronology in so short a time.

"I told Johnson to station himself in Baker Street," Holmes continued, taking off his coat and hat. "He was outside in Baker Street when Girthwood arrived. If you also will recall, when Girthwood left, I went to the window and pointed at him three times with my pipe."

"A signal to Johnson to follow the man," I declared.

"Yes," said my friend. "Please take a chair at the table. We should make these plates appear to be our own. Did you say that Mister Stephenson had called in my absence?"

"Yes, just as Miss Adler and I finished breakfast. But back to Shinwell Johnson."

"Yes, of course. Well, Johnson followed Girthwood back to his rooms and rang me a second time to inform me of the man's location."

A knock came at the sitting room door.

"Enter," said Holmes.

Mrs. Hudson came into the room. "A Mr. Starkey, sir," she said with a touch of disdain.

"Is he a short, weasely, young fellow with a tattered silk waistcoat?"

"That's the one."

"Send him up, Mrs. Hudson, if you will. Oh, and one more instruction…"

"Yes, Mr. Holmes?"

"Once you bring him here, please retire to your room and bolt the door."

"Mr. Holmes, is—"

"There is no need for worry," said the detective. "I am merely becoming more protective of those around me as my active career draws to a close. Go now, please, and bring up this Mr. Starkey."

"As you wish," said a disappointed Mrs. Hudson.

"I truly doubt we have much need for alarm," Holmes assured me. "But have you your service revolver stored somewhere?"

"It is in the writing-desk but unloaded, as you directed. Shall I quickly get my ammunition?"

"I think not," said Holmes, joining me at the table. "We have better arguments at present than an Eley's No. 2. But allow me to finish my tale before our visitor ascends the stair. Having ascertained Girthwood's base of operations—he has rooms at the Waymore—I made a point of ostentatiously nosing about. I then paid another visit to the offices of Mr. Crabbe, which produced nothing new, then set back for Baker Street. Along the way, I acquired this young fellow"—he motioned toward the door, whence we could hear the tread of approaching feet—"who trailed me home with all the furtive clumsiness he could muster. I had no absolute certainty he would call at 221, but here he comes now."

"Mr. Holmes," said our landlady. "Mr. Vic Starkey."

Our visitor was but a youth, perhaps not even twenty years of age, and Holmes's description of him as weaselly was most apt. His muted yellow waistcoat was silk but ragged beyond belief and in combination with his dirty brown pants and jacket produced an unpleasant vision. A dusty billycock remained perched upon his pale head.

"Greetings," said Holmes evenly, rising from the table as Mrs. Hudson quickly closed the door and retreated down the hall. "Will you take a chair by the—"

"What I'll take won't be a chair!" snarled our caller, the weasel suddenly trading places with a runt of a badger. "Just hope I don't take both your lives in the bargain!" he cried, pulling a knife from his coat.

"Doctor," said Holmes evenly, "please refrain from any writing just yet."

"What's that?" said the young man.

"Nothing," replied Holmes. "After Dr. Watson and I finished our meal here, he was going to—"

"So you're the croaker," said Starkey, staring at me. "And you," he continued, turning toward my friend. "You're Holmes, the bogey."

"And you must be Starkey, the whizzer."

"Vic Starkey ain't no whizzer!" protested the man. "Haven't lifted pockets since I was ten. If you two are looking for Barney, then say otherwise, eh?"

"I'm not wanting to fight you, but if you don't pick pockets, then what do you pick?" Holmes asked calmly.

"Pickings," said Starkey, waving the knife ostentatiously. He began to laugh disdainfully. "I pick pickings. I blag what I choose."

"What do you want here?" asked Holmes, stepping slowly toward the young man.

"I heard you got dabble here yourself," Starkey replied. "And halt that! Stop, or get a taste of the chiv here. That's it. Don't advance no farther. And you stay in that chair," he ordered me sternly.

"Mr. Girthwood sent you, did he not?" asked Holmes. "He told you we have property stolen from him that he wants back. Is that the story?"

"I don't needs to tell you nothing."

"Did you learn your manners in that district known as the Jago,[5] Mr. Starkey?" Holmes inquired.

Our visitor smiled and brandished the knife again.

"Tell me, where do you live now?" Holmes continued. "The Jago, after all, has been torn down."

"Hoxton, mostly. I live in Hoxton. You got a better place to recommend?"

"Hoxton, eh? Tell me, have you ever worked with the likes of Cupperly, Warren, or Uncle Bill Briggs?"

"No, never had the pleasure or the honour—yet. Two of them is all away, anyway."

---

5   The Jago is a fictional East End slum described in Arthur Morrison's 1894 novel *A Child of the Jago* and generally thought to represent the real district then known as the Old Nichol.

"In the jug?"

"That's what I heard about Cupperly and Warren. Maybe when they gets out, you'll give me a reference, eh? But for right now, I'm wanting the dabble."

"I'm afraid you'll have to describe it," insisted Holmes.

Starkey's eyes narrowed. Motioning with the knife, he directed Holmes to move away from our table.

"As you wish," said the detective with a smile. "But, if you please, a description of Mr. Girthwood's property?"

"Black bird," Vic Starkey muttered. "A black bird statue's what I'm after, and no mind about whose it is. The man what paid me—and I'm giving no names—he paid me enough dropsy so as I believe it's his."

"Could more from us change your mind?"

"I don't want no rent from you," Starkey said with a laugh. "And they all used to say you was Saint George and more. There was days when you had everybody in the old Jago trembling, Mr. Sherlock Holmes, but I guess you're no more what you were than the Jago is now, eh? Look at me, nineteen, and who wants to pay me rent? Sherlock Holmes. Ha!"

Holmes shook his head. "The more common the criminal, the greater the bluster."

The ragged youth laughed so hard that he was forced to sigh, and in that moment of relaxation, Holmes's left foot snapped sharply into the air, kicking the knife from Starkey's hand. I heard a cry of pain then saw my friend turn round once to his right, and as all of time seemed to expand in my perception, his left shoe wheeled in a graceful orbit of his body, only to strike sharply upon our visitor's chest.

The sense of eternity popped as might a bubble. Starkey stumbled backward and then surged forward to the table where I sat. Again, I heard the shout of pain, and then I realized it was coming from Holmes. Looking up, I saw Starkey, with eyes wild, holding tightly onto the table edge and shaking his head to recover his senses. At once I grasped a fork and plunged it into the back of his right hand.

The youth screamed and frantically flailed his fists about. I darted from my chair, throwing it into Starkey as his wild blows missed me. Scrambling toward my writing-desk, I looked back to see Holmes writhing on the floor, clutching his leg. Starkey's motion had regained some method, and amid constant cursing, he careened toward the hearth, where his dagger had landed.

"I cannot reach my crop!" cried Holmes. "Stop him, Watson!"

Acting rather than thinking, I grasped the most immediate object—a thick pile of foolscap that was my latest set of manuscripts. Striding forward toward the coals as Starkey reached down for his blade, I swung the mass of paper in a low arc and landed a blow that was enough to send our lurching assailant to the floor. As my sheets scattered across the room, I took the slightly bent fire iron from its stand near the hearth and struck the young man a vicious blow upon the knee. As he seized his joint in agony,

I ran—still clutching the iron—to my writing-desk, took up my old service revolver, and held a steady bead upon the enemy.

"Well done!" cried Holmes, who had crawled to the edge of the room to seize his riding crop and now sat with his back to the wall, massaging his outstretched left leg with his free hand. "I congratulate you for, at last, putting that foolscap to good use, Watson."

"Holmes," I said nervously, edging closer to both him and the still-writhing Starkey. "Are you injured?"

"Somewhat," was his reply. "Though it is self-inflicted and largely to my pride. At my age, I must not permit several years to elapse between exercises of baritsu."

"Shall I help you up then?" I offered.

"No, keep your revolver trained," said he, crawling closer to the fire. "I shall call Mrs. Hudson after performing one last urgent task."

"And what is that?" I asked, keeping careful watch of Starkey. "Recovering the knife from his reach?"

"No," said Holmes, reaching the hearth. "Saving, against my better judgment, a good portion of your manuscript." He reached out and pulled several pages of foolscap from the dwindling fire and patted out the flames. "There," he said. "I have made the ultimate sacrifice so that you may continue to torment the reading public. Now for the knife," he added, taking the dagger in hand and lightly tossing it across the room so that it landed at my feet.

Keeping a vigilant watch on our visitor, I kicked the knife into the corner behind me.

With great but careful effort, my friend rose to his feet and limped across the room and rang for our landlady. "Mrs. Hudson!" he called loudly down hall. "All is well! Please attend us!"

Leaning on the doorway frame, Holmes surveyed the disorder and then fixed his attention on Vic Starkey, now sitting sullenly on our hearth rug, holding his bleeding hand. "I'll do what I can for you, Mr. Starkey," the detective offered.

"And I'll remind you that I am a doctor," I added.

"They can give me a carpet or a stretch," muttered the youth. "Throw me in the Scrubs, if they like. I won't break! Not Vic Starkey!"

"Well, I shall ring up Hopkins, if I can," said Holmes, limping to a chair as I heard Mrs. Hudson's door open at the end of the hall. "And, in either case, we shall tell one of the agents outside to go for a policeman."

In the ensuing minutes, that is what occurred. In due course, Vic Starkey was taken away, and Holmes rang up Stanley Hopkins. Our sitting room was restored to its usual state—"Disordered, but by your own doing," was how Mrs. Hudson described it—and Irene Adler emerged at length from what I now considered her prison cell.

"I heard a struggle," were her first words. "Was anyone hurt?"

"Injuries were suffered," said Holmes with a smile, "but all is well for the moment."

"Did you gain any news of Robert?"

"No," my friend replied. "But we do know the identity of Mr. Girthwood's quarry."

"What is it?" the woman asked.

Holmes set himself down on the sofa and stretched out his left leg. "The statue of a bird," he said. "A black bird."

CHAPTER EIGHT:

Four Interviews

"This means we must now pay our respects to Jasper Girthwood," said Holmes as he turned Vic Starkey's knife round in his hands. Then, with some discomfort, he set the blade down and shifted his weight upon the sofa, where he lay, his left leg elevated by means of several pillows. "Watson, might you ring up the Waymore? Ask that someone there convey to Mr. Girthwood the message that we wish to pay a call at half-past three."

"Of course," I said and strode to the telephone.

"Do you care to join us?" the detective asked Miss Adler, who sat stiffly in the basket-chair.

"Must I?" she said. "I thought your position was to deny my presence here."

"I now tend to believe that ruse will not be productive and that you would be safer in our company rather than here. And—Oh, Watson! Make certain that it is conveyed to Mr. Girthwood that we here do not have the object he seeks. He has that by my word. Miss Adler, are you willing to make that same declaration?"

"That this black bird object is not in my possession? Of course I am."

Holmes nodded. "Have you knowledge of its whereabouts?"

"I do not know the statue's location," said Miss Adler at once.

The detective smiled. "Did you know of its existence before its mention by Mr. Starkey to Watson and me?"

"I told you earlier that I knew there was something that both Robert and Mr. Girthwood sought."

Holmes did not respond to her failure to directly answer but merely shifted his weight upon the sofa again and turned toward me. "The message has been relayed, Watson?"

"It has," said I, putting down the telephone.

"Very well. We shall all journey to the Waymore to see Jasper Girthwood once I am rested."

"Mr. Holmes," said the woman. "Do you intend for me to participate in the interview?"

"Only if you wish," my friend said. "Knowing your aversion to Mr. Girthwood, I suppose you might choose to not even leave the cab, to which I would not object. You may decide your own fate in that regard."

Irene Adler did not respond immediately. Instead, she, yet again, retired to her room. During the ensuing time, Holmes rested, hands across his eyes, and I restored my scattered manuscripts to their original order.

"And so the centre of the case is a statue," I said to my friend. "Truly, I wonder if there will be four more of them and whether we shall be forced to break them all."

"What said you?" asked Holmes, eyes still covered.

"I was comparing the black bird statue to the five Napoleon statues."

"There were six, and they were busts," was his idle comment. "And while it is possible, I do not think the dabble will be ripe for breaking."

"Dabble?"

"Criminal argot for stolen property. Mr. Starkey used the term, if you recall. No, unlike the Napoleons, I am inclined to believe that the value lies with the statue itself, though that value is likely hidden nonetheless."

"How so?"

"I doubt Girthwood would have asked someone possessing such an immoral compass as young Vic Starkey to fetch an obviously valuable statue and return it to him. Had its value been self-evident, Starkey would have been expected to simply vanish with it. Moreover, our assailant described the bird as black." Holmes uncovered his eyes and stared at the ceiling of our room. "I ask myself whether an unadorned black statue of a bird would, in itself, inspire murder, and my response is to doubt it, unless the artifact has hidden treasure or is the symbol of personal passions. Or both, which is perhaps the most probable."

"You just alluded to murder. What murder?"

Holmes turned his face toward me. "Earlier in the week, just before this case was brought to us, I commented to you upon the murder of a Greek art dealer in Paris."

"I fear I have no such recollection."

"The remark was uttered in the course of our debate over Mr. Finney," my friend said. "By the way, I suppose I must congratulate you on your recent good fortune at the track. Trust me when I say that the remark causes me perhaps more pain and embarrassment than my leg at present. Next time, Watson, you must allow me to purchase the molasses."

"Done. I believe now that I do recall the incident—of the Paris murder, I mean."

Holmes turned his entire body and braced one elbow against the sofa, so as to support his head in one hand. "Art, violence, Paris—those attributes are common to both that case and ours."

"You believe they are connected with one another?"

"In most investigations such as the current one, the definitely certain must take precedence over the merely possible. Still, the comparison is intriguing, and I am tempted to reverse the relation. How I yearn for details of the Parisian murder beyond what the press can supply."

"You are considering sending someone to France?"

"No," replied Holmes. "Only I should go there and then only in the gravest of situations; for the moment, I must remain here in London. I shall have Johnson wire the Prefect of Paris in the morning, however."

"Holmes?"

"Yes?"

"You have suggested to Miss Adler that we abandon the fiction that she left Baker Street."

"I believe Girthwood is now certain she is here, and casual admission of the same would represent a boldness that might serve us well in dealing with the man. Yes, I am now inclined to change my strategy and admit to him that she resides temporarily at 221."

Holmes rested for a while longer then left the sofa and spent several minutes limbering up his strained joints. At length, Miss Adler came down again, declaring herself to be in better spirits than before and ready to accompany us, and so, within the hour, we three finally set out under a blue-and-white sky in a four-wheeler, for the Waymore Hotel.

"I do believe we are being followed," I said shortly after our departure, as we turned into Oxford Street.

"That is your belief and my hope," answered Sherlock Holmes. "And I do hope you can observe the driver of the pursuing vehicle to be none other than Shinwell Johnson."

Looking closely at the hansom following in our wake, I saw the driver was, indeed, Johnson himself. I gave him a nod that went unacknowledged and returned my attention to my companions.

"Upshaw and Mercer are inside his hansom," said Holmes in a distracted tone. "You may also wish to check the identity of our own driver."

With a contortion that threatened me with injury rivalling that of my friend's recent mishap, I saw that it was the pale-faced Langdale Pike, another of Holmes's agents, at the reins. He grinned sardonically and then gave his attention to the traffic once more.

"Stannard and Hollins remain outside 221 itself," continued Holmes. "Though the precaution may be unnecessary. With Mr. Starkey in custody for his assault, I expect Jasper Girthwood may, once again, be alone and unassisted in London."

We proceeded without further conversation to New Oxford Street and then Holborn, where Irene Adler took delight, after an absence of years, in seeing that area's black-and-white gabled houses. We then turned left to invade Bloomsbury where, after skirting the British Museum, we encountered the Waymore Hotel. Holmes and I left the four-wheeler, while Irene Adler hesitated.

"If you are uncertain, I suggest you remain in the vehicle," said Sherlock Holmes, hand held against his hat in the heavy breeze. "I shall instruct Mr. Pike to drive you round for a time and then return here. Moreover, Shinwell Johnson and his crew will continue to follow you. All shall be well."

Miss Adler agreed, and Holmes gave instructions to Pike. As the four-wheeler and hansom sped off, my friend and I entered the lobby of the Waymore. There, supported by the largest chair in the room, sat Jasper Girthwood.

"A warm welcome, Mr. Holmes, and to you as well, sir," the man said, straining to rise from his seat. "We meet as old friends now, do we not? By gad, I love hospitality," he declared, as if the effort of getting up were itself a gift of affection. "Take those chairs there, gentlemen, please!"

We three sat down in unison, and Girthwood pulled out his watch. "Precisely half past! Punctuality in all things, sir," he said, returning the timepiece to the pocket of his huge black suit. "If a man can't keep his time, how can he keep his place, eh? Now then, what do you desire in the way of drink? I can call a man at any time."

"Perhaps in a moment," said the detective, speaking for us both. "I believe I have something that may be yours."

"You do?" whispered Girthwood. "What?" The immense young man looked suspiciously back and forth at Holmes and me. "You certainly can't be carrying it. Did you leave it at the desk?"

"I do indeed have it with me. It is this," replied Holmes casually, taking Vic Starkey's knife from his coat pocket and setting it upon a nearby table. "I said it may be yours. Then again, perhaps it is the property of an associate."

Girthwood leaned back, assumed a distracted air of gruffness, and set his hands upon chair rests that were only a tad less plush. "Whose did you say it was?" he asked. "I did not hear a name."

"A Mr. Vic Starkey. I will give him credit for not admitting it, but I strongly suspect he is your associate."

"I readily admit he is my agent, sir, as I know you have agents, such as your friend here. I say that straightaway, with no intention of muddying the waters. And a damned fool agent Mr. Starkey must have been." The man contemplated the knife. "Are you telling me that he actually used that? Did he attempt to threaten you, sir?"

"Both of us, in fact."

Girthwood looked at me. "My deep apologies."

I acknowledged him with a curt nod.

"Your gesture is accepted," added Holmes. "Fortunately, a passing messenger-boy disarmed Mr. Starkey, and Dr. Watson convinced the lad to allow us to have it."

Girthwood stared at Holmes for a moment and then burst into loud laughter. "Good! Very good! Regardless of venue, sir, you are precious! Indeed, priceless!"

"I thought to keep the knife," said Holmes, interrupting our host's joviality, "believing it might, in fact, be yours."

Girthwood and Holmes sat in silence, each contemplating the other, as I sat and watched. At length, Girthwood said, "No, sir, it is not my knife, not my knife at all. What Mr. Starkey did was regrettable; indeed, it was shocking. But as you yourself noted, Mr. Holmes, I am new here. I place my trust in certain people, and they... disappoint me."

Girthwood took a small snuff-box from another pocket and opened it. "Fine silver," he said, contemplating the container. "Not as exquisite as the one on your mantel, to be sure, sir—a piece for which you could get a pretty penny, if I may say. If Tiffany's or Lambert's have not fully appraised it yet, you must allow me that pleasure." Girthwood took his snuff then closed the box and put it back in his pocket. "My," he said after a loud sneeze, staring at Holmes's chest. "That's a fine emerald tie-pin you've got there as well, sir."

"Thank you. It was given to me by a late, very great lady."

"You truly are the collector and connoisseur, Mr. Holmes. When all this dreadful business is finished, we must tour London's jewellery establishments together. Have you, perhaps, the time today? I understand there is a marvellous showroom at Elkington and Company."

"In Regent Street, yes," said Holmes. "But let us return to the knife."

"Mr. Starkey made a sorry choice," Jasper Girthwood muttered, looking away. "I shall scold the boy for it. By the by, how long will he be in jail?"

"That is not mine to determine, and I do not know if the matter will even be referred to the assizes."[6]

Girthwood's expression betrayed a lack of comprehension.

---

6   Assizes, or the courts of assize, were periodic criminal courts, which heard the most serious cases. Minor offenses, on the other hand, were dealt with in so-called magistrates' courts by justices of the peace. This court system was revised in the early 1970s.

"You received Dr. Watson's message concerning the black bird?" Holmes continued.

"That you don't have it, yes. And you don't?" The man looked at me with a coy smile. "Neither of you?"

"No," said Sherlock Holmes.

"And I believe you, sir. I can tell the truth in men as well as gems, and by gad, I think this time your testimony is true—that braggadocio about the messenger notwithstanding. And, perhaps, unlike our previous conversation," Girthwood continued with a sigh. "When you were less than truthful about the whereabouts of certain...clients?"

"My profession can be a difficult business," replied Holmes. "Truth must, at times, be a weapon."

"Oh, yes, it's dog-eat-dog out there, sir," said the other man. "Arf," he muttered after a pause and then laughed heartily. "So tell me, now that we are no longer lying to one another," Girthwood added, his eyes narrowing as he leaned forward as much as his belly would allow. "Do you know *where* the bird is?"

"No," said Sherlock Holmes.

Girthwood stared Holmes in the eye. "I accept that," he said, leaning back and again grasping his chair to assume a magisterial air. "Tell me, have you any idea *what* the bird is?"

"I take it to be an *objet d'art*, whose immense value is disguised by, I fancy, a coating of black enamel."

Girthwood's eyes widened, and his manner deflated. He joined his hands together and looked down at them. "Why did you arrange this appointment, sir?" the man asked. "For what practical purpose did you call it?"

"You have yet to ask me if I know *whose* statue it is."

"Ownership can be a purely metaphysical concept, Mr. Holmes. Accept that when it comes to the black bird, physical possession alone is the only true test of consequence."

"I observe that it is a test you yourself fail to pass."

"For the present only, Mr. Holmes. For the present only."

"If Mr. Starkey represents your best mustering of forces," the detective said graciously, "I fear nothing will change."

"I have others at my disposal."

Holmes merely smiled.

"Yourself, for instance," Girthwood continued. "You realize, sir, that I was quite serious yesterday with my offer to hire you."

"I told you I am already in the service of another client."

"Yes, but that is to locate Robert Hope Maldon, isn't it? With all those agents you claim to have, surely you can handle more than one investigation at a time? Find Maldon for your anonymous client, and find the bird for me."

"Given the direction my current investigation is taking, I am quite certain such an arrangement would lead to difficult conflicts of interest. Under the circumstances, I cannot consider your offer."

"You're correct about the bird being valuable, Mr. Holmes," the large man said. He gave a nasal laugh. "You cannot comprehend how correct you are. If you accept my offer, the commission alone would guarantee your future. Why, you might as well refuse a knighthood or a dukedom."

"I refused a knighthood only last year," said Sherlock Holmes. "And as for a dukedom, well, I fear that is not in the offing. Even if it were, my answer would still be a firm no."

"A pity," Girthwood said with a deep sigh. "The word inevitable always saddens me."

"Though, when combined with the word victory, I find it most invigorating," said Sherlock Holmes.

Girthwood laughed yet again and then waved one hand as if it were a closely tethered balloon. "Well, then off with you, sir. I've had my fun trying; I can tell you. When the game's afoot, the blood runs fast."

"I have often conveyed much the same sentiment to Dr. Watson here in almost the same terms," Holmes replied, rising from his chair. I followed my friend's lead at once. "If we are, indeed, each well experienced at the hunt," Holmes continued. "Perhaps we shall meet again in the field."

"Either there, Mr. Holmes, or in Hades."

Without another word, my friend turned to leave. Once more, I took my cue from him. Discreetly looking back as we departed the hotel lobby, I saw our antagonist pick up the knife and clench it before gently returning it to the table.

"I do not see our two vehicles," said Holmes once we had regained the street. "Come, Watson, let us cross and then proceed northward some small distance."

I followed my friend's directions, bending my shoulders against the wind before commenting upon Girthwood's intolerable rudeness.

"Pure swank," said Holmes in agreement. "And little more."

"Do you not view him as a serious enemy?" I asked.

"The man does not yet seriously inconvenience me," said Holmes. "Let alone hamper my plans. I feel no loss of liberty, and my situation is by no means an impossible one."

"A simple no would have sufficed," I observed as we halted and turned round to espy our companions when they should pass.

"I was borrowing your own words, Doctor. Or, at least, those your pen placed in the mouth of Professor Moriarty."

"Ah, of course," I said, understanding why the phrases had seemed familiar to me. "We may only hope that this problem will not be your final one."

"Well played, old fellow. But to respond to your comment, I doubt the apocalypse looms. You know, Watson, you should never have resurrected my fictional persona," Holmes abruptly remarked as he shielded his eyes from the sun's glare to search amid the bustle of King's Crossing for our cabs. "I'd rather that my literary alter ego still were buried beneath the pages alongside our dearly departed professor."

"You were most efficient in rescuing my recent efforts from the fire," I said crisply. "I should say your fictional persona possesses strong survival instincts."

"Your tongue is as cruel as your pen, Doctor," my friend replied with a puckish smile. "Halloa, I believe Miss Adler's cab is in sight."

Hailing our four-wheeler and nodding inconspicuously to Shinwell Johnson aboard the trailing hansom, Holmes approached the vehicle and boarded it; I followed in his wake. Pike touched his hat's brim as we boarded.

"I have seen some streets in this portion of London that I have not visited for years," said Irene Adler at once. "I had quite forgotten about Gordon Square."

"I am glad your jaunt was entertaining," Holmes remarked in a friendly way. "How went your interview?"

"Sadly, the occasion entertained no one. I conveyed to Mr. Girthwood those points I wished to impress upon him," my friend said. "Unfortunately, the man himself remains intractable."

Holmes turned away to stare at the passing buildings and comment upon them for the benefit of Miss Adler. I sat and listened as well, and little more of consequence was said by any of us for the remainder of the trip back to Baker Street. Within sight of 221, I realized that the hansom driven by Shinwell Johnson was no longer following.

Our four-wheeler halted, and we three debarked. Holmes conversed briefly with Langdale Pike, while I escorted Miss Adler through our front door. Inside I found our agent Hollins passing time in the waiting room. "Pleasant day, Dr. Watson," the stubby fellow said. "Stannard is out back. It's been quiet; I can tell you. There was a ring of the telephone that Mrs. Hudson dealt with. She'll tell you about it. I'll be going out, I suppose, now that you're back."

The man briefly repeated the same to Sherlock Holmes as my friend entered 221. Our landlady appeared almost at once and confirmed Hollins's report.

"The man did not identify himself," she said as she took Miss Adler's hat and coat. "And his voice was muffled, as if through cloth. Most rude, I thought."

"What did he say?" asked Holmes.

"He asked if Miss Adler were here, and I informed him she was not, whereupon he gruffly suggested I wasn't telling the truth and cut me off."

"Hum," the detective said. "We shall take to the sitting room, Mrs. Hudson."

Holmes and I parted with our hats and coats, and then we three ascended the stair. The detective and I entered the sitting room, while Irene Adler ascended to her quarters, where she dispensed with her own hat and coat before coming down to rejoin us. Together, we sat round a newly invigorated fire.

"It was Robert who called," Miss Adler asserted. "It was he to whom Mrs. Hudson spoke."

"Perhaps," replied my friend.

"Who else would suspect that I am here?" said Miss Adler. "Of course it was he! I do so wish I had been here to speak with him."

"I shall be most gratified to see him in the flesh," Holmes countered as he surveyed his day's mail, which Mrs. Hudson had left upon a table. "Nothing of consequence," he remarked, rising to set the small collection of letters behind the jewel-encrusted snuffbox. Idly, the detective rubbed the wound in the mantel caused by his jack-knife, which, for so many years, he had used to fix his unanswered correspondence in place above the fire.

"Do you not believe Mr. Girthwood seeks Robert also?" Irene Adler asked suddenly. "Despite your earlier comment to me, I—"

"Mr. Girthwood desires the black bird above all else," answered Holmes in a distracted manner. "However, perhaps your fiancé has the bird, in which case Girthwood would see him as a means to an end."

"Robert told me to wait," said Miss Adler. "That, Mr. Holmes, is what I shall do." With that remark, Irene Adler asked to take leave of us and once more seek quiet solitude above. Holmes waved his hand in a gesture of preoccupied indifference as I escorted our guest as far as the sitting room door.

"Take care of your friend," she whispered to me. "He frets much. Somehow, I know the man on the telephone was Robert, and that knowledge has calmed me. Now I know all will come right."

"Of course," I said, supporting her optimism while privately questioning its foundation. She closed the door behind her, and I turned to find Holmes digging his Persian slipper out of the coal scuttle.

"I do not sense these waters are necessarily deep, Watson," my friend said with irritation as he withdrew shag from the slipper and pushed it into his pipe. "And yet, why do I feel as if I were drowning?" With apparent impatience, he tossed the slipper aside.

"But surely all goes as you wish, does it not?" I consoled him. "You sit, as always, at the centre of your web, pulling the strands. Will not Robert Hope Maldon come to us and perhaps bring with him the statue?"

"I fear, Watson, that I am not so much the spider as the sloth," my friend said loudly. "Please recall that we were employed originally by Lord Monsbury, who was concerned with corporate shares rather than statues. And consider, old fellow, that most of our time has been spent here at Baker Street, passively awaiting events, rather than actively pursuing matters in the field, my own boasting to Mr. Girthwood notwithstanding."

"Your assessment is too harsh," I offered.

"Pshaw," said Holmes in a loud voice. "In my old age, I do not grasp the bull by the horns as I once did. Each day I become more the image of Mycroft, engaging only that which comes to me in my armchair."

"I doubt you could ever become your brother's twin," I replied. "But, surely, there are aspects of the case that make you take heart?"

"I do not know the whereabouts of young Hope Maldon," said Holmes, again in a sharp tone. "Instead, I must have him come to me. I seek shares. Instead, I am bothered with a bird statue of supposedly great value to some but of no interest to my client. I crossed paths with Mr. Girthwood in order to gain some advantage. Instead, I learned next to nothing from him."

Dejectedly, he took to his armchair and, at last, lit his pipe.

I turned suddenly upon hearing a creak on the stair outside our room.

Holmes held up one hand and smiled, extinguishing and then discarding his vesta. "It is nothing," he said softly.

"Eavesdropping?" I whispered.

My friend nodded.

"And your comments?" I said quietly as I took to the basket-chair next to him.

"They were misleading in attitude, though not entirely in content. I do believe we have been far too bound to 221 here, but then, we labour under the burden of having Miss Adler's security to consider. And somewhere in these shallow waters," he added. "There may, indeed, be deep pools."

"And so you do not despair?"

"Oh, certainly not. I adhere faithfully to my philosophy."

"Which is…?"

"Formulate a hypothesis," said Sherlock Holmes. "And then question it."

At that moment, our telephone rang.

"Watson, please answer, if you will. Should it be from the house of Lord Monsbury, politely inform them I am out and that we are getting very close to a resolution of the case. For all others, should I be wanted, I am in."

It was, in fact, Stanley Hopkins. I handed the telephone to Holmes, who spent several minutes recounting for the inspector our progress in the most general terms, still excluding any mention of Irene Adler and failing to include Jasper Girthwood by name.

"Had Hopkins anything of interest?" I inquired when the conversation had ended.

"I am not certain which of us was less educated by the other. The Yard has latched onto nothing new in the Hope Maldon affair, though, of course, I should have been surprised if they had."

"The cabinet minister, after all, asked them to refrain from investigation and defer to you."

"Just so."

Our telephone rang again.

"Same instructions, if you will, Watson."

This time I found myself speaking to Diarmund Stephenson, whose voice gave way to that of Lord Monsbury himself. Obeying Holmes's request, I informed the earl that the detective was out in pursuit of the old man's son and that we held high hopes for success.

"Tell your employer I want to speak to him!" demanded Lord Monsbury. "This wait is unendurable! Good day, I tell you."

With that, my conversation with the earl ended. I reported its meagre substance to Holmes, who put down his pipe. "I suppose that I must go round in person to inform Monsbury of our progress, though I expect he will not use that particular word to describe it. I shall ring up his man, Stephenson, within the hour to arrange it."

Moments later, for the third time within a brief span, the telephone sounded. The caller this time was a man unknown to me, to whom the exchange had connected the wrong household by mistake.

"You know, Watson," said Holmes with a sigh. "I believe I can now understand Solicitor Crabbe's antagonism toward that device."

CHAPTER NINE:

Unexpected Arrivals

Holmes rang up Diarmund Stephenson, both to arrange an audience with Lord Monsbury and to acknowledge that I had passed on the information the young man had given me. My friend then departed for the interview at Lennox Square, and it was perhaps an hour later that I finally heard Irene Adler's tread on the upper stair. Setting down my volume of sea stories, I prepared to greet her.

"May I enter?" the woman asked through the open sitting room doorway.

"But of course," I said, rising quickly. She elected to sit in the basket-chair and, once there, emitted an enormous yawn.

"I fear I slept," said she, "and suffered continual dreams of bells ringing."

"Perhaps it was the telephone," I said in jest.

The woman gripped the rests of her chair. "Did Robert call again?"

"I fear not," I responded, now regretting my attempt at humour.

"Who rang then?"

"Scotland Yard and Lord Monsbury's household."

Miss Adler slowly nodded, remaining silent for some time. At length she said, "I know I shall see Robert soon."

"I fervently believe that also."

"Doctor, how stands this matter in the mind of Mr. Holmes? Is he close to a solution?"

"I do not know," I told her, keeping in mind my friend's earlier performance for her when she had silently stood on the other side of our closed sitting room door. "I fear, Miss Adler, that this may be one of those rare occasions when Sherlock Holmes is uncertain of finding a solution, because he cannot define the problem. But Holmes is not his best objective judge," I quickly added to forestall any distress on her part. "I have seen him wrest victory from situations far darker than this one appears to be at present. Then, too," I continued. "He does not always share his closest thoughts with me during the case itself. The man usually knows more than he lets on."

"Yes," she said, suddenly brightening. "He does, does he not?"

Wishing to take the woman's mind off her troubles, I attempted conversation concerning America, especially the nature of trout fishing on that continent, a subject about which she predictably knew nothing. This led, in a brief span of time, to her becoming the listener while I expounded on the broad category of genus Salmo. Realizing, perhaps too late, that I was treading on her graciousness, I apologized for my long-winded nature and commented upon the lateness of the hour and the absence of Holmes.

"I should think that not unusual, Doctor."

"In the early days, Miss Adler, it was, if anything, the usual custom. Now, in his later years, as he terms them, he has adopted somewhat more bourgeois hours, if only somewhat less Bohemian habits."

"And yourself?" she said. "Have you never considered domesticity? I mean not to flatter or seem forward, but surely more than one pair of eyes has flashed your way?"

"I am several years widowed," I told her directly. "Please, it does not signify," I added quickly, before any apology could leave her lips. "But, I am affianced again, you see."

"I am so happy for you, Doctor. I shall be eager to meet your future wife. Will she soon call here? Might we call upon her?"

"I fear she is in Plymouth," I answered. "She has had the need to attend to family matters there often these past months. I do not expect her back in London before the middle of next month."

"I see." The woman looked round our sitting room and asked, "Was it here that a significant portion of the courting occurred? This bastion is so formidably male, I must say."

"My residence and practice in Queen Anne Street is perhaps more friendly to both genders," said I. "When my fiancée has been required in the west, however, I have stayed here in Baker Street."

"As a cushion against loneliness?"

"Yes," I said after a moment's hesitation. "Yes, I suppose that is one reason." I looked round the room, taking in the hearth, the windows, and the familiar pattern of the wall-paper encircling us. My portrait of Henry Ward Beecher, now hanging framed in Queen Anne Street, had been supplanted by some ghoulish indigo-and-blue depiction of a beggar, and where my picture of General Gordon had reigned, Holmes had placed what was to me an incomprehensible painting of a mountain by some Frenchman of note. Still, sitting there in the fading afternoon, hoping that winter's final frost had come and gone, I could not be certain I did not sense the ghosts of Jefferson Hope, Jonathan Small, and others, including my own dear Mary.

"Oh, Dr. Watson," I heard Miss Adler say. "I have not caused you sadness by my remarks, have I?"

I looked over at her perfect face surrounded by a halo of auburn and smiled. "Of course not," I insisted. "If Holmes is entering what he terms his later years, then I must have passed the same threshold some time ago. No, Miss Adler, an old man was allowing what is left of his mind to wander. I believe I have—"

At that moment, the house door opened and closed.

"He has returned," said Irene Adler.

We turned to face the sitting room door and awaited the detective, who came up the stair with a steady pace.

"I believe I have forestalled Lord Monsbury's temper for yet another day or two," my friend said after returning our greetings. Looking in the mirror, he stared at his teeth and straightened his collar. "The man is unrealistic in his demands. Mark this, Watson—he shall never attain his wish to be premier. The members of his party may, most of them, be mad but surely not that mad."

"You were kept by him for some time."

"If you seek to have me assume all the responsibility again in the eyes of Mrs. Hudson, so be it, Watson. But, yes, you may privately blame the earl, as well as two injured horses, which brought traffic in New Bond Street to a complete halt. Poor creatures," he said, warming himself by the fire. "Surely these new motors we see now will put an end to their exploitation."

"And our sense of hearing as well?" I offered.

"Is aural discomfort comparable to the suffering of thousands of animal souls?" my friend said wistfully. "And do not forget the burden placed upon noses and shoes. But I am prepared to go down and accept my scolding from Mrs. Hudson," he continued, his mood now entirely shifted toward the jovial. "I shall see what sort of meal I can salvage for us." With that, Holmes strode toward the sitting room door then paused and turned to face our guest. "Oh, Miss Adler," he said with a beatific smile. "Are you much in the habit of dangling colourful cloth for the public benefit?"

"What?" said the woman.

"You have a bright blue kerchief hanging in your window upstairs," the detective said. "Is it for the pleasure of the pigeons that flock upon the roofs of Baker Street? Or, perhaps, it is meant to comfort the starlings that we now occasionally see roosting in buildings?"

The woman stiffened in her chair. "It is for my memory of Robert," she said. "It is one he gave to me."

"I see," Holmes replied.

"And do you take the observation of my window as one of your principal obligations?"

"I did not observe it directly," my friend replied. "It was noticed by one of my men guarding 221. He passed word of it to me, which is what prompted my question. I have sent the agents home, Watson," he added. "With both of us here, I believe the house is secure for the night." With that remark, Holmes then turned and descended the stair.

"I do not have his trust," she said. "I suppose, under the circumstances, I cannot."

"It is his calling," I quietly stammered. "To be a sceptic, that is."

"That is true." Miss Adler leaned back and covered her eyes with the back of one hand. "I, meanwhile, must remain certain that this will all pass in time."

For the present, time had brought first the return of Sherlock Holmes and then the arrival of our evening meal, which was again seasoned with hearty conversation. Holmes recounted for Miss Adler the details of several cases long past, from the adventure of the unsalaried clerk to the mystery of the blind man's strabismus. At length, he took the occasion to once more cast friendly aspersions upon my literary efforts, suggesting, by what I must admit were devastating parodies, how I would have presented particulars of the affairs just mentioned. As riposte, I attempted to goad Holmes with dismissive remarks concerning Tibetan theology, but my friend merely declared he would rather debate the issue in any life other than this one.

When our meal was finished and Mrs. Hudson had cleared the table, we three settled into our now-familiar stations round the hearth—Miss Adler claiming the sofa, Holmes in his armchair, and I filling the basket-chair.

"Have you no questions concerning the progress of the present case?" Holmes asked at last of Irene Adler.

The woman looked him squarely in the eye. "I am certain that when you wish to share your answers with me, you will do so," she said.

Holmes glanced about as if for one of his pipes but, finding none within reach, clasped his hands together instead. "I have no answers," he said. "Perhaps some will come to me in time."

"Perhaps," the woman repeated.

Holmes nodded and then excused himself to once more find interest in his commonplace books. Miss Adler immediately rose and bade us a good-night. "Doctor, sleep well. Meanwhile, I will retire to my hopes," she said, turning to Holmes, "and my kerchiefs."

"I wish you a good night," said he, not looking up from his pages.

The woman left, closing the sitting room door behind her, and it was with some irritation that I returned to reading, finishing my book perhaps half an hour later. My friend had not stirred during the entirety of that time.

"Holmes," I said at last, "could you not show Miss Adler a bit more courtesy and respect?"

The detective looked up. "What? Why, I show her enormous courtesy and respect at every moment."

"But your obvious lack of trust—"

"Is an obvious show of respect, Watson. Have I not been quoted by you—in print, for the entire world to read—that I believe she surpasses all of her sex in craft and intelligence?"

"Holmes, she is still a woman!"

"You mean, Doctor, that she is *only* a woman, which is to say that she should be treated as a ward—which, I should say, is the complete reverse of respect."

"And baiting a person is a form of courtesy?" I countered.

Holmes took his head in his hands. "Oh, for a world without the baggage of social camouflage." He sighed. "Watson, believe that it is no reflection upon our association, which I treasure, when I say that I long to cohabit with a species possessing more than four limbs."

"You refer, perhaps, to those bees you've waxed on about these past many years?"

"Yes," he said wistfully. "And well put, by the way."

"Yet they are socially rigid in the extreme, are they not?"

"That is true."

"Then do you not contradict yourself when—"

I was stopped in the middle of my sentence by a piercing scream. I flew from my chair but, even so, found myself lagging Holmes as we ran up the stair.

"See to Miss Adler's room!" cried my friend as he rushed past her door. "Then follow me to the top!" he added as he ascended farther, toward the lumber room door.

I flung open the door to the maid's quarters and found the room orderly, with Miss Adler's possessions arranged neatly but the woman herself gone. Noting that the window appeared sealed, I ran up the stair to join Holmes. Bolting through the lumber room doorway, I saw, in the gloom, the bay window, open and framed by two figures. One was that of Miss Adler, who lay slumped at the windowsill, sobbing. Above and opposite her, his hand resting upon the frame, stood Holmes, gazing down into the night.

"What is it?" I asked. "What has happened?"

"They fought!" said Miss Adler in a distraught voice. "They fought, and Robert pushed him!"

"Doctor, pray see to her," Holmes said to me in a voice that was soft yet distant.

Stumbling in the dark, past the boxes in which Holmes stored surplus books and other memorabilia, I approached the pair. Miss Adler kept repeating the same words she had already uttered. "Here," I said, gathering her shoulders in my hands and assisting her onto her feet. As she rose, I glanced out the open lumber room window and believed I could discern some large object upon the stone walk below.

"He flung him off!" sobbed Miss Adler. "He just flung him off!"

Holmes at last appeared to move. In the moonlight, he gave the window frame a brief examination then reached down and lifted a glove from off the dusty lumber room floor. It was, to the best I could discern in the dim light, light brown in colour.

"It's his glove!" said Miss Adler. "Robert's glove!" She seemed to curl up in fear in my arms, and it required all my will to guide her out of the room and toward the stair.

"Holmes?" I said. I turned to face the detective, who stood silhouetted against the window as he slowly put his hand into the glove, his long fingers not quite able to fit. Then, more loudly, I repeated my call.

"Coming, old fellow," he replied. He quickly removed the glove before rushing past me, and as he did so, Miss Adler seemed to gain a greater degree of poise.

"I will follow and not be a burden," she said urgently. "Come, Doctor," the woman told me, as if now she herself were leading me. Trailing Holmes, we descended to the sitting room, where the detective instructed me to settle Miss Adler upon the sofa. Mrs. Hudson, alarmed by the noise, had already been waiting on the landing to meet us.

"Please attend her," Holmes asked of our landlady. Then, to Miss Adler, he inquired, "You will feel safe here while the doctor and I go below?"

The woman nodded then seemed to almost lose consciousness as she sank onto the sofa.

"Come, Watson," said my friend, after he had grasped a lantern.

We rapidly descended the stair and, without coat or hat, strode to the rear of 221 and exited into it dark back yard, shielded in part from the night sky by Baker Street rooftops. As we stood in a mist pierced only by Holmes's light, two or three voices called to us from nearby windows. Holmes replied by requesting that someone summon the police and then shone his lantern upon a body that lay face down upon the stone walk. It was as still as the upturned hat sitting nearby, and the corpse's legs pointed back toward 221.

"His condition, Watson?" said Holmes, holding the lantern as if he were a statue himself.

I bent down and searched for a pulse, though from the state of the man's skull, I knew at once what I should find.

"He is dead, Holmes." I briefly stared at the body, and then I rose to my feet, grieving for Miss Adler. "How can we tell her?" I asked, turning away. "This will crush everything within her."

"What?" said the detective, and I looked round to see that he was in the midst of examining the body.

"Holmes?"

"Think you this is Lord Monsbury's son? Your tears are premature, I believe. Recall what Miss Adler herself told us above. Here, my survey of the back side is complete. Assist me in turning the body over, if you will."

Years of medical service at once asserted itself, and I dispassionately helped my friend expose the battered face. Even in the light of Holmes's lantern, I could see it was not that of a twenty-four-year-old man but rather the damaged visage of someone far older.

"Yes," said my friend as he bent to look down. "I thought it might be him."

"You know who this was?" I asked. "I do not—"

"You never glimpsed him during the case in question," Holmes said. He rose to his full height of more than six feet. "And I saw him upon only one occasion but for great enough duration to recognize him now. This will, at least, set the public record correct in its essence, if not the exact chronological details."

"Explain yourself, please," I said impatiently. "Who is this man?"

"Why, Godfrey Norton, of course," Holmes replied, his hawk-like nose accentuated in the dim light. "The now truly deceased husband of our guest."

"Norton?!"

"Yes," said Holmes as others approached down the alley. "But only to us, Watson. For the moment, he is an unknown person, presumably a burglar, who appears to have fallen while travelling the roofs of Baker Street. We ran outside when we heard the screams and found the body, only that and nothing more. You comprehend?"

"Of course."

"Good. I fancy this must be the police coming. Please be responsible for the interview—present the facts as I have just instructed you while I go inside and see to Miss Adler."

"Holmes?"

"Yes?"

"Am I to mention her?"

"Do not volunteer the fact of her presence. If they ask for the particulars of 221, tell them only of the two of us and Mrs. Hudson. Should the police wish to enter the house, fetch me first. I suspect, however, that mention of my name will provide all the protection you will require."

"Very well."

"We might also speak tomorrow to Stanley Hopkins," Holmes added quickly. "But for the moment, I should like to maintain simplicity in our relation to the police."

"I understand."

"Here they are now. See to it, if you will."

Holmes handed me the lantern and retreated into 221 while I met three police constables, who had been gathered by the local folk, many of whom now crowded round the body as well. My explanation was as Holmes had instructed: we had heard a scream and a crash, come out to investigate, and found the body of a man we did not know. Upon giving my name, two of the three constables recognized me as Holmes's assistant and biographer before I could even mention my friend, whereupon they gave me a considerable degree of deference. When asked if they wished to interview the detective himself, they all declined vigorously, expressing no desire to bother one they held in such great esteem. It was, perhaps, nearly an hour before all matters were attended to, including the arrival of a wagon for disposing of the body. When, at length, I re-entered

221—bolting the door behind me—I found Mrs. Hudson preparing water for tea. I inquired after Miss Adler.

"The dear remains shaken, as we might expect—all of us, that is, except Mr. Holmes," she said with more than a touch of irritation in her voice.

"Did she—"

"I tell you, Dr. Watson," our landlady continued. "I've never understood the way he treats my house, but I can tolerate it. Mr. Holmes is a great man and, during most hours, a kind and generous man, so I let those things pass—"

"Mrs. Hudson, how—"

"Though he treats my house callously," she went on, talking to me as the water heated. "Though he treats things roughly, yet I can dismiss it, seeing in him what I do. But the way he can treat *people*!" She turned her now-florid face to me. "The poor dear up in that room is at the end of her wits, I tell you. You remember how I saw the terror in her eyes on that first day? I told you both about it. I saw—"

"Mrs. Hudson—"

"I saw what was in those frightened eyes of hers! She's a dear one, I can tell you that. She's right and square, no matter what Mr. Holmes seems to think!"

"Mrs. Hudson, I believe the water has reached a boil."

She turned and quickly removed the kettle from the heat.

"Go up there," she ordered me as she settled the vessel back down with both hands. "Tell the dear woman I'll be up in a bit with some special tea that will soothe her. And try…" she added as I turned to leave. "Try to talk some little speck of human kindness back into that man!"

I hurried up the stair and entered the sitting room, where I found Holmes alone, planted in his armchair before the fire, his hands wrapped in each other as if in prayer. "How is she?" my friend asked.

"I do not know," I replied. "Has she retired to her room again? I can—"

"I was referring to Mrs. Hudson," the detective said gently, staring into the coals.

"She will be bringing some tea shortly for Miss Adler."

Holmes nodded.

"Our guest has gone up then, has she?" I asked, to end the awkward silence.

Again he nodded.

"I shall wait by the door and direct Mrs. Hudson to the maid's room then."

My friend remained motionless.

"Holmes, might I fetch you your shag?" I asked, seeing the Persian slipper lying across the room from him. "And if you will direct which pipe you—"

"I am fine, Doctor," said he, leaning back in his chair and grasping an armrest with each hand. "But I appreciate the thought, old fellow," he said in a somewhat distrait tone. "I assume the business with the police was uneventful?"

"Uneventful, yes. Your reputation oiled the gears of bureaucracy immensely."

"Did it?" Holmes said, almost with a tone of self-reproach. He smiled wanly in the wavering light, crossing his arms and stretching his legs toward the warmth. "I fancy I hear Mrs. Hudson. Help her, Watson, and then return when you can, and we shall discuss tonight's events."

"Very well. Holmes?"

"Yes?"

"Forgive me for asking, but do you know anything of Miss Adler's composure?"

"It has been several minutes since I last saw her," said my friend, his posture still unchanged. "I assume she has quieted."

I thanked him and stepped out to meet Mrs. Hudson, who had reached the landing. There I offered to take the tray from her and help attend to Miss Adler.

"Thank you, Doctor, but this I can do by myself," she told me. "Nothing against you personally, but this isn't a time for men. If you wish to see to anyone, choose the one in there," she said, nodding toward the sitting room. With that, our landlady proceeded up the stair toward the maid's room.

I watched as she ascended and then entered Miss Adler's quarters after knocking. The door shut behind her, and I returned to the sitting room, where I found Holmes still perched before the coals. He acknowledged my presence by the slight turn of his head.

"Ready, Watson?"

Silently, I approached and, pulling the basket-chair close to him, sat down.

Holmes smiled grimly in the light of the fire. "How shall it be, Watson? Dialogue or pure exposition?"

"Did Miss Adler say anything at all?"

"Ah, dialogue. Well, yes," my friend answered. "Before our conversation was terminated by Mrs. Hudson, she informed me that it was her fiancé who hurled Godfrey Norton to his death."

"He was here then?"

"That is his glove," said Holmes, pointing to it upon a nearby table. "It was still warm when I picked it up." In the full light, I could see that it was tan in colour.

Holmes continued to recount their conversation. "Miss Adler admitted that the kerchief in her window was actually a signal to Robert Hope Maldon, conveying that it was safe for him to contact her. He did just that, she confessed, tossing small pebbles at her window from the roof. Once she had quietly opened her window, she silently directed him to the lumber room above. While we were still in the sitting room, Miss Adler discreetly ascended to the second floor, where she opened the lumber room window for him."

"Why such an approach?" I asked. "Why did he not come to the front door and ring the bell?"

"A good question, Watson, and one to which I did not receive any suitable answer. In any event, Hope Maldon chose the lumber room as his path of entry. He gained access to the open window by means of the plane tree. According to her, they enjoyed a brief embrace after days of separation, when who should follow Hope Maldon in through the window but Godfrey Norton himself. There were words—the precise content of which I, again, had no opportunity to learn—and the two men struggled. One glove was pulled from Robert Hope Maldon's hand, but he, in turn, pushed Norton away. Such force was used that Norton was hurled out the window and to his death upon the stone walk. Miss Adler screamed. Hope Maldon scrambled out the window and away across the rooftops or down the plane tree; I was not allowed by Mrs. Hudson to ask which it was."

"The presence of Godfrey Norton is most astounding, if tragic," I remarked.

"Oh, I have long believed it was only a matter of time before he arrived to play a part in our little drama," said Holmes. "His death, however, is a most unfortunate development."

"Why did you expect him?"

"It has been obvious that one more character lurked somewhere offstage."

"How so?"

"Recall that young Hope Maldon's rooms at Breton Mansions were entered through the court window. Prior to this evening, who could it have been?"

"Jasper Girthwood?"

"Mr. Girthwood is barely able to negotiate the stairs of this house, let alone its roofs and windows."

"Girthwood's henchmen then."

"Girthwood, to this point, has had no henchmen in London, excepting the pathetic Mr. Starkey," said Holmes. "No, the intruder at Breton Mansions was someone else. Until tonight Godfrey Norton was, I admit, merely a possible candidate."

"And considered possible for what reason?"

"For the fact that both Irene and Godfrey Norton were reported in the newspapers as having died together in an avalanche. If one escaped that fate, why not both?"

"But why did Miss Adler not tell us of his survival? And would that not affect her plans with young Hope Maldon?"

"As to your latter question, I expect it does—or did—complicate matters greatly. As to the former, she did not say. I expect she will claim it was to shield her husband from the king of Bohemia."

"The king would have had Norton murdered had he known the man still lived?"

"I am not so certain of that conclusion, but I suspect Miss Adler is, yes."

"So its truth is uncertain?"

Holmes yawned. "I leave it for the ghost of Pilate to contemplate the nature of truth at the moment," he said. "You may join him in discussing it if you wish. For myself, it is now to bed. We shall get no more, true or false, from Miss Adler tonight, and perhaps we might fabricate some additional evidence for Hopkins when he comes round tomorrow, as he surely will."

"Do you believe it is safe for us to retire?"

"I sent word to Langdale Pike earlier, while you were occupied with the police. He and Upshaw will arrive shortly and take up positions to the front and rear of 221 tonight as a precaution. Good night, Watson," said Holmes, rising to his feet and striding toward his room. "See to the coals, if you will, old fellow."

CHAPTER TEN:

The Quarry and Its History

W hen I descended the stair the next morning I found, as usual, the sitting room occupied. The inhabitant was not Sherlock Holmes, however, but Irene Adler.

"He has not yet arisen?" I asked in astonishment.

"He has already left," the woman said. "I woke early," she continued. "And Mrs. Hudson kindly provided me breakfast and suggested I warm myself here." She looked down at the hearth and then idly smoothed her dress with one hand. In her lap was *The Martyrdom of Man*.

"You are still attempting to read that?" I asked, fearful of raising the subject of the previous night's tragedy.

"Yes. Mr. Holmes did recommend it, did he not?"

"Holmes recommends a great many things, not all of them advisable."

"You do not approve of the book?"

"It is too long-winded for my taste."

"Perhaps it is," Miss Adler said. "Nonetheless, I shall stay with it."

I considered reaching for my Arcadia then thought better of it and took to the basket-chair. "Do you require anything to calm your mind?" I asked, trying obliquely to acknowledge her grief. "I could go down to the chemist..."

"No, Doctor, but thank you. I shall see all this through relying upon my own resources."

We sat opposite each other for a moment, and as she failed to return to her book, I said at length, "We, of course, did not know your husband...was alive...at the time."

"You must now find me as untrustworthy as Mr. Holmes has always seemed to," the woman replied in a hesitant voice. "If only you could understand—"

"But I do," was my immediate response. "I do understand! You would not have wanted the king of Bohemia to know of Mr. Norton's survival."

"But Mr. Holmes does not believe that, does he?"

"We discussed the matter last night."

"And what did he say?"

"He expected you to give the reason that you just conveyed to me."

"But he does not believe it, does he?"

I struggled to make some answer.

"I have not led the most honest of lives, Dr. Watson." She turned again toward the hearth. "You know that, yet you show the extreme kindness of never alluding to it. Still, I have been dishonest. I have been dishonest with you and Mr. Holmes."

"Shall I attend to the coals?" I asked, feeling myself to be a most uncomfortable witness to Miss Adler's unfolding confessions.

"Please leave them; I am fine. Perhaps one honest thing I did do was forswear any attempt to blackmail the king of Bohemia. Godfrey and I—"

The door to 221 opened and closed below us. Almost at once I heard the familiar bound of Holmes upon the stair.

"Ah, you have both arisen," said the detective, tossing off his coat and hat. He stirred our fire with the bent iron then stood to one side and leaned upon the mantel. "Did you chance to read the note I left for you?" he asked Miss Adler.

"I did."

"May we now resume our conversation of last night under those conditions?"

"Yes," the woman said, setting aside her book. "I have been ready for some time."

I suddenly felt the outsider in their conversation.

"Good," remarked Holmes. "It would seem—"

My friend was interrupted by the telephone.

"So early in the day," said Holmes as he strode across the room to answer. "I fancy a time will come when shopkeepers will endeavour to sell merchandise with this instrument. Halloa, this is Sherlock Holmes…Yes, I did. Of course…That will suit, yes…It will be most welcome. I completely agree…Good, we shall await you."

"Hopkins?" I asked as Holmes turned away from the table.

"Jasper Girthwood," he said. "Our portly friend will pay a return visit to Baker Street in two hours."

"For what reason is he calling?" the woman asked.

"The same reason as before. He proposes, in his words, to 'pool our resources' in the hunt for the black bird. Once again, Miss Adler, I must—"

"Ask the full truth of me."

"In all honesty and with no sarcasm, that has been my only request of you these past few days," he replied.

Miss Adler clasped her hands together. "It was Mr. Girthwood who discovered the existence of a valuable statuette in Paris. Of its true nature and final value, I cannot say, save that Mr. Girthwood felt compelled to steal it and proposed that my husband, Godfrey, join him in that deed."

"And so this Girthwood truly was, in fact, an associate of your husband?"

"He was, for the several years that we spent in America. Mr. Girthwood and his activities were one reason for my estrangement from Godfrey, who readily agreed to this most recent proposal from Mr. Girthwood. For reasons I do not know, they both asked me to accompany them. You must believe me when I say that I would never have agreed to such a thing if Godfrey had not promised, should I comply, to grant me the divorce he had denied me these many years."

"And this was prior to your meeting Robert Hope Maldon," said Sherlock Holmes.

"Oh, indeed. I had repeatedly asked for dissolution of our marriage, but Godfrey had refused. Though initially I had brought property to our union, given the nature of the law, I had no way to regain it and no hope of obtaining my full independence."

"And so you agreed to participate in the theft of this valuable statue."

"Yes. Godfrey and Mr. Girthwood booked us on a voyage across the Atlantic. It was during that transit that I met Robert. By the time we docked in England, the two of us were quite in love. I explained my situation to Robert—all of it, Mr. Holmes, from before the king of Bohemia to the present. I spared no detail—"

"Yes, but please go on," said Holmes.

I made a great stir while shifting position in my chair, and the two of them turned toward me.

"Do you wish perhaps a glass of water?" I asked of Miss Adler.

The woman smiled and shook her head. "Robert seemed less shocked at my history than I had expected," she continued, turning back toward Holmes. "He was kind and understanding but, as I learned, also a bit dishonest himself. Even when I told him of the scheme to steal the black bird, he expressed not dismay but rather a serious interest in joining the enterprise."

"And did he? Join, that is."

"In a sense. Robert announced he could contribute some small amount of money to finance the scheme in return for a share of the profit. Godfrey and Girthwood were, of course, shocked and angry that I had confided in Robert, but in the end, they had no choice but to accept him as part of the venture, though they insisted that his share of the return come from my original portion."

"Did your young man say whence he obtained his capital?"

"No."

"Hum. And all four of you then travelled to Paris?"

"No," said Miss Adler. "That is where the plan unravelled."

"How so?" asked Holmes.

"Robert quickly became as obsessed with the statue as Mr. Girthwood and grew dissatisfied with what he saw as the meagreness of our portion of the profit. He arranged for the two of us to leave early for the Continent, without Godfrey and Mr. Girthwood knowing. I did not know of these plans until the last moment, when Robert revealed to me his intention to steal the statue for us alone. I became distraught at his confession; I could not see how the pair of us might escape the wrath of both Godfrey and Girthwood. It was at that point that I believe I mentioned you as a possible protector for the pair of us. I thought I had succeeded in dissuading Robert from going ahead with his plan, but he deceived me."

"How so?"

"He pretended to have been swayed by my arguments once we arrived in Paris and left the hotel, he said, to wire Godfrey in London that our premature departure was a mistake. Instead, he went to steal the black bird, sending to my hotel room a brief letter admitting the same and instructing me to return to London and wait until he might come for me."

"And that is what happened?"

Though speaking to my friend, Miss Adler stared at me as she continued. "Yes. I was unable to stop him! I went to the shop where the statue was supposed to be, but by that time, terrible events had transpired there. The building was in flames, and as police swarmed round, I learned a murder had occurred there as well."

"A murder?" said Holmes. "Tell me, do you recall the name of the victim?"

"No," said Miss Adler. "I do recall that it was the owner of the shop, a Greek by nationality."

"Could the name have been Charilaos Konstantinides?"

"Perhaps."

"I have just given you the name of an art dealer recently murdered in Paris," my friend said, casting a suggestive glance in my direction. "The printed accounts have been rather horrific indeed. Konstantinides was most brutally murdered, his shop ransacked and then set afire. Do you believe your young man capable of such acts, Miss Adler?"

"Never."

"Yet you saw him push your husband to his death last night."

"That was an accident! They were fighting, grappling with each other! The dear simply pushed Godfrey away. He didn't mean for him to die."

"Well, we are getting ahead of ourselves, are we not? The shop was robbed, the owner murdered, and your fiancé was nowhere to be found. Pray, continue, if you will."

"From that point on, it is largely as I told you before," Miss Adler said. "I returned to London immediately."

"You did not wait for your husband and Mr. Girthwood?"

"I feared what they might do! I believed I had to find Robert before they did. I had nothing but the possessions I have now and, in my worried state, could think only of calling upon you for assistance, though I had no guarantee you would come to my aid." The woman looked down, close to tears. "I used invention to try to gain sympathy, I admit. I had no idea what you might do if you knew the full truth."

Holmes slowly strode across the room. "And may I now return to the unfortunate events of last night?"

"Yes," the woman said. "I believe I am capable of discussing them calmly."

Holmes nodded. "Please do so then."

Miss Adler took a moment to compose her thoughts and then began. "Once I realized by his written message that Robert had supposed I had come to you in Baker Street, I thought to display the blue kerchief in my window—it was a signal of assurance between us, as you surmised, an indication that all was well and safe. I could only wait, hoping he would either ring up Baker Street again when I might be present or that he would attempt to contact me in person. It was the latter course that he chose."

"By throwing the pebbles at your window," Holmes said.

"Yes, I looked down and saw Robert standing in the back yard. I motioned for him to go up to the lumber room window, which I indicated I would open. I did so, though I feared I would be detected."

"You underestimate your ability in the art of stealth," Sherlock Holmes said quietly.

"Robert climbed the tree," she continued. "He was able to step to the open window from there."

"Yes, it is a rather easy route. I have used it once or twice myself."

"I do not recall that," I said from my chair.

"It was before we shared these digs, Watson, in an era when I was capable of such athleticism." My friend strolled back across the room and again took up station before the mantel. "I frequently went to St. Bart's with my pockets full with samples to test, and I sometimes forgot the key to 221. As a precaution, I frequently left that lumber room window open, so as to eventually find my way to bed. But forward, please, Miss Adler. You and your fiancé were now reunited."

"He told me he had failed to steal the statuette. Someone else had reached the Greek's shop earlier. Whoever that person was had evidently claimed the piece and murdered Konstantinides. Frightened, Robert had immediately left. At that point in his story, he was interrupted."

"By Godfrey Norton."

"Yes. He had followed Robert's path up and into the house. 'That's a good story,' he said. 'Now make me believe it.' Robert, however, acted impulsively. He did not say anything; he merely lunged out at Godfrey. They struggled near the open window. Robert lost one glove and then obtained an advantage in position. He pushed very hard, and Godfrey flew over the sill and out. I screamed, and Robert left through the window and then sprang to the tree, down which he scrambled to the yard. I then lost sight of him. The rest you witnessed personally."

"No one heard or saw Hope Maldon run away from the scene," Holmes said after a moment. "Given the lateness of the hour, that is, perhaps, unsurprising. Well, you have given me something to digest. I fear, however, that I can no longer play the innocent before Mr. Girthwood where you are concerned. The only question for us now is to determine if you should be present during the next interview with the man."

"I will not face him!" she replied sharply, turning again to stare directly at Holmes.

"Then the matter is settled. I suggest you retire to your room, as you have so often before."

At the scheduled time, Jasper Girthwood appeared for the second time in our Baker Street sitting room. Once more, he occupied the sofa as we faced him, with Irene Adler again in hiding above.

"I understand a man died here last night," Girthwood said immediately after greetings were exchanged. "I am told that man was Godfrey Norton."

"That is true," replied Holmes.

"Dreadful thing. I play the game seriously, sir, but I need no reminders of its seriousness. Now then, shall we put our minds to conciliation, sir?" the man said. "Shall we lay out all the cards, this time with every one face up?"

Holmes nodded. "Let us begin," the detective said, "with Godfrey Norton himself. Were the two of you in league with one another?"

Girthwood let out a great sigh. "No," he said. "Mr. Norton and I were once allied. Indeed, we were part of an even grander cabal dedicated to a worthy aim. That conspiracy came undone, sir, because of treachery on the part of half its members."

"And you and Norton constituted the other half?"

"Only momentarily," the American said. "The first treachery prompted Norton to leave me as well. Normally, I wish no man dead, sir, but I will not mourn that recently departed individual."

"I understand," said Holmes. "Well then, let us continue with the bird."

"A fine place to continue, indeed," answered Girthwood. "The bird shall be the prime topic, I daresay. Tell me, Mr. Holmes, have you any familiarity whatsoever with the Order of the Hospital of St. John of Jerusalem?"

"Later styled the Knights of Malta?"

"Good, sir. More than that, indeed—very good!"

"Some years ago I had the need to research certain mediaeval tracts, which referred to them on occasion. They were forced from Rhodes in the early sixteenth century—"

"In 1523, to be precise," interrupted Girthwood. "They were driven out by—"

"The Ottomans," said Sherlock Holmes. "And they then settled, I believe, in Crete."

"Magnificent!" said Girthwood heartily. "By gad, sir, when I think of the years we've already lost not knowing one another. Oh, I must say, you're the top, sir!"

Holmes and I exchanged raised brows.

"Yes, the top," Girthwood repeated with a laugh. Then his demeanour changed abruptly, and he asked, "Do you know what occurred then? To the Hospitaliers, I mean, after their arrival in Crete."

"I believe Emperor Charles V of the Hapsburgs granted them stay in Malta."

"Yes! By then it was 1530, and Charles gave to the order not only Malta but Gozo and Tripoli as well. Still," the man said in a hushed voice, raising one plump forefinger, "this was a gift of occupation only, you understand. The islands still belonged to the Hapsburgs, and were the knights to leave, all three would revert at once to Charles. In recognition of this, Mr. Holmes, the Order of St. John was required each year to give to the emperor the gift of a falcon."

"A living falcon?" I asked.

Girthwood looked at me with an odd expression, as if truly contemplating my presence for the first time. "Why, yes, that was, in fact, the intent. A ceremonial tribute, you see," he continued, waving his stocky arms. "But at that time, as you must realize, Mr. Holmes, the knights were chest high in wealth, and so they determined that the tribute that first year would be no mere living bird, with dirty feathers and a beak demanding to be fed, but rather a jewel-encrusted golden statue of a falcon. From each eye to every talon, sir, not one square inch of the outside was without a gem, and on the inside was nothing but the purest of gold!"

Holmes reached for his briar pipe.

"Perhaps you think the story apocryphal," declared Girthwood. "Perhaps you consider it myth, what I, as an American, should call bunk. If it's not in your histories or encyclopaedias, you dismiss it, eh? Well, I tell you that it will be found in no fewer than four references."

"Hum," remarked Holmes languidly, filling his pipe with shag. "I do seem to recall some oblique reference to such an object in a work of Paoli."

"Yes, the unpublished supplement to *Dell'origine ed Instituto del Sacro Militar Ordine!*"

"That was it," said the detective, smiling as he lit his pipe. "I believe that it was... perhaps...seven or eight years ago, and I remember I had the deuce of a time reading the manuscript, for it was in a code, which—"

"In code? But that would make it the original in Paoli's own hand, sir! And that copy is in the personal library of the—"

"I was in Rome at the time, engaged in a singular affair involving stolen cameos," said Holmes. "Discretion forces me to ask that we return to the main thread of your tale."

"Yes," said Girthwood, eyeing my friend with what seemed to be newfound respect. "Yes, of course. I shall then continue, sir. Gad, the places you've been, eh? Well, this statue of a falcon, the figure of which I speak—one foot high—was sent to Emperor Charles in Spain on board a galley commanded by a French member of the Order of St. John. But neither he nor the bird ever reached Spain! A buccaneer out of Algiers, known as Redbeard, captured the galley and took the bird to Africa. There it stayed for over a century, until it was carried away by an English freebooter named Verney."

Holmes took the pipe from his mouth. "Did you say Verney? Sir Francis Verney, perhaps?"

"Why, the very same, sir. You are familiar with this man?"

"I have a degree of interest in his family, which has a distant French branch—the Vernets.[7] I recall, however, no mention of the falcon in Lady Verney's *Memoirs*."

"Indeed, there is none," agreed Girthwood, his eyes narrowing. "So you've read that also. Tell me, sir, are you ever what you seem to be?"

"Life itself is but a walking shadow, Mr. Girthwood."

"What's that mean? You lose me."

"Pray, return to your story."

Our guest exhaled as if confused. "Certainly, sir. Well, as you say, there is no mention of the statue in the *Memoirs*, and Sir Francis did not possess the bird when he died penniless in Messina in 1615. But the bird unquestionably went to Sicily with him; for over one hundred years later, it was there when the abdicating king, Victor Amadeus, presented the statue to his wife as a gift. The author Carutti verifies that act in his account of the monarch." Girthwood looked cautiously at the detective and asked, "Have you ever read Carutti, sir?"

"No," said Sherlock Holmes. "I cannot say as I have ever come across the name."

"Ah, yes," replied our portly visitor with satisfaction. "Well, Carutti places the bird in Sicily at that time. Tell me, do you find these details tedious?"

"Details themselves are never tedious," remarked my friend. "It is the conclusions drawn from them which either bore or enthral. Pray, continue."

"Well, sir, the falcon ironically passed next to a Spaniard, the father of a future count. As far as my research shows, it stayed with that family until the end of the Carlist War, when one of them took it into exile, to Paris, where it was lost. By this time, Mr. Holmes, the bird had acquired at least one covering of black enamel, which made it appear to be nothing more than a common statuette. My own guess is that it was the Spaniard's hand—a precaution during the Carlist troubles, you see."

"It retains this covering to the present day?"

"That is my understanding. In disguise, Mr. Holmes, it was batted about the gutters and byways of Paris for years, until several months ago, when an art dealer obtained it by chance."

"Charilaos Konstantinides," said Holmes, holding up his pipe to study its silhouette against the window light. "The Greek art dealer recently murdered."

---

7   Holmes's grandmother was the sister of Horace Vernet, the French artist.

"The same, sir. You never miss a point, do you, eh? Yes, quite the man you are. Well, it was, indeed, Charilaos. He wasn't sure what he had, but he had an inkling that something of value lay under that coating of enamel. I had corresponded with him frequently, and when, in a letter, he described the bird he'd found, I realized what it had to be and knew I must obtain it for myself. Wasting no time, I booked passage from New York across the Atlantic for myself and two associates."

"Godfrey Norton was one," said Holmes.

"Yes," replied Girthwood. "I believe you know the other—his wife. Along the way, we gained another compatriot—young Mr. Hope Maldon, the man whom I understand you are seeking. Well, the voyage did not agree with me, I must say, and so upon arriving in London, I was forced to remain there longer than I'd planned before going on.

"It was during that time that Mrs. Norton and Mr. Hope Maldon saw fit to scurry ahead to Paris, with the intention of taking the statue for themselves. I was understandably outraged, sir, as was poor Norton. And then, three days later, to compound matters, what should I read in the *Times* but an account of Charilaos's own murder! The details of the story were monstrous, if I do say so myself. I went to Paris immediately, but not much remained of my old friend."

"I take it the statue had been removed from his shop by that time?" asked the detective.

"I know it was not there, in whole or in part, following the murder," our guest said. "Well, figuring that somehow my two disloyal associates had absconded with the bird, I returned to London, where Norton had remained. He believed that his wife might come to you for assistance. In the course of our discussions, however, our own alliance fell apart into argument. Norton abandoned me, vowing to find them on his own. We parted enemies, a fact I now regret," Girthwood added. "Although he himself is no longer capable of feeling the same."

"Apparently he succeeded in his quest," said Holmes. "But at the cost of his own life."

Girthwood stopped in the act of pulling a cigar from his pocket. "Oh? So Mr. Maldon and Mrs. Norton are here?"

"Not at the moment," replied Sherlock Holmes.

"I see," Girthwood said, his eyes narrowing. "Were you referring to one or the other or both?"

"Both."

"So they are not in this house?"

"They are not...here," said Holmes.

Girthwood smiled with amusement. "Well, that's neither *here* nor *there*, I suppose," said Girthwood, resuming his motions. He lit the cigar. "I've now given you the history of the Hapsburg falcon, sir. It doesn't rival that fellow Gibbon in depth or wit, I suppose, but the sweep is nearly as grand, is it not?"

Holmes shook out his briar, placed it upon the table, and made a steeple with his fingers. "Tell me," he said. "Do you believe Robert Hope Maldon has the statue at present?"

"If he does not, then Irene Norton does."

"Or some other person," suggested Holmes.

"If it is another person, I may have no hope of recovering the falcon," said Girthwood. "It is Mr. Hope Maldon or Mrs. Norton or nothing, insofar as I am concerned."

"You realize," said Sherlock Holmes, "that to the extent that I become involved with this statue you speak of, I must see it back to its rightful owner."

"And who might that be, eh? The present king of Spain? The Austro-Hungarian emperor? I believe I've already told you, sir, that rightful ownership is an invalid concept where the falcon is concerned."

"You said several minutes ago that you had to possess this statue," said Holmes. "What were your original plans to obtain it?"

Girthwood circumspectly trimmed the ash of his cigar. "I'm afraid you venture too far afield there, Mr. Holmes. You take a proprietary view of your own means; I have the same perspective on mine." The man looked about the room. "Is there anything civilized to drink here, sir?"

"Dr. Watson perhaps might offer you a glass of his Beaune."

"Ah, splendid! That would be most appreciated!"

Holmes motioned to me, and I rose to pour a modest glass for our visitor.

"Excellent!" Girthwood said, his doughy fingers encircling the offering. "Perhaps I failed to take full measure of you earlier, sir," the portly man said, looking up at me.

I returned to my chair, catching Holmes's bemused look.

"I believe you were discussing your means of acquiring the falcon," my friend said.

"No, sir," replied Girthwood, clicking his lips, "I was, in fact, avoiding it. The subject is not germane to our discussion. We need merely note that I wanted the statue. Means are irrelevant."

"Mr. Girthwood," said Holmes. "I fear means are of the utmost relevance. Mr. Konstantinides was murdered, and so our conversation encompasses capital crimes."

Girthwood took a deep sip of the Beaune before replying. "Are you suggesting that I am responsible for the murder? Because if you are attempting to assert that point, I'll have you know that—"

"I mean to imply no such thing. I am merely underscoring the need to, as you said, lay all the cards face up."

Jasper Girthwood disposed of his cigar's remains, set his empty glass upon the table, and laced his fingers over his enormous stomach. "For the third time, Mr. Holmes, I am offering to pay you to recover the falcon for me. Your fee, you must realize, will be almost beyond calculation."

"My fees, as I am wont to remind people, are upon a fixed scale. I do not vary them, save when I remit them altogether, though in your case, an exception could, no doubt, be made. Still, I must, for a third time, refuse the crown you offer."

"You will not reconsider?"

"How can I reconsider it, Mr. Girthwood, when I have never seriously considered it once?"

Our rotund guest frowned and, in a manner best described as a childish pout enacted by a grown man, rose and took his hat and coat in hand. "You have made me most unhappy, sir. I had hopes our talk would lead to something far different, and you disappoint me greatly." He placed his hat upon his head and shuffled to our sitting room door. "You shall hear from me in the next few days, Mr. Holmes," he continued as he left. "But it will be by indirect means."

"That is some cheek," I said to Holmes as the man reached the bottom of the stair and the house door closed. "After all, he did send that Starkey fellow here, did he not? Should we not go to Hopkins with a complaint? Should we not read that last comment as a—"

"A direct threat," completed my friend. "Yes, Watson, we should consider it such, but I am still not inclined to grant Scotland Yard any greater role in this matter than it has already, which is virtually none." Going to the bow window, he looked out into Baker Street then strode to the sofa and felt it with an outstretched palm. "Still warm," he said, with an air of disgust. "Watson, I'll retire to my room now. See that I am not disturbed, please."

"You prefer that I leave the sitting room?"

"It is of no consequence. I suppose, however, that you should inform Miss Adler it is once again safe for her to come down."

CHAPTER ELEVEN:

Shifting Courses

It was perhaps an hour later that Holmes emerged from his personal quarters into the sitting room, where I sat at my writing table. Despite my assurances to her, Miss Adler had remained, as she so often had, sequestered quietly alone on the floor above. My friend came to the window without a word, glanced at my work, and smiled. Striding across the room in his mouse-coloured dressing-gown, he sat in the armchair and stretched out his legs.

"Ha! I wonder who the worst man in London is now," the detective said, resting his head upon the back of the chair so that his gaze fixed upon the ceiling above. "Moriarty, Moran, Merridew, Milverton, Milligan…Hum, is there something evil about that portion of the alphabet?"

"Not since you've finished with it, I should imagine. Is this the beginning of more reminiscences?" I asked, dipping my pen and holding it aloft. "I am ready."

"By that tone, one might believe you think reminiscing to be a vice, Doctor." He motioned toward my paper. "You are guilty of the sin as often as I. Indeed, you commit yours to paper."

"And I am compensated handsomely for them," said I, "both yours and mine." I smiled and set my pen onto the foolscap to continue.

"There was an American named Barnum who had something to say about your activities of these past many years, Watson. The remark concerns the naïveté of the public."

"You have delivered that quotation to me frequently over the years," I said while finishing a paragraph. "Twenty-seven times during our association, if my count is correct."

"Doctor!"

I clicked my palate in dismissal, and we smiled briefly at one another.

"I realize this announcement is sudden," my friend declared in a suddenly serious tone. "But I fear I shall be emigrating as I threatened to do as this affair began to unfold, though the move is temporary. Old fellow, I must travel to Paris."

"Why?" I asked. "What has changed matters so dramatically that—"

"The death of Godfrey Norton for one," replied the detective. "For another, I have received an answer to the telegram Shinwell Johnson sent to the Parisian authorities." He motioned toward the mass of papers lying upon the mantel.

"When did that arrive?" I asked.

"This morning. I met the messenger as he was about to ring."

"Are you certain you are required on the Continent? Cannot Johnson himself go? Or Langdale Pike, perhaps?"

"No, Watson, there are fine points of detail concerning the Konstantinides murder that have a crucial bearing on Robert Hope Maldon's whereabouts, and neither agent would be equal to the task, I fear."

"And so the presence of the master is desirable?"

"Yes," said Holmes, rising to seek out his clay pipe. "But as my brother, Mycroft, is loath to travel, he cannot attend to it, and so I must stand in his place."

"What of the continuing siege of Baker Street?" I asked. "Do you expect me alone to protect Miss Adler? I do not believe I can possibly—"

"I do expect that of you, old fellow. What other person has never disappointed my expectations?"

"But what might Girthwood now attempt?"

"As I have noted, the fellow is, at heart, of a vicious type," said Holmes, coming to my side with his clay pipe in hand. "Yet he is, in practice, a youthful bungler and a bungler without allies in a strange land. You, on the other hand, will still have the assistance of our host of agents, as well as your own personal resources. No, Watson, I do not think Mr. Girthwood poses a fatal threat for the time being, though he needs to be carefully watched."

"And you truly believe that travelling to Paris is a necessity?"

"I do, as much as when you first asked that question but a moment ago. Trust me when I say I would not leave were it not so."

"When do you depart then?"

"Today."

The imminence of my friend's leaving took me sharply aback. With an attempt to sound unalarmed, I asked, "And what do you believe will come of your visit?"

He found his Persian slipper of shag and smiled. "*Nous verons.*"[8]

---

8   "We shall see."

Lighting his pipe, Holmes vanished into his room again and emerged some time later, fully dressed. Taking his hat and coat in hand, he announced his intention of going out to make final arrangements for departure to the French capital.

"My passage is already booked," he said. "A few minor loose ends must be attended to, however, before I am off to Paris. In the meanwhile, should anyone call or ring for me, take what message you can, but do not mention my trip to the Continent."

"Not even to Miss Adler?"

"Exempt her from your vow of silence. Oh, and as before, allow no one above the ground floor."

"Of course. Are there any other instructions concerning our guest?"

"She has shown the capacity to tend to her own needs," Holmes said as he strode toward the sitting room door. "I expect she will know what to do and when to do it."

With that, my friend left the room, departed 221, and set out across Baker Street. I spent the next several minutes alone, writing at the window, before I heard Miss Adler descend to the sitting room.

"Mr. Holmes is out," she declared as a statement of fact rather than a question. "I heard the house door and assumed it was he leaving."

"You are correct." Gathering my wits, I came straight to the matter. "In the wake of all that has recently happened, he has fixed upon journeying to Paris himself."

"Oh?" she said in surprise, taking to the basket-chair. "He has not yet begun that trip, has he?"

"For Paris? No, he is in the midst of making the last of his preparations. I do not see the need, myself. I am not, however, in possession of all the relevant facts."

"When is he to cross the Channel?"

"Today, if he is to be believed. In truth, Miss Adler, I confess that I'd rather he not go, if for no other reason than that it leaves only me to assist you."

The woman sat quietly thinking then said, "If Mr. Holmes deems it necessary, we must not question the decision. And as to my safety, Dr. Watson, I declare my complete confidence in you. You shall prove a faithful guardian; I do not doubt. And you will have all Mr. Holmes's agents at your disposal, will you not?"

"Yes, that is true, as Holmes himself kept assuring me," I replied, perhaps more to calm my worries rather than hers.

"I am certain it will all come right," she responded. "And I know Mr. Holmes believes his course of action is the right one."

"I assure you he is doing his best for your——"

"I know that, Doctor. As I have remarked before, he is the best at what he does."

At that moment, as I had done so often in the past two days, I suggested ringing Mrs. Hudson for a bit of food, an idea that my companion accepted. And so, minutes later, we were presented with a delightful set of fried herrings. As our provider departed the sitting room, I passed a plate of lemon quarters to Miss Adler and then briefly looked into the sugar bowl.

"Do you always perform that act?" my dining partner asked. "I have seen you at it previously."

"I beg your pardon?"

"The sugar bowl," the woman said. "You peek inside before starting almost every meal. Why so?"

"Yes, it is a little ritual of mine, I suppose," was my reply. "In the early days of our association, Holmes's domestic habits were not yet adjusted to account for a fellow boarder. He would, not infrequently, store dry chemicals in the sugar bowl, as well as other inappropriate locations."

"He continues in that habit?"

"Oh, no. This bowl has contained nothing but sugar for well more than a decade, but I still make certain."

"For luck?"

I shrugged. "I suppose it is my little charm, yes," I said casually, not admitting my silent wish upon the bowl—that Holmes be delayed in his departure for France.

Miss Adler and I continued to talk amiably together, she steering our conversation to topics unrelated to her current troubles, matters as light as the joys of cycling and the public's recently revived interest in the game of gossima. After we had finished the herring and Mrs. Hudson had cleared our table, I asked Miss Adler's leave to return to my writing.

"The last thing I should wish to do is to keep you from your work," the woman said. "Indeed, I fear my presence alone might be a distraction."

"Your presence would, if anything, be an inspiration," I boldly said. "Perhaps I might ask your advice in the matter of turns of phrase?"

"As you wish," she said, smiling broadly. "I shall read by the hearth again, if you will permit."

"It is not for me to allow or disallow," I said. "Please recall that we are both guests here at 221. Though, if it will not offend, let me express a wish that you discard that drab book Holmes gave you."

"*Martyrdom of Man?*" she replied. "Oh, I did eventually put that down, Doctor, though I would rather you not tell Mr. Holmes. I found this instead yesterday," she continued, pulling a volume from the shelves. "It is a quaint historical romance."

"Oh, yes," I said. "It is a favourite of mine, a true epic worthy of greater public attention. I am acquainted with its author, you know."

"Truly?"

"Yes. There is another work of his there on the same shelf. I recommend it highly as well."

"Thank you." The woman sighed. "I must say, I should not think Mr. Holmes would enjoy such works as these."

"Oh, he doesn't. Those books there, the group from which you pulled the present volume, they are all my own, you see."

"They remain here at Baker Street? Why are they not at Queen Anne Street with you? Have you no room for them?"

"It is an embarrassing confession," I said. "But my future wife has no great affection for them. And, as I frequently find myself here at 221, Holmes generously allots me some space on his shelves."

"Your wife does not enjoy historical literature?"

"She does not enjoy literature at all, considering it rather frivolous," I said timidly. "She is of a more practical turn, you see. Her family's business claims a great portion of her attention, as well as her brother's, following the death of their father."

"Does she not enjoy, for instance, the theatre?"

"No."

"And probably not opera then, either."

"That is correct."

"I could not imagine life without either. But then, I have been on the stage. Does she not take even a little joy in music?"

"Oh, yes," I said at once. "She especially enjoys those little mechanical music boxes. She is fascinated by what she calls their 'intricate tinkling.' I have given her three during our courtship."

"How wonderfully nice of you," Miss Adler said.

I smiled back at her, feeling somewhat uncomfortable and suddenly melancholy, and excused myself to return to my composition while Miss Adler again took up her fictional narrative of the Hundred Years' War. Sometime later, I thought to ask her advice on punctuation.

"Oh," she said with a laugh. "You're the writer, not I! In any event, is that not the purpose of editors?"

"Yes, I suppose they must have some reason for being."

She smiled. "Is that another of Mr. Holmes's stories you are working at?"

"Well, yes," I replied. "Of course, it is one of *my* stories about *his* exploits."

"Exploits in defence of British law," she added solemnly.

"Not in all cases," I said thoughtfully, looking down at my nearly completed manuscript. "I should rather say in defence of people rather than law. Indeed, in this instance I am writing about, Holmes—and I—most assuredly broke several statutes. I beg you, though, not to mention that fact to a soul." I paused and then added, "You see, Holmes defends not so much the letter of the law as the spirit of justice."

"He will take it upon himself to choose people over the law, as you just said, then?"

"Depending upon the particular people and the particular law, yes."

We then spent more than another hour in each other's quiet company. On two occasions, our silence was broken by the telephone, which I had begun to think of as yet another fellow lodger in Baker Street. The first person with whom I conversed was Stanley Hopkins, who requested I inform Holmes that Scotland Yard had nothing new of value in the Hope Maldon disappearance and asked that my friend ring him back promptly. The second was Diarmund Stephenson, who rang, he said, on behalf of only himself, for information about his missing friend. Regrettably, I was forced to admit I could offer nothing, a response which led to several minutes of my commiserating with the young man. It was just as the conversation ended—Irene Adler having since retired to her room— that Sherlock Holmes returned to 221.

"All aspects of my passage are arranged," were the detective's first words upon re-entering the sitting room, a message that turned my anxieties into fears. "Please excuse me while I assemble my things," he said.

Before Holmes vanished into his room, I informed him of my telephone interviews with the inspector and the secretary.

"I shall ring up Hopkins presently," my friend replied. "Perhaps I shall toss him a few unimportant items he may pursue; that should make him feel he is putting his time to some use. As for Stephenson, I should like you to personally cultivate that young man when he rings or calls again."

"You think it likely he will?"

"I shall be greatly disappointed if he does not. He claims to be a good friend of Mr. Hope Maldon, and there is the chance that the latter may now try to contact Stephenson rather than Miss Adler. If that happens, we must know of it." And with that comment, my friend strode into his room. I stared out the bow window, wondering what I should do now.

Within the hour, Holmes stood at the door to 221, prepared to depart. Beside him sat a large valise, his only baggage.

"Two agents will be outside at all times," he told me in the company of Mrs. Hudson and Miss Adler. "I shall return as swiftly as possible and, in the interim, advise you all of my progress by telegram."

"Will this bring us closer to finding Robert?" asked Irene Adler.

"I cannot say," Holmes told her. "Your fiancé knows where you are. His first attempt at reuniting with you ended in tragedy, and we can only wait for him to seek you out here at Baker Street once more. If he does not, then it is we who must seek him out. That is, in part, why I travel to Paris," he said. "To establish a trail from there."

"Might we who remain do more than simply wait at 221?" I asked.

"I fear, Doctor, that the answer must be no. I have placed messages in all the agony columns; perhaps Mr. Hope Maldon will catch sight of one and act upon it. Whether that happens or not, your duty remains the monotonous but necessary one of sitting and waiting. In my absence, Watson, you shall, of course, be in full command. Act decisively, but do nothing rash. Be prudent, but do not allow that quality to paralyze. And," he said, putting one hand on my shoulder, "above all, Watson—"

"To mine own self be true?"

My friend's eyes widened almost imperceptibly. For a moment, he stood speechless; then he slapped my back and gave a hearty laugh. "No, old fellow, no." Turning his billycock hat round in his hand, he continued. "Adherence to that precept is part of your very character; you need no advice in that realm. No, what I was going to say was, at all costs avoid the use of force. If, heaven forbid, Girthwood attempts violence, do not meet it with your own. Do you promise me that, Watson?"

"Of course."

"Good. Well, I am off to Paris," said he as he strode out the door of 221.

"I hope this journey proves valuable," I declared to him as we followed. "We can expect you to return to London, can we not?"

"Of course," replied Holmes with a smile as a four-wheeler appeared round a nearby corner. "Never fear." Then, taking my hand, followed by that of Miss Adler, and, finally, bowing to Mrs. Hudson, he turned and quickly walked off into the rush of Baker Street, toward the horse-drawn vehicle.

"I shall serve you two a good dinner of chicken soufflé tonight," said Mrs. Hudson as she waved good-bye to the detective. "And a supper that will be at a civilized hour for a change." We three re-entered 221, and then Miss Adler and I, together, ascended the stair to the sitting room.

At the landing, I turned to my fellow lodger. "I should expect you to desire your usual time alone," I said. "Shall I retire to my quarters and leave you the sitting room, Miss Adler?"

"Doctor, I expected you to continue writing at your desk."

"My work in that vein is finished for the day," I said. "In truth, I feel rather weary and desire a nap. The sitting room is yours. Please instruct Mrs. Hudson to wake me should I fail to come down for dinner."

"As you wish," the woman said as I began to climb the stair. At my door, a sudden thought occurred to me, and I continued to the upper storey of the house. At that acme, I entered the lumber room, more sedately this time, and I navigated the maze of boxes holding Holmes's old newspaper files, nearly stumbling over his rusting portable basin and now rarely used collection of chemical apparatus before I espied, in the far corner, the item I sought. Negotiating round several more boxes and an ancient, worm-eaten wooden chest, I reached the object of my search. The cobwebs that enveloped it were no match for me as I pulled the dull metal pole from its recess.

Stepping back to one of the few open spaces in the lumber room, I held it as one might a cricket bat and slowly made as if to swing it at some imaginary foe. The casual observer would expect it to be light, but the end was heavily weighted, a fact which had been crucial during the case in which Holmes had encountered it. And, I reasoned, in a moment of emergency, any potential weapon would be most welcome. I left the room with my prize and closed the door and then descended the stair to enter my own quarters, where I set the dusty aluminium crutch at my bedside.

"Better more weapons than fewer," I told myself as I removed my coat, recalling also that Holmes's riding crop still lay against a wall of the sitting room. And there was also the slightly bent fire iron at the hearth, I remembered, as I searched for my latest number of the *British Medical Journal*. It also occurred to me that Holmes had secreted a singlestick somewhere in his own room.

I found the copy of the *Journal*, placed it upon my bed, and sat down beside it. "And there is my revolver," I whispered. My promise to Holmes aside, I glanced toward a corner of my room and saw the Eley Bros. ammunition box still there, undisturbed. "But only as a last resort." I removed my shoes with some effort and then swung my still-clothed body onto the bed. It was there, with the *Journal* spread across my chest, that I awoke later to the sound of Mrs. Hudson knocking at my door.

I came quickly down for supper, apologizing to Miss Adler for my hastily assembled appearance, for I had feared Mrs. Hudson's wrath should I have taken more time to prepare.

"You are as dashing as ever," said Miss Adler in disagreement, and I fear I may have blushed while questioning her opinion. Any notice of my embarrassment was quickly forgotten, however, as we both took interest and delight in the soufflé Mrs. Hudson had prepared. Following my customary look inside the sugar bowl, performed this time with an exaggerated self-conscious air meant to amuse my guest, Miss Adler and I resumed the threads of our afternoon discussion.

"I do rather prefer the name gossima to table tennis," she said. "The latter is so uninspiring."

"Yes," I said, savouring our landlady's knowledge of seasoning and spice. "Gossima is such an airy name—it recalls the word gossamer, does it not?"

"The game itself is hardly of that nature, Doctor. You said you had played often?"

"Oh, many times, and I became rather skilled at it, I must say. Some time ago, when I still resided here in Baker Street, I attempted to persuade Holmes to clear out an area in the lumber room, so that a gossima table could be placed there."

"A request he opposed, no doubt."

"Unfortunately, yes."

"Mr. Holmes is not the one for games and sport."

"He would agree with you," I said. "But you both would be quite wrong. He is an expert at boxing and fencing, and he is skilled, if not recently practiced, in several Eastern arts of attack. Then, too, he has joined me for fishing expeditions now and then. He has also admitted to playing golf at least once, and I have seen him put down several opponents in lawn tennis. It was after the latter that I suggested gossima, you see, believing that if he enjoyed the one, he might wish to substitute the other on rainy days."

"But he did not."

"Alas, no, but for the feeblest of reasons."

"Which was…?"

"Oh, he was somewhat fond of lawn tennis for itself, but he particularly enjoyed examining the court afterward to study and interpret the impressions made in the grass by the players and the ball. He searched in vain for analogous scuff marks after a single match of gossima at the house of an associate of mine, but he found nothing to satisfy him. That caused him to lose interest rapidly."

"Hence, no gossima table at 221."

"Regrettably, yes."

"Well," she said, placing her napkin upon the table. "Mr. Holmes would not be across the water yet, would he?"

"He is the one who can quote from Bradshaw's,[9] not I, but I do not believe he would be that far yet, no."

"Doctor, would it alarm you if I said I should like to go out tomorrow?"

"Out? Where?"

"Just out. When we all went about—before Godfrey's death—before, when I rode about in Bloomsbury, my spirits were very much lifted. I feel a prisoner here; please do not take offense at my statement, for I know I have made myself the prisoner." She looked at me with grey eyes that, in their intensity, had oddly shed much of their grief and worry. "Do you believe I have stayed too much in that room above? Tell me truly."

"I can hardly pass judgment on that."

"Please, Doctor! I wish you to do so. Do you not think some excursion tomorrow would be a welcome relief to both of us?"

"It would, indeed, be a relief, but it also would be most unsafe."

"We ventured out only recently," Miss Adler replied. "For a time, I was alone."

"You were escorted by at least three of Holmes's agents," I told her.

"You said earlier that Mr. Holmes himself discounts any further threat from Jasper Girthwood," argued the woman. "What other obstacle is there to our enjoyment of a bracing spring day in London?"

"Perhaps we could entertain the thought," I said, merely to forestall further discussion of the topic. "I believe, however, that it would be best to again have one or two agents along for protection."

"Oh," said Miss Adler with mild dejection. "Should it be thus, I do not know whether I should wish to go or not. I had in mind a pleasant outing, not a military expedition."

9 George Bradshaw published the most popular railroad timetables during the Victorian era. By Edwardian times, his name was applied to any such set of schedules.

"And I have in mind your safety."

"Of course you do. With the terrible burden of responsibility you feel, what other perspective could you possibly entertain? Still, there were no mishaps in the street before, were there? We were not confronted. We were not threatened, were we?"

"No," I reluctantly admitted.

"We are under no cloud. Tell me, Doctor, do you feel we are under a cloud at this moment, other than one of your own making?"

"Perhaps not," I said at last, staring at my empty plate and feeling the warmth of a satisfying meal. "Certainly, I sense no such cloud at all when in your company. But would it not be unseemly?" I said, taking a different tack. "Forgive the directness of my words, Miss Adler, but your husband has been dead less than twenty-four hours."

"Do you see any black, other than my neckband?" the woman asked sharply, raising her arms to display the pale blue of her gown, the same one she had worn when I first saw her in the sitting room. "There is none, is there? I suppose you have probably silently questioned my apparent lack of grief, have you not?"

"Miss Adler, I—"

"Have you not?"

I gave an embarrassed nod.

"Recall that I have wished to be addressed not as Mrs. Norton, or now Widow Norton, but rather as Miss Adler. Godfrey was my husband in the eyes of the law but not in my heart—not for many years. I regret his death, yes, as I would regret that of any person, but I do not mourn him any more than I do the countless others who passed on that very same day."

"I was thinking of propriety, madam," I stammered.

"We have already passed into a new century, Dr. Watson, one that may choose not to carry the baggage of its predecessor. Do not become too chivalrous for my sake, or else you will find yourself living in one of your friend's romances rather than merely reading from its pages."

"I shall consider it," I said curtly, masking my uncertainty as to how I might proceed with a woman speaking in such a temper. I felt rescue at hand when Mrs. Hudson appeared to clear our table.

"Dr. Watson and I were discussing the wisdom of going out tomorrow," Miss Adler said boldly to our landlady. "What might you think of such a suggestion?"

"Oh, it would be wonderful," Mrs. Hudson replied as she gathered up the plates. "In truth, I had considered putting the same to you only this evening, but here you've gone and thought of it yourselves."

"This man of the house believes it may be unsafe," Miss Adler declared.

"Why, no. The dear needs some air, Dr. Watson. Surely a man in your profession can see that? Where's your power of diagnosis, sir?"

"Miss Adler's fiancé might arrive here at 221 at—"

"Any moment," said Mrs. Hudson. "Yes, that he might. And if he does, do you not think that I and Mr. Holmes's men can do what is right?"

"Of course you can," I said with some irritation.

"Bear in mind, Doctor, that my service to Mr. Holmes is longer than yours and uninterrupted, save for his own absence after that Professor Moriarty business."

"I, of course, have full confidence in you," I replied coldly, taken aback by the landlady's boldness and stung by her implied assertion of superiority. Moreover, I sensed a conspiracy between the two of them. "Trust is not the issue."

"Then take the lady out," insisted Mrs. Hudson.

Inwardly I fumed, yet at the same time, I found myself caught in wonder at Miss Adler's odd turnabout in attitude. From a self-imposed confinement, she now proposed to tour the byways of London. There was a purpose here, and it occurred to me that only a bluff might tip her hand. And so I determined to change my own course as well. "Then I yield. I should be pleased to take her out," I said impetuously, "if that is what she wishes."

"You agree?" said my fellow guest, her manner transformed at once into that of sweet, feminine joy.

"Will it be breakfast tomorrow at your usual time then, Doctor?" asked Mrs. Hudson as she left the sitting room.

"Yes," I said, without looking at her, questioning at once what I had done and wondering what Holmes would think of my impromptu gambit. "That will suit."

Miss Adler guided our remaining conversation to the subject of the next day's itinerary, and by the time I scattered the coals in the sitting room hearth we had agreed to include a walk along the Embankment, a meal at Simpson's, and a tour of the City.

"Bart's would not be far," I suggested as I escorted her up the stair.

"That is a hospital, is it not?"

"St. Bartholomew's Hospital," I told her. "It is joined to the University of London, where I took my degree."

"I should be so glad to view the place where your professional career began."

"Oh, Bart's is the site of a personal beginning as well."

"It is?"

"Yes," I replied, stopping at her door. "It was in the chemistry laboratory there that Holmes and I first met."

"Indeed! Well then, we certainly must add it to our list of sights. Dr. Watson," she said, stepping toward me, "I do thank you so much for acceding to my wishes concerning tomorrow. You truly are the most understanding and generous of men."

"That view may be questioned," I said. "I believe I question it myself."

"While modesty is a virtue, self-incrimination is not." She clasped my hand. "You give me a wonderful gift, and I do so look forward to it all. I wish the sun would set this moment, only to rise an instant later, so that we might begin at once."

Looking at her face and her hair, I was half tempted to believe that she was capable of working such an astronomical miracle. Uncertain of any other comment I might make, I followed the only course that came to mind. "Good night, Miss Adler," I said, applying gentle pressure to her hand before letting go. "Good night," I repeated and then quickly retreated to my own room. I prepared for bed, once more picked up the *British Medical Journal*, and made certain my old service revolver—unloaded—lay nearby at the ready. Then, extinguishing the light, I proceeded to bed, where I lay awake for some time, contemplating my own lack of self-confidence. Sometime before midnight, I heard Mrs. Hudson's stately tread on the floor below as she retired for the night. For several minutes more, I thought of Holmes's room—vacant, as it must have been during my friend's long absence following his duel with Professor Moriarty. At last I felt the first gentle tugs of sleep and sometime in the night dreamt it was I who had faced that late master of Continental crime, locked in deadly hand-to-hand struggle there above the roaring torrent of some Morphean Reichenbach.[10]

---

10   The Reichenbach Falls of Switzerland are the site of Holmes's final confrontation with Professor Moriarty, who fell to his death there. At the time, Holmes was presumed to have perished as well.

CHAPTER TWELVE:

Revelation and Pursuit

It was at eleven in the morning the following day, one blessed with a suddenly mild temperature following an overnight frost, that Mrs. Hudson entered the sitting room to announce that Diarmund Stephenson had arrived to pay another call. Irene Adler and I were about to leave 221 for our trip about town, but I bade my companion stay in the sitting room while I descended to receive our caller.

"A very good morning, Mr. Stephenson," I said pleasantly, intending to be true to Holmes's request that I cultivate Lord Monsbury's secretary. "You are well, I trust?"

"I am; thank you, but what of you, Dr. Watson?" the young man asked with concern. "You appear to be limping, sir."

"It is but an old war wound, one of many," I said, thinking to myself that Stephenson would have been a child at the time of my military experience. "I was struck by a jezail bullet, you see. It's mended in its own way, mind you, but the area throbs at times during the changing of the seasons. It is an ailment to which I've grown accustomed. Being a man in your prime, Mr. Stephenson, you've yet to experience the aches of old age. One becomes inured to such things; it is nothing, I assure you."

"Still, perhaps we'd best sit down," he said, attempting to lead me into the waiting room. I humorously rebuffed his well-intended desire to help and invited him to take the same chair he had enjoyed last time. I sat down opposite him.

"I do not mean to hurry you," he said, "but it is not my wish to keep you long here, either."

"No matter. May I offer you something to drink?"

"Thank you, no."

Believing I knew his purpose in coming to Baker Street, I determined to get straight to the point. "I fear I cannot give you today any more information on the Hope Maldon investigation than I could yesterday. There can be——"

"Is Mr. Holmes about?" the man asked. "If you are presently engaged, Doctor, I can talk to him instead. To be quite honest, Mr. Holmes is, once again, the person I desperately require."

"How so?"

"He is not in then?"

"He is out of the house at present," I replied circumspectly, "on the trail of your good friend."

"Can you tell me the hour of his return?"

"I fear I cannot."

"Yes, of course," Stephenson said thoughtfully. "The rugby and cricket business."

"I beg your pardon?"

"Mr. Holmes likened detection to cricket rather than rugby when my employer asked a similar question of him the other day."

"During our interview with Lord Monsbury?"

"Yes. It occurred just as I was entering the room. But that's neither here nor there, Doctor. Tell me, what type of man is Mr. Holmes? Would you term him compassionate?"

"I will utter to you the same phrase I wrote to the whole world ten years ago. He is the best and wisest of men."

The young man nodded as if to himself alone. "Dr. Watson, I hope I do not offend when I say that I would rather be addressing Mr. Holmes himself at this moment, but as he is absent and you are his associate, I beg you to hear the confession I am about to give."

I shifted position in my chair. "Does this pertain to the disappearance of your friend?"

"It pertains not to his disappearance directly, no, but I suspect that it may affect Mr. Holmes's investigation of Robert's whereabouts."

"Hum," I said, edging forward. "You may rest assured of my discretion and understanding."

"I believe you, Dr. Watson, and so I am willing to tell you this most terrible thing: two weeks ago, it was I who removed the shares from Lord Monsbury's study."

"What? Why?"

"I did so in order that they might serve as collateral for a debt I had incurred," said Stephenson. "That debt has since been honestly paid without difficulty, and the shares have been returned to me. I shall restate that they were used as collateral only. I never sought to employ them to gain any material advantage for myself. I always intended to put them back as swiftly as events would allow. Pardon my demeanour, Dr. Watson. It is not easy—admitting to such a thing, that is."

"Of course. You are certain you wish nothing to drink?" I asked.

"Quite certain, thank you."

"Tell me more, please. Did you not fear your actions would soon be discovered?"

"I was well acquainted with Lord Monsbury's ways, Doctor, as I told you before. He had taken inventory of his wall safe only two days previous, and by habit, he should not have looked again for another two months, by which time I knew I could return the shares. For some reason my employer broke with custom and examined the contents of the safe again too soon."

"It was a foolish act on your part," I declared.

"I know! I had convinced myself, however, that it was an innocent one that would harm no one. Of course, I knew at the time that I was violating the trust the earl had placed in me, but I had led myself to believe that lack of detection would render the act a trifle."

"Why do you make this confession to me and not to the Earl of Monsbury?"

"I know I have transgressed, Dr. Watson. My hope—please do not tell me it is forlorn—is that Mr. Holmes might put things right without the earl discovering my error in judgment."

"That is all you consider it to be, sir? An error in judgment? Lord Monsbury is your employer and—"

"In fact, he is more, sir," said the young man. "Lord Monsbury is my natural uncle, Dr. Watson. My father was his brother, the late Sir Wyatt Hope Maldon."

I paused to consider this revelation. "Your uncle?" I said at last. "You are his brother's son?"

"Yes."

"Yet your name is Stephenson."

"My mother was not Sir Wyatt's wife."

"I see."

"Sir Wyatt provided for my mother and me," said the young man. "He saw to my education and, before his death, asked that his elder brother look after me. Lord Monsbury more than complied with my father's request in allowing me to become his secretary."

"And the earl is, of course, aware of your origin?"

"Oh, yes. He knew of me before I was born. The ties of blood are strong in him, you see, as they were with my father. If the earl were simply my employer, I suppose I might get up the courage to admit my mistake and accept my fate, but given that he is my uncle and given all he has done for me, I cannot. It would break his heart, I fear."

"You may be angered by this remark, young man, but I found your uncle's heart to be something much less than compassionate when his own son was discussed."

"You refer to Robert?" Diarmund Stephenson shook his head slowly. "You misunderstand, Dr. Watson. The earl has no fatherly love for Robert, because Robert is not his son."

Once more I sat in numb contemplation. "What do you say?"

"Lord Monsbury is not Robert's father."

"The earl knows this as well?"

"He suspected it from the moment that brown-eyed Robert was born. Robert's mother, you see, had blue eyes."

"Yes," I said after a moment's reflection, recalling the tinted photograph at Breton Mansions. "And the earl himself is blue-eyed as well," I added, remembering the watery gaze that had transfixed me at Lennox Square. "And you just alluded to the fact that Robert Hope Maldon's eyes—"

"Are brown," completed the young man. "The earl became enraged at his first viewing of the babe, and I am told by the more senior servants of the household that Lady Monsbury confessed her sin the same day as the birth. Lord Monsbury essentially disowned Robert from that moment, in all the realms that matter. Oh, the child was raised in the household as a scion of the Hope Maldon family, for the sake of appearances, but the earl never showed him a whit of affection. Alienation occurred between Lord and Lady Monsbury as well, of course. I have been told that it hastened her death, after which the earl lost all animosity toward his deceased wife and transferred it to Robert, somehow blaming him for her passing."

We both sat in silence for a moment before I said, "You have placed great confidences in me, young man."

"I have, sir. May I now ask that you place the same in me?"

"How so?"

"The investigation that Lord Monsbury has charged Mr. Holmes to pursue—does it concern the shares or Robert or both?"

I stared at the earnest face and rambling hair of the man before me for what seemed a very long time then cast discretion aside. "Formally, it concerns only Robert," I told him. "Though in the mind of Lord Monsbury both are intimately entwined."

Stephenson nodded, again as if for his own benefit. "I feared that would be the case. The earl blames Robert for the missing shares, yet he is completely innocent of their theft. Our situations within the household have such an odd asymmetry," he added wistfully. "Robert has the family name but not the blood and affection, while my condition is just the reverse."

"Were these familial relations common knowledge between the two of you? Did others know?" I asked.

"At the time that I entered service at Lennox Square, no one save the earl himself had knowledge that I was his nephew," Stephenson answered. "Awhile after assuming my duties as Lord Monsbury's secretary, I learned of Robert's origin from the older servants. Moved by the similarities—and the differences—in our situations, as well as a genuine affection for him, I eventually revealed my true identity to Robert some time ago."

"The knowledge did not affect his attitude toward you?"

"No," said the man. "If anything, I believe it brought us closer together."

"You said earlier you wished that Sherlock Holmes might put things right," I continued. "Had you anything specific to suggest to my friend?"

"Nothing, I fear, other than to wish that perhaps he might be able to convince the earl that his inventory had been mistaken and that the shares had remained in the safe all this time. Would Mr. Holmes think that possible?"

"I cannot express his opinions for him, though we might expect that if your uncle has returned to the safe many times since his initial discovery, a fabrication such as you suggest would be rather unconvincing."

"Oh," said Stephenson, crestfallen.

"If it is some encouragement to you, however, I should relate that upon at least one occasion similar to this, Holmes orchestrated the very type of ruse you propose. You say you now have the shares back in your possession?"

"Yes. They are hidden in my quarters at Lennox Square."

"I see. Well, I am uncertain when I shall be able to communicate with my friend in the next several days, but at the first opportunity to do so, I shall convey to him what you have revealed to me and offer your suggestion as a possible course of action."

"I am very much in your debt, sir, far more than I can say."

"We'll see it through," I told him, giving the young man an avuncular tap upon the knee. "Any debt you've incurred will have no collateral, I assure you."

He smiled faintly at my weak jest, and then we both rose together from our chairs. "I know this must appear a non sequitur, but please tell me," I suddenly said. "Did Robert Hope Maldon ever mention to you his intention to wed?"

"Robby? Oh, heavens, no. Not that he isn't a quick one about the ladies. No one likes a fresh face more than he—but marriage? I have never heard the word upon his lips, Dr. Watson."

"Even after his return from America?"

"Oh, then I'm afraid I cannot help you there. I suppose he might have met his match on the other side of the water, but I do not know about it yet," Stephenson admitted. "You see, I've not spoken to Robert since his departure for America. We had set up a dinner engagement by letter, but owing to his disappearance, it did not occur." The young man smiled meekly. "One reason I was looking forward to seeing him was to hear firsthand of his experiences in the United States and Canada. My mother settled in Nova Scotia when she entrusted my upbringing to Lord Monsbury, and I hope to someday visit her—she lives in a village just outside Halifax."

"It is pleasant country, and I am certain you shall someday have that joy. Let me bid you good-day then, and thank you for the information you have provided me. I assure you I shall make every effort to turn this matter in your favour."

"Again, I thank you with all my heart, Doctor."

We shook hands, and I saw him out the door. Then, after slowly ascending the stair, I opened the sitting room door and asked Miss Adler if she was ready to leave.

"Yes," she replied from the window. "You were detained for some time by Mr. Stephenson. Is anything the matter?"

"No," I said. "He wished merely to learn of any news of our investigation. I could, of course, tell him nothing." I quickly surveyed the sitting room. "You are certain about this journey?" I asked, hoping that at the last moment her mind might change yet also remaining curious about the reason for her desire to roam beyond 221.

"I am certain for myself," the woman said as she left the window to approach me. "But I still question your need to go with me. Though I do desire your company, your limp gives me cause to—"

"It will be fine," I told her, as I had repeatedly throughout the morning. "If anything, I have found that a brisk walk helps loosen it. Trust an old veteran who has come to terms with his battle scars."

"Very well. Let us go," she said and then took my arm as we descended the stair and bade farewell to Mrs. Hudson. Leaving the house, we encountered our agent Mercer, who stood outside by the kerb, ready to follow. Although agreeing to a jaunt about London, I had held firm in my insistence that we not go alone, and reluctantly, my companion had agreed.

Once in Baker Street, Irene Adler puckishly suggested we board the bus, but in her company, I would have none of it and, instead, whistled for a hansom while Mercer signalled for his own. After pausing to discuss contingencies with the agent, I returned to the first hansom, in which I joined Miss Adler.

"To Holborn," I called to the driver, who urged his horse on at a pace I immediately thought much too brisk. "I say, could you please slow the cab?" I asked him.

"You think I'm fast?" the cabby replied sharply. "You should have seen me go before the war, when I had Big Ramses. The army, they took all the good horses out of London when it was time to fight those Boers. It was then—"

"Please slow down!" I asked again, as the hansom made a precipitous turn. "I won't have such reckless—"

"I'm doing just what the lady paid me to do!" protested the driver.

I looked in astonishment at Irene Adler, who turned away. Then, looking behind us, I saw that our dashing hansom had outrun Mercer's cab, which was no longer in sight.

"Tell me now," I said sternly to my companion. "Tell me the meaning of this."

"I must have none of Mr. Holmes's agents about me," the woman said, facing me with her intense grey eyes.

Our hansom ran over a piece of debris, jostling us both in the cab. "And what am I, madam, other than my friend's principal agent?"

"Unlike the others, you, I believe, can be your own man," she replied. "You, Dr. Watson, can transcend the act of merely following orders."

"Much to my discredit," I said, now regretting my decision to allow this trip.

"I would have gone without you knowing, had you not agreed."

"Oh?" I said angrily. "That is the extent of your gratitude?"

From outside the cab came the harsh cries of a cyclist, whom we had nearly run down.

"Well?" I continued. "Is this how you repay all we have tried to do for you?"

"You must believe me, Doctor, when I say this journey is most urgent."

"How so?"

"I cannot divulge that yet, not even to you."

I sat silently, looking forward as our cab sped on. At first I felt only anger but no serious alarm, for I had informed Mercer that Holborn was to be our destination, but after a few minutes, I realized the hansom was not heading in that direction.

"I instructed the driver to take us to Trafalgar Square," said the woman, perhaps sensing my realization. For a brief moment, she placed a hand on mine. "Doctor, please. I do not seek to disappoint."

As she let go of my hand, I said, "I disappoint myself."

"Because you believe in me?"

"No," I replied as we rushed on. "Because I wish to believe in you when I do not."

In time, our driver called out Trafalgar Square. Wordlessly, we departed the cab, and in continued silence, we took a slow walk round Nelson's Column before entering the Strand.

"It is much as I remember it," Miss Adler suddenly said with a light air, as if our conversation in the hansom had never occurred and no sense of betrayal separated us. As we were engulfed by the street's world of shops, theatres, and restaurants, she proclaimed, with forced joy, "It has been so long."

"I prefer the way it used to be," I said curtly. "Before it was widened time and again."

"Things change," she told me, offering her arm, which I took stiffly in hand, so as not to create a spectacle of discord for those milling about to witness. "Cities change," Miss Adler continued, "as well as people."

"Am I to know where we are going from here?" I asked, looking back in hopes of seeing Mercer arrive in his cab.

"Oh, Doctor, please do not be angry. Can you not wish to believe in me a bit longer?"

I looked at the woman whose arm I held and inwardly considered whether I could piece together that trust, which had been so rudely shattered. "I wish that I could wish,"

I said, using a logic which I now, in retrospect, find baffling. "But will it be coyness until then, Miss Adler?"

"Do not call it that, please!"

"Well then," I said, forcing myself to assume a light-hearted tone as well, "I shall try." I gazed round. "Have you ever seen it at night, Miss Adler?"

"The Strand? Oh, many times, Doctor. It is a kaleidoscope then."

"Yes," I said with a hollow laugh. "I believe I've used that very same word myself. Somewhere nearby, unless it was demolished, is the hotel where I stayed before sharing Baker Street with Holmes."

"Certainly, you did not want for entertainment in those days," my companion replied, indicating our surroundings.

"It was little comfort to me then," I told her, thinking back to that time. "Indeed, I thought my life comfortless…meaningless, for that matter. I had no one, save for my poor bull pup, and life on eleven shillings and sixpence a day was no picnic, I can tell you. A lean lounger and an idler, following in my family's uneven tradition—that was my description."

"It is not the portrait I see before me today. I perceive instead a solid, well-groomed man of firm chin, the picture of accomplishment and respectability."

"Ha! I fear I was the very opposite when I resided here."

"And then you met Sherlock Holmes."

"Yes, and that reminds me that we must not fail to take in Bart's," I said while passing the iron gate before Charing Cross Station. We then continued down to the Lowther Arcade and spent time at the American Exchange before approaching Simpson's, where it had been our plan to dine. In bypassing Holborn, we had arrived earlier than expected, but we each found ourselves not reluctant about expressing our desire for food.

"I did not take you from any work today, did I?" Miss Adler asked as we passed the imitation-marble entrance columns and strode across a floor of coloured tile and small trees growing in their tubs until we were seated near the huge dumbwaiter that dominated the centre of Simpson's great dining room.

"What work?" said I. "My practice in Queen Anne Street is looked over by an associate, and my latest story is ready to be sent to my editors. I can afford to be on holiday."

"It is better than eleven shillings and sixpence a day, is it not?"

"Oh, yes," I replied, admiring the plated wine coolers that adorned each corner of the massive dumbwaiter. "It is a most wonderful feeling to be chronicling Holmes's cases again. If I may, I wish to recommend the fish dinner here."

"Thank you," Miss Adler said, gracefully adjusting the placement of her black-cushioned chair and withdrawing a napkin from its empty glass. "You ceased writing for a time then?"

"For a few years," I said. "Holmes encouraged my literary silence, as he did so often back then, but in truth, the demands of my practice were as much to blame. My first new tale was published only last year, and I have a contract for several short stories that will begin appearing soon."

"And you enjoy that."

"Oh, yes. I find, in the end, I could even say that I love it."

"Which do you enjoy more, living the adventures or writing about them?"

"I don't know," I told her. "I suppose writing about them allows me to relive them, does it not?"

"Well, I am happy for you in any case. I trust that though your fiancée frowns upon the books you read, she does not intend to stop you from writing books yourself."

"Why...no," I said, staring at the curtains and mirrors encircling much of the room. "Of course she does not...I believe."

We both chose the restaurant's fish dinner and enjoyed it immensely then left Simpson's to continue our promenade as far as Doctors' Commons, where we turned into Wellington Street to approach the Thames before making our way back toward the west, along the granite of the Embankment, passing beneath the shadow of Cleopatra's Needle. All the while, I searched for Mercer in hopes the agent might chance upon his escaped charges but to no avail.

Miss Adler and I paused frequently to take in the slow glide of river traffic, and just short of Charing Cross Station, which very much held my companion's fascination, we hailed a cab to ferry us into the City, which Miss Adler had evinced a strong interest in seeing. Passing the Temple and then St. Paul's, our driver deposited us in Cannon Street.

"Shall we walk on to Bart's?" I suggested. "It is just on the other side of Newgate."

"I should very much like that," Irene Adler replied. "But could we not wander about here first? Is not Upper Swandam Lane nearby?"

"I am not certain," I replied, pausing to get my bearings. After a moment's hesitation, I accosted a passing clerk and got directions.

"Shall we see what lies in Upper Swandam?" Miss Adler suggested.

"As you wish," I said. "I assume that destination must be your ultimate goal."

Miss Adler only smiled absent-mindedly, and I followed her on, my leg once more throbbing mildly. We quickly found Upper Swandam Lane, where Miss Adler's course seemed less a distracted meander and more the determined search I had been expecting.

"I take it that our journey concerns either your young man or the black bird," I said as we paused opposite a stalled furniture van, whose driver was treating his horses in a manner that made me impatient to leave the scene.

"A moment, please, Doctor," the woman whispered.

"I plead for your confidence, Miss Adler," I said as we stood near steps that had been whitened by pigeons. "I have shown great trust in you, rather more than Holmes's might have wished me to. Can you not reciprocate?"

Just then the van began to move and in so doing revealed to us a small lane off Upper Swandam.

"That's it!" said Miss Adler. "Fresno Street! Come, Doctor."

My patience tried by her failure to acknowledge my remarks, I followed her nonetheless down the narrow pavement, almost to its end. "Miss Adler!" I said loudly, not caring what impression it might give others nearby. "Miss Adler, please halt, if you will!"

The woman stopped and turned round. Her gloved hand pushed her hat down farther onto her head while the other hand gripped the front of her coat. Irene Adler's face exhibited a look of shame as she approached.

"Oh, Dr. Watson, do forgive me!" she said. "It is your leg, is it not?"

"It is not my leg which troubles me most," I insisted. "It is your continued treatment of me. You speak of confidence and trust, yet you do not offer any of your own. Will you not tell me—"

I stopped abruptly, noticing that my companion's attentions were suddenly directed behind me. I turned about and saw at the far entrance to Fresno Street, beyond a throng of passers-by, the outline of a huge man in an Astrakhan coat and bowler. Behind him stood men of a sort I had no wish to be near.

"Doctor?" said Miss Adler.

I looked back at the woman to see her staring frantically into my eyes.

"Come slowly," I said, taking her arm as I made a hasty examination of the lane. "We shall go in here." With rapid steps, we entered a tea shop of the Aero Bread Company.

"I am Mr. Price of the Yeast Council," I declaimed to those inside. "Show me to the back of your establishment."

"What, sir?" said the thin male attendant.

"The council has instituted mandatory inspections of premises such as these! Now get us to the back, or have you something to hide?"

"Here, we've nothing to hide," said a woman who emerged from the rear of the shop. "This way," she directed. We followed her through a door to the back side of the building, where Miss Adler and I found a door giving access to an alleyway. "All appears well," I said in a peremptory manner to our escort as we rushed past her and down the winding, narrow corridor, thence to a thoroughfare that was Cannon Street itself, with the Cannon Street Station just opposite us. I hailed the first hansom I saw and then, after quickly assisting Miss Adler into the cab, offered the driver two crowns to find the fastest way back to Baker Street. We tore past St. Paul's and into the Old Bailey, skirted Newgate, and went on, ironically, toward Holborn, leaving behind St. Bart's, unvisited.

I frequently braved possible injury while attempting to glimpse if any vehicle was following ours, but I saw none. All the way to Oxford Street, I assured my fellow passenger that we were, indeed, safe.

"Foolish," I heard her say to herself. "You were right. I am foolish."

At last we were racing past the dun-coloured houses of Baker Street, where I quickly settled with the driver, tossed him an extra crown to his disbelief, then shepherded Miss Adler under the fanlight of 221 and on into the waiting room. Half-consciously, I noticed that Holmes's agents were not in attendance.

"Mrs. Hudson!" I called. "Pike! Hollins? I say, where are you?"

"Your men 're in a place where they won't come when called," replied a flinty voice from the top of the stair. I looked up in horror as a tall, rugged man in an overcoat and slouch cap slowly descended.

"Who are you?" I demanded. "Where is Mrs. Hudson?"

"The woman? She's with 'em," said the man as he reached the ground floor and stopped to lean back upon the railing, the brim of his cap almost covering his eyes. "They're all fine, they are. They're just…shall we say…indisposed." The intruder stroked a dirty chin and smiled broadly, revealing a gap in his discoloured teeth on the upper left side.

"Your name, sir?" I asked sternly.

"Briggs," he replied. "But you can call me Uncle Bill. And don't go reaching for the door now, miss!" he told Miss Adler sharply. "Georgie! Shep!"

From the back of the house came two men, neither of them even thirty years of age, both dressed in shabby attire.

"Will you boys make a nice frame for me portrait here?" he said, and the pair stood on either side of us.

"Real nice!" Briggs said with mock admiration, holding up his hands, the thumbs and forefingers forming corners. "Picture perfect of the pair it is!"

"You would be best advised to leave at once," I said calmly, cursing the distance between myself and the service revolver in the sitting room above.

"Oh, I'm going eventually, never fear," Briggs answered. "And you're coming with me, right after we talk to Mr. Girthwood himself."

CHAPTER THIRTEEN:

Captives

"Who are you to order us about in our own house?" I said sternly. "We'll have naught to do with threats."

"You'd not do to ignore them, if I was you, sir," said Briggs. "You act as directed here, and by all that's fair, no harm 'll come to either the two of you. That's a promise what comes down from the boss himself. But understand, you see, that for now, you need to go up them stairs, right brisk now."

"And if I do not wish to do so?"

"Oh, I'm beginning to think that your mouth ain't quite knowing what your brain must by now, sir," Briggs replied. He walked up to me and, taking a long steel pin from his lapel, he used it to pick his teeth, revealing again the missing canine. "Your brain knows that upstairs is where you wants to be, so shouldn't your mouth be in agreement?"

"You need some help, Uncle Bill?"

"No, Shep," Briggs replied, slipping the pin back through his coat. Then suddenly, he took me by my own lapels. "You wants to tell me you're dying to go up them stairs, now don't you, sir?"

My eyes caught the animal fury in his, and I steeled myself to meet it squarely, though I could sense that great strength lay in his hands. I was about to speak when I felt another, more gentle grip take my right arm.

"Come, Dr. Watson," Irene Adler whispered in a low tone. "Let us join in the amusement and go up the stair."

"We are not required to yield," I said, as much to Briggs as to her. "And this is hardly an amusement."

"Discretion, Doctor!" the woman implored. "Do not fight when the fight is useless. For my sake, please!"

"Take the lesson," Briggs rasped. "Listen to the lady."

And, for the sake of Irene Adler, I rejected confrontation. Briggs sensed my silent submission and, keeping his insane stare fixed upon me, slowly released his hold on my coat and stepped back, allowing Miss Adler to guide me toward the stair. Now taking her arm in mine to assume the lead, I climbed resolutely with the woman to the sitting room, where Briggs had us sit upon the sofa while his two men stood by the door and he sprawled in Holmes's armchair like a ragged monarch.

"You realize Sherlock Holmes will have this house surrounded within moments," I said calmly.

Briggs blew a gust of air in amusement. "Oh, truly? He going to direct that manoeuvre from some Frenchy cancan house, is he?"

"What does that mean?"

"It means your Mr. Holmes ain't here, don't it?" said the ruffian, pulling a folded telegram from his coat pocket. "I got in my hand a message from the fellow himself. Plucked it from the messenger and tipped him for it, too; by God I did. And what does that great snoop of a detective say?" Briggs declaimed.

He squinted at the piece of paper as he fumbled with it. "Do the police in different voices, I can. Oh well, right, Mr. Holmes Esq. here says he got over to Frenchy-land, learned a whole lot, and he's on his way back now, even as we're speaking so cosy to one another. But just between you and me, sir and lady, by the time he gets back, it'll be to surround an empty house. Some adventure, that. Maybe you could write it, eh, sir? Ha!"

"I fear the title is already taken." I sat back and, with the others, waited quietly for several minutes, the steady ticking of Holmes's Swiss clock the only sound. Then the door below opened, and I heard a now-familiar strain upon the stair. Within a moment, the sitting room doorway was engulfed by Jasper Girthwood.

"Well, Briggs, that's good," exclaimed the portly man. "Both of them in tow! Marvellous, sir. I knew you were the man for me, I did. Astounding what good help can do to change one's fortune. Now then, Dr. Watson," Girthwood said, removing his bowler. "A pleasure, sir. And, my dear Irene, how are you? So far from home, aren't we?"

The woman sat straight and unmoving; there was no suggestion that she might ever speak again.

"No word of greeting?" Girthwood said, his eyes heavy-lidded and his expression smug as he wheeled about the room in his Astrakhan coat. "Not even for me?"

"You know this man well?" I said. "Well enough for him to speak of—"

Miss Adler turned to me. Her outward resolve did not fade, yet in her eyes, I sensed a collapse of spirit, and in a hushed voice, she said, "He is my half brother."

"Yes, and so let us act as if we were at least half a family and say hello," the large man said.

"I should give you but half that word, sir," the woman replied.

The heavy man pressed his lips together, clenched his fists, then relaxed them and struck a philosophical stance. "Well, one can't have everything, and something is better than nothing. You know quite well what I want, Irene; there's no more to be said. Perhaps a little trip with Briggs here will change my older sister's perspective, Doctor. Do you think so?"

"You presume to remove us from this house?" I said.

"Ha!" Girthwood said with amusement. "You are ever the indignant squire, aren't you? I must compliment you on the Beaune, however." He moved his arms like flippers in his great coat, his expression now grim. "Is nothing simple in the world? Why cannot people bow to simple logic?" He glanced toward Briggs. "See to it as planned and swiftly."

"We shall, sir," was the ruffian's answer.

"None of the responsibility for this unpleasantness lies on my shoulders," Girthwood declared as he stomped from the sitting room.

"You heard the boss," said Briggs as his employer left the house. "Get up, and let's be about." He signalled for his two young accomplices to be ready.

Miss Adler stood up.

"You cannot succeed in this," I declared, remaining seated.

"Oh, I believe we're all going to succeed quite well," said Briggs. "Ain't we, ma'am?"

Irene Adler stared him full in the face and whispered, "I suppose you will. Say what you must, and we shall comply."

"You heard the lady," Briggs declared. "Get up, sir, or is your bum now getting as disagreeable as your mouth was just a bit ago?"

I looked at Miss Adler and saw desperation in her eyes. Once more, I yielded on her account and silently rose to my feet.

"That's the attitude to have." Briggs tapped my shoulder and smiled. "You could do well to take your lady friend here for an example, my good doctor friend. Now get going!" he snarled and turned round to leave.

"May we at least gather some personal items?" I asked.

"Uncle Bill?" said one of the raw-faced underlings.

"Calm yourself, Georgie," said Briggs, turning round again, this time to face me with narrowed eyes. "The gent here's a croaker. He knows what broken bones be like. And you do know, don't you, Doctor Squatson—Watson?"

Miss Adler took my arm. "Come, Doctor," she said. "There is no choice. We must!"

Nervously, I covered her hand with my own. "I will go," was my response after a moment. "But I wish to take some things if I may."

"Don't want no baggage here slowing us down."

"They are just some personal effects. They are there in my desk. If—"

Irene Adler gripped my hand tightly. "No," she whispered. "Perhaps we should simply go now. You can always get them later, Doctor, when all this is past and we return."

"But I—"

"Please!" the woman begged. "No. Mr. Holmes would wish us simply to go."

"But to so completely acquiesce—"

"We must acquiesce," she said. "I believe we shall be safer if we do."

"Because that man Girthwood is your brother?" I said with disdain.

She bowed her head. "Perhaps, Dr. Watson. Please, let us simply go," she said again, lifting a worried yet brave face to me. At last, with reluctance, I agreed, and we followed Briggs down the stair, his two accomplices behind us. At the bottom, I paused the door to 221.

"Where is Mrs. Hudson?" I asked sharply. "And our agents? What have—"

"I told you long ago. They're well taken care of, sir," said Briggs, nodding toward the back of the house. "Quite safe they are, never you mind."

"I demand to see them!"

Briggs smiled, again baring the gap in his teeth as he approached me. He brushed my lapel with the back of one hand and then abruptly once more took violent hold of my jacket. "I am getting well up and sick of your constant demanding! You don't demand nothing, you don't!" He growled as if he were a crazed ape who had acquired speech. "You folks here are members belonging to the passive tense, you are! Don't never forget that! Here!" Briggs said, letting go of me before stepping to the door to open it. "Out now," he ordered. "Real dainty like and real quiet, let's not make no fuss, if we know what's best for the health!"

I made no further attempt at obstruction, and we were escorted out the door of 221 and toward a pair of waiting hansoms. Traffic was light, and there were no familiar faces about.

"I'll remind you again, no commotion, if you please," Briggs said softly into my ear. "You can't see them, but there are weapons on our persons, Doctor. No telling what could happen when a man gets excited. Women and children first, you know."

Miss Adler was put into the nearest hansom with one of Briggs's assistants, while the other mounted the cab to drive it. Briggs escorted me into the second vehicle, whose driver—a third young ruffian—had been tending both vehicles and now mounted his own. "Inside," barked Briggs, and he climbed in after me.

"In a minute, Johnny!" the man said to our driver. "Just a precaution, this is, Doctor," he remarked, pulling out a large kerchief, which he tied about my eyes. He then coaxed me to lean forward and place my hands behind my back before binding the wrists together with cord. "There we are. A mite uncomfortable, perhaps. Still, you're nice and tight there, sir. Johnny!" he cried. I heard him give the top of the cab two sharp raps. "Up and away with us!"

I lurched backward as the hansom started into motion.

"Aye, relax, Doctor," Briggs said as he braced me with unexpected gentleness. "We've got a bit of a trip ahead here. Enjoy the ramble, though I suppose there's less fun without the sight of it; ain't that the case?"

"If you say so, then so must it be," I muttered.

"There's the spirit," the man replied with another hearty laugh. "It took you long enough to come round to being cooperative, but oh, yes, you're in the spirit at last!"

For the first few moments, I was able to sense our route in my mind, but a quick series of turns soon made any attempt at memorizing the path a futile one. After minutes of listening to Briggs whistling a familiar tune I could not quite place, I decided to try diplomacy and guile.

"And so you are in the pay of this Girthwood fellow, are you, Mr. Briggs?" I asked.

The man ceased whistling. "Well, Doctor, if you are engaging me in a little discussion, one professional man to another as it were, then I would have to tell you that your statement is ever so true, it is. American he be, and they always pays well, so's been my experience."

"If money is your principal motivation, Mr. Briggs, I can assure you that Sherlock Holmes could pay you far more. If you were to release—"

"Ha!" Briggs blew wind from his mouth. "I never have met a croaker who could carry on much of a conversation, and you're no exception, are you? Look here: Mr. Girthwood's promised me a huge sum, he has. Says he's got a line on an article of fabulous value, he calls it. I'm happy with my chances as they are. Then, I got my pride, just like you do. Your Mr. Holmes ever talk about me?"

"I confess I am not certain. Perhaps."

"Well, he put me away once, and that's immediate disqualification, I say. Him and me are moral antipathies or something that sounds very much like it. I'm not engaging in any business with one who put me away; do you understand that? So take your bribe elsewhere, Doctor. When I breaks the law, it's done with honour!"

I did not reply and simply sat as Briggs resumed his whistling for a moment; then he stopped.

"Do you mind the tune, Doctor?" he asked.

"The whistling, you mean? No," I replied tactfully.

"If music be the belly-timber of love, chirp on, I says," Briggs remarked with a laugh that resolved itself into a hacking cough.

"I cannot place the melody, though it sounds familiar," I added as our cab rattled on.

"Some carpaccio of Pagliacci, they tells me," Briggs replied idly. Our hansom rolled along for many more minutes, which I eventually estimated to have been perhaps thirty. At last we stopped.

"Now, Doctor," said Briggs in a calm voice. "I have to step out briefly to run me an errand. Remember that my boy Johnny is up top driving, so don't get no ideas about trying to take matters into your own hands, which are tied, anyways. And, of course, we've still got the lady in the other cab, right?"

"I understand perfectly."

"Good," the man replied. "I think this here jaunt has been good for our friendship, don't you? Be back in a moment."

Momentarily I wrestled with the rope binding my wrists, but to no avail, and so I waited until I heard the hansom door open and smelled the aroma of Briggs's ragged coat beside me. Then came the sound of two raps on the roof of the cab. "Away, Johnny!" Briggs called out, and once more, we rattled along still more anonymous London streets.

The hansom carried us on for perhaps another five minutes before stopping.

"Well, here we are," Briggs said. "Home at last. Now remember, Doctor, all obedience and cooperation, right?"

I was led out of the cab, still blindfolded, and escorted along what I felt to be a cobbled walk and into a building, which had the feel of a house.

"You're not alone, sir," Briggs told me. "Speak to him, missy, and tell him you're here."

"I am at your side, Dr. Watson," came Irene Adler's voice.

"You are unharmed?" I asked.

"Yes, completely so, though I am blindfolded with wrists tied, as I gather you are."

"And we means to keep it that way for just a while longer," said Briggs. "If you don't mind now, straight on ahead here." He guided me by the shoulder through what I took to be a room to what we were told was a stair. I ascended slowly and haltingly.

"Are you there still, Doctor?" asked Irene Adler.

"Yes, he is," answered Briggs for me. "That's it, Doc. You're doing a whale of a job, you are. Two more. There you go. Good. Now straight ahead here."

We were led into an unheated room that smelled of incense, with perhaps the hint of stale tobacco. In the distance, through what I assumed were windows, I heard the muted drone of London traffic but could find nothing unique registering upon my senses that might identify the locale. Hoping to act as I might imagine Holmes would, I found myself with no conclusions to show for my effort.

"Now into this chair, if you please," Briggs commanded, guiding me. "And the lady, too. That's it."

"You are still well?" I asked urgently. "No harm has been done you?"

"None," was the reply I received from her.

"And may you stay so," said Briggs. "Provided you remain nice and quiet. If not, we'll have to stopper your mouths, won't we? You talk low if you want, but somebody will be nearby—trust to that. Remember, no yelling—we want you to stay whole, and you want to stay whole, right?"

"Yes," said Irene Adler at once.

"Good," said Briggs, and a door shut.

Miss Adler and I sat there in silence for several moments. Then, not knowing what more to think, I once more asked Miss Adler if she were well.

"I remain quite unharmed, Doctor," she said. "Do not worry on my account."

"And so this Girthwood fellow is not a mere business acquaintance of Mr. Hope Maldon or your late husband," I said. "Rather, he is your brother. Perhaps Sherlock Holmes would have appreciated that knowledge," I said tersely.

"He is my half brother," she corrected, a hint of shame in her voice. "My father died when I was young, and my mother remarried. Jasper was the child of that second union."

"But why did you not—"

"I know I should have informed the two of you, Dr. Watson! I know all too well now." Her voice was strained. "I could not—dear Dr. Watson, at times I do not wish to admit to even *myself* that such a creature bears any relation to me. Forgive me, please. I did not believe"—her words suddenly stopped.

"Miss Adler?"

"Forgive me, Dr. Watson."

"Of course," I whispered, seeing the futility of pursuing the argument. And so we sat for several minutes, Miss Adler now and then shifting in her chair while I continued to turn over in my mind any possible way by which I could deduce our location.

We were in a house, I felt certain. It was a first-floor room. From the sound of traffic, I knew the street to be at my left. We were still in London; of that I was certain also. But what else might I glean? I asked myself. How would Holmes approach the matter?

After unnumbered minutes, I had no answer; all remained blank to me. At length, I found my will faltering and my consciousness floating, and at some moment, I must have fallen asleep from fatigue, for I awoke to find the background light through my blindfold gone, and I gathered we had entered the night. It was then that I heard a door open and sensed light blazing against my blindfold.

"You folks all right?" came a man's voice, which I recognized as that of Briggs's man Shep. "I say, are you doing well, ma'am?"

"I do not suffer," Irene Adler's firm voice announced.

"Nor myself," I said. "Though, I must say, I should prefer there be a fire to warm us. What do you want?"

"I am to use the telephone now," the accomplice said. "I will ring up the man who hired Uncle Bill and then have you speak to him so that he may know you are safe and being held as instructed, sir."

"We are hostages to be exchanged for the black bird then; is that it?"

"Don't know nothing about no bird, sir. I just know that I am to ring up the man and have you speak to him."

"And if I should refuse?" I asked the unseen, young criminal. "Then what? Will you set hands to me?"

"I won't," Shep replied. "But Uncle Bill's downstairs, and if you don't cooperate, I'm to fetch him, and he'll rough up not only you but perhaps the lady as well."

"You're swine! All of you!"

"Ordinarily, sir, I'd consider breaking your thumbs for that remark, but Uncle Bill's my leader, and he said there's to be nothing rough from me. My hands are kind of tied like yours—metaphorically speaking if you will—but Uncle Bill's ain't. He can eat twenty like you alive without blinking and still be wanting his dessert, if you know what I mean—and I think you do."

I did not need several minutes to ponder the truth of the man's statement and slumped in my chair to wait as the accomplice proceeded to establish a connection.

"Now I'm going to hold it for you, sir," said Shep in my ear before answering. "Just a moment here...Hey there? Yes, here he is, sir."

I could feel the telephone next to me, and in my ear was the tinny voice of our obese adversary.

"Well, Doctor, you are relaxing in comfort, I trust."

"I do not suffer," I said, repeating Irene Adler's phrase. "Though I am bound at the moment."

"Yes, well, necessity and all that. But I will not hold you longer—in this conversation, that is. I merely wished reassurance that Briggs was still holding you as desired. Good day to you then."

And with that, the exchange, such as it was, ended.

Shep took away the telephone and I heard a click. Then there were footsteps, and a door closed. After a few seconds, I sensed that Miss Adler and I were again alone.

"Dr. Watson, you are there?"

"Yes, Miss Adler."

"You spoke with my brother?"

"Yes, but he said nothing of substance."

"I see."

"Shall I describe St. Bart's for you?"

"What?"

"Should I convey what you would have seen today, had we been allowed to proceed to St. Bartholomew's?" I asked, believing that such idle conversation would ease her anxiety.

"No," she said. "Thank you, Dr. Watson, but no. I wish to be left alone with my thoughts, if you please."

I leaned back in my chair then paused as I heard muffled voices on the floor below. Then a steady tread began ascending the stair. One step, two, three...Half-consciously, I counted them, up to fifteen, sixteen, and ending upon seventeen. Then, at that moment, the hint of stale tobacco, which I had been inhaling underneath the aroma of incense, crystallized within my consciousness as the signature reek of Holmes's shag.

Coincidence can intrude upon conclusion, as my detective friend had remarked to me more than once, but still I impulsively leaned over toward my fellow hostage as I heard the door to our room begin to open with a now-familiar squeak.

"Miss Adler!" I whispered.

"Yes, Doctor?"

"Miss Adler, I believe there is a good chance we may still be at 221! Do not think me mad, but I believe it possible!"

"Don't doubt yourself for a moment, Watson, for you are the sanest of men," came the voice of Sherlock Holmes next to my ear.

CHAPTER FOURTEEN:

The Object at Last

"What is this?" I said as my blindfold was removed, revealing Briggs standing before me.

"Well, Watson," replied the man in Holmes's voice. "I must admit you are not entirely speechless, but three words are really not much, you know."

"I...we...Briggs..."

"Very good, old fellow! You've doubled the exposition! Here, allow me the honour of untying you."

My hands were released, and I massaged my wrists where the ropes had pressed into my skin. I stiffly rose and removed the blindfold from Miss Adler before loosening her bonds. Looking up into Briggs's eyes once more, I now perceived for the first time the persona of my friend behind the criminal facade.

"Oh, dear," sighed Holmes. "At my age I am simply not up to these long performances." Smiling, he took a denture from his pocket and slipped it into the space of the missing canine, which, I now recalled, the thug Matthews had knocked out in the waiting room at Charing Cross Station years before.

"We have been at 221 all the while," I said.

"Of course. Can you conceive a safer place?"

"And Briggs?"

"The last remaining principal from my dwindling clan of alter egos," said Holmes, removing the wide-brimmed hat and pulling a wig from his scalp. "One unknown to you, Doctor. Yes, Uncle Bill Briggs had built up a rather sizable reputation among the criminal class, and I hope this escapade will not expose his real identity. However, to ensure your safety, Watson, it was a sacrifice I was more than willing to risk."

"My safety? I don't know that you necessarily contributed to that cause, Holmes. You were rather rough with me, twice taking me by the lapel and—"

"Yes, well, it were a bit of fun, eh?" he said in the voice of his creation. "But then, I believe *you* knew from the first act who Briggs was, did you not?" he asked, turning to Miss Adler.

The woman opened her mouth as if to speak, hesitated, and then slowly nodded. "I did not realize it immediately, but by the time we ascended the stair, I thought I knew. It was for that reason, Doctor, that I urged compliance."

"We may only hope the proportion of females who turn to crime does not significantly increase in the years to come," said the detective, pulling off false eyebrows. "Their intuitive ways would, I think, have a stultifying effect upon those who would follow me in the profession."

Holmes stepped over to a table, where I saw thin sticks embedded vertically in a platter of sand. Faint, curling wisps of smoke rose from their burning ends. "I shall extinguish them in a moment," said my friend. "They have sat for nearly a decade unused. As I brought them all the way from Lhasa, I thought I might as well finally employ them."

"To mask the scent of your shag," I said.

"Rather, to cover the aroma of your Arcadia mix, old fellow."

At that point, Georgie entered the room.

"Holmes!"

"Do not fear, Watson. They are all—Georgie, Shep, and Johnny—on our side. They are also most familiar with 221, though I'd wager you would not recognize any of them now."

I thought for a moment as the young ruffian stood and stared at me, and then I said, "Old Baker Street Irregulars?"

"Yes, Watson. A changing band of youths," Holmes told Irene Adler. "They used to act as messengers, spies, and ferrets in the early days of our practice." He chuckled, a distant look in his eye. "To this day, I can't say as Johnson, Pike, and their compatriots have ever exceeded my expectations as well as those scruffy boys of so long ago."

"And which one were you?" I asked the man I had known only as Georgie.

"Oakes, sir."

"Hum," I said. "The name is familiar, though I confess I cannot recall your face."

"I'd be most surprised if you could do that, sir, what with all that being over twenty years ago. I must say, though, that you've not changed much."

"How have you fared in the meanwhile, lad?"

"I do foundry work in the south of town, sir. One of the top men there, even if it is me saying so. I ride the tram in each morning from Kentish way, where I've a wife and two girls. Mr. Holmes, do we turn things over to your real agents now?"

"Yes, and tell Mullin and Smith that I shall be down presently to thank them and see you all off. Your assistance was most valuable."

"Right, sir," said Oakes, touching his cap. "Quite wonderful to see you again, Dr. Watson." The young man turned and started down the stair.

"Good lads, all of them," said Holmes, who continued to remove more elements of his disguise. "Both in the old century and on into this new one."

There were more footsteps upon the stair, and in the doorway appeared Mrs. Hudson and the agent Hollins. I delighted in seeing our landlady again, but she declined the attention.

"If it will suit, Mr. Holmes, I wish to be off to bed. The hour is already getting late, and——"

"Of course. Pray, keep to your quarters in the morning, if you will."

"I'm unlikely to be as decadent as that, sir."

"Mrs. Hudson, I believe our small affair will reach its end early tomorrow," said Holmes with a supplicant air. "Perhaps you will consider seriously my suggestion?"

The landlady eyed my friend harshly. "Will that finale include some of the rough and tumble?"

"There is a distinct possibility of that, yes."

"We shall see," said Mrs. Hudson with resignation. "I shall insist on providing you all with breakfast beforehand, of course, but I may then remain closeted while your drama concludes." She pushed past Hollins and retired for the evening.

"The house is secure, Mr. Holmes," declared Hollins.

"Inside and out?"

"Yes, both front and back."

"Good. I shall be down shortly," said Holmes, and with that, Hollins descended the stair, leaving the detective once more alone with me and Miss Adler. "I hope the two of you will forgive my insistence upon real discomfort. Girthwood desired verification by telephone that you were ensconced in Briggs's criminal lair, and I wished that everything, including your anger and apprehension, seem genuine. I do hope you forgive me for rattling your emotions so. It was rather callous of me."

"At times the business of this agency necessitates the like, does it not?"

"Good old Watson, ever the trouper!"

"You never travelled to Paris," said Irene Adler, speaking for the first time in several minutes.

Holmes nodded. "There were intriguing details of the Konstantinides murder that warranted investigation, but, in fact, I did send Shinwell Johnson for that purpose. I trust, Miss Adler, that you have borne your own ordeal well?"

"You say you never left London?" I said.

"No," Holmes replied. "I did not travel, having in the meanwhile obtained employment with our Mr. Girthwood."

"He took you on as Briggs?" I asked in astonishment. "How?"

"It was simplicity itself. I merely set as my goal the failed burgling of his hotel room."

"What?"

"We knew he was a stranger in London, apparently without henchmen following the embarrassment of Mr. Vic Starkey, and that he would seek out other men in desperation. I allowed him to catch me as Briggs in the act of ransacking his rooms at the Waymore. As he confronted me, I"—Holmes changed once more into his alter ego—"I begs him to lay off, as I was an honest thief merely trying to make a grand life of it. And I points out how he might could use me, seeing as he appears to be a gentleman of the trade himself."

The detective loosened his kerchief as he resumed his normal voice. "Well, he seemed truly taken aback by the bravado of it all and declared this must be, in his words, the top. Yes, he took to me on the spot, and I made certain that I was the man for him."

"And you seized control of Girthwood's plans from that moment."

"Of course. That was my objective, was it not? I convinced him that I and a band of associates could capture the two of you as ransom for the statue. I insisted that I have a free hand, and he complied as a good fellow."

"Holmes, Girthwood followed us into the City."

"Yes, more of that later. To continue, after the two of you left Baker Street for your walk down the Strand, I called at 221 with former Irregulars Oakes, Mullin, and Smith—or, as you knew them, Georgie, Johnny, and Shep. I explained everything to Mrs. Hudson and our agents here, who all then graciously hid in the back of the house and awaited your return."

"And Mercer in the cab?"

"I had previously told him to volunteer for the task of following you, should you choose to tour the town, and to not worry should he lose sight of you and that should such occur, to return to Baker Street and wait outside. When I called at 221 as Briggs, he was there and subsequently joined the others."

"And so you *expected* Miss Adler and me to leave during the day."

"At this moment, Girthwood thinks you are still held captive, though he believes you to be at a different locale," said Holmes, ignoring my comment. "I, meanwhile, arranged the false telegram, which I showed to Girthwood as well as yourselves, leading our portly friend to believe that I was returning from Paris."

"And is Girthwood to ring you up upon your supposed arrival?"

"He may do that once the lines are open. Alternatively, he may call in person tomorrow. We shall see."

"And where *does* Girthwood believe us to be at this hour?" I asked.

"In the criminal hideout of Uncle Bill Briggs, as I thought I mentioned moments ago."

"But what if he wishes to speak to you as Briggs?"

My friend smiled. "I merely told Girthwood to wait at his hotel until I contacted him as Briggs, making the argument that should the authorities be brought into the matter and attempt to bring pressure against him, he could truthfully claim to know nothing of your whereabouts. The man has weight in a literal sense, Watson, but against a forceful mind, his own is quite pliable. He accepted my somewhat specious suggestion without objection. But enough of these details. Are you game for a night ride across town, old fellow?"

I glanced to the window and noticed that more time had passed than I had believed. "Now?" I asked, staring at the darkness outside.

"Yes," my friend replied, striding toward his room. "Or, rather, a few minutes from now, once I've had the opportunity to fully change. I shall be out presently."

My friend exited to his room. Slowly, I walked round the sitting room, which now seemed to me lifeless in the absence of a fire, save for the still smouldering sticks of incense. I glanced over at Irene Adler, who sat quietly in the basket-chair, staring into the dark hearth.

"We can rejoice," I said, concerned by her long silence after our release. "All is well, after all."

"Perhaps."

Moments later, Holmes emerged once more as Holmes, carrying his Swiss clock, which had been lodged in his quarters. He restored it to its usual place, and its ticking once more graced the sitting room. The detective then noted that he had not had time to remove a day's growth of beard and asked if I would ride with one so uncouth. I answered in the affirmative, whereupon he looked at the clock and then turned toward the woman. "You may go up and get what sleep you can," he suggested to her. "There are agents inside and out, and Girthwood believes you elsewhere; you will be safe."

Irene Adler nodded silently. As Holmes turned his back to extinguish the sticks of incense, our guest rose and left without offering even the briefest good-night. Moments later in the waiting room, Holmes and I stood dressed in hats and waterproofs, facing Hollins.

"Recall my admonitions concerning the use of force," Holmes said to his subordinate.

"Of course, sir."

"I believe we can assume Girthwood is, at this hour, asleep, dreaming of a particular bird. Still, we should cover all possibilities. Dr. Watson and I shall return within two hours."

My friend and I walked out into the night, where Mercer had already summoned a hansom.

"Fresno Street, just off Upper Swandam Lane," Holmes told the cabby. "It is in the City, north of Cannon Street."

"I'm well aware of its placement, sir," our driver replied with a yawn, and almost at once, we set off at a steady pace into the drifting miasma of London.

"Holmes," I said urgently, even before our cab had reached the end of the block. "I've a number of important facts to relay."

"Begin the enumeration, Watson," replied the detective as our horse's hooves echoed off the relatively deserted pavement.

"Jasper Girthwood is Miss Adler's—"

"Half brother. Yes, I know. Briggs was there listening, was he not?"

"Oh, but of course. Well then, Diarmund Stephenson confessed to me that it was he who removed the shares from Lord Monsbury's study."

"He alone?"

"Yes. It appears to have been unrelated to the disappearance of young Hope Maldon. The boy is the natural son of the earl's late brother—Stephenson is the earl's nephew, I mean."

"Truly? Well, those are unexpected facets, though, of course, given the situation in the earl's household, my suspicion naturally fell upon him at once. Did he tell you why he took them?"

"He was forced to supply collateral for a debt he had incurred. He has the shares back in his possession now, however, and—"

"Wishes us to set matters right?"

"Yes."

"Well, that's easily accomplished, isn't it?"

"Holmes, I must in addition tell you that Robert Hope Maldon is not the natural son of Lord Monsbury."

Holmes's eyebrows rose. "Hum. Well, that perhaps explains the familial antipathy."

"Yes. Stephenson related the background to that as well. Holmes?"

"Yes?"

"Are we, by any chance, travelling now to obtain the statue of the black bird?"

"Of course we are."

"It is in Fresno Street."

"Yes."

"Miss Adler went there to seek it out?"

"You deduce correctly," my friend said. "It was that act, which you so adroitly coaxed into execution, that revealed to me where it was."

"My behaviour strikes me as incompetent rather than adroit," I said, leaning my head back. "I should not have allowed the journey, but I believed the woman had a purpose in mind and set myself to discover it."

"And so you did, old fellow. Come now," he said, grasping my arm. "If you plead incompetence, then so must I."

"I did not follow your directives."

"I did not direct you to remain in Baker Street, Watson. I gave only general instructions for my trusted second-in-command to use as a guide."

"But you told Mercer not to pursue us. You knew I would agree to let her go out."

"No, Watson, I merely hoped you would, and by so doing, you fulfilled my true wishes. If you had not, we would not now be making this journey, bringing us closer to the end."

"Then why not simply direct me so from the beginning?"

Holmes leaned in my direction. "Watson, in all the years of our association, I confess I have found only one deficiency in you as a member of this agency."

"Oh?"

"Old fellow, you are a most hopeless actor."

"What?"

"You are too bluff and honest," he continued as our cab clacked over the cobblestones. "I hope you will not view me as conceited when I say that I am a somewhat accomplished thespian."

"Well, you certainly made me fear for my life earlier this evening."

"I can dissemble even when it comes to character," the detective went on. "Miss Adler has been upon the stage," he added wistfully. "And she possesses that same ability. You, on the other hand, lack the capacity to feign an untrue heart. I truly hoped that you would escort Miss Adler out of Baker Street in search of the falcon, for I was certain she knew where it was or would be. I could not, however, directly ask you to do so for fear that your manner would betray my presence behind the scenes. Similarly, when you were held captive and interviewed by Girthwood, it was essential that he truly believe your fear and anger. And so the deceit, old fellow. I suppose," he said, leaning back beside me, "I should beg forgiveness from you yet again."

"Nonsense," I replied. "I quite understand."

My friend looked me in the eye. "I know you do, Watson. Believe me when I say that I never viewed my actions as deceptions where you were concerned. I merely wished to put you, as it were, in a position where your own abilities would see us through. And so they have. I value you as a partner in my work, Watson, more than I think I have ever had the good sense to convey in all these years."

"Quite the contrary, Holmes," I replied. "I am honoured to stand by you—or sit by you as I do now—and I am most grateful that young Stamford brought us together."

"Young Stamford," sighed Holmes, leaning back again. "By now should there not be some on this island who know him as old Stamford?"

I smiled. "No doubt there are."

"Where did the lad wind up? Do you know?"

"He has a practice of moderate success in Potters Bar, but I believe he has his sights now set upon adventure. He is applying to be a member of Huddleston's next expedition to the South."

"Stamford in Antarctica. Well, perhaps he can acquaint the penguins with one another."

"And where, precisely, in Fresno Street is *our* bird, Holmes?"

"It awaits us as the Aberdeen Shipping Company."

"Have you done business with that firm previously? The name is familiar."

"Yes, I've utilized their services now and then. Moreover, I believe it played a minor role in one of the cases you wrote of in your first or second brace of stories. The St. Clair matter. Do you recall it?"

"Yes, of course, but I know that I do not recall seeing the establishment in Fresno Street today."

"Well, you had several distractions at the time."

"Yes, Jasper Girthwood for one. He followed us there with some thugs. I suppose they were old Irregulars as well, weren't they?"

"No, they were men from Whitehall."

"What?" I said as we continued to race down Oxford Street.

"Moreover, the man you mistook for Girthwood today in Fresno Street was, in fact, my brother, Mycroft, decked out in Astrakhan and bowler. He did not enjoy parading about thus, I can assure you. He enjoyed having to get out of his chair in the first place even less."

"You set him after us?"

"Yes, and while he found the effort of venturing out-of-doors most odious, the Holmes blood is notoriously thick. Moreover, I promised I would investigate for him some trifle at the Russian embassy. It seems a young military attaché by the name of Kemidoff has gotten himself into a rather embarrassing situation."

"And so you had your brother frighten Miss Adler into cutting off her attempt to retrieve the bird at the last moment."

"Yes. In that way I knew its approximate location. I had, as previously mentioned, gathered that Miss Adler did not have the statue but did know where it was or soon would be."

"In a more grand manner, I suppose the ploy was somewhat similar to the ruse you employed against her in your first encounter."

"The false alarm of fire?" said Holmes, referring to "A Scandal in Bohemia."

"Precisely."

"Hum," said my friend. "I had not considered that. Well, Watson, I'm through with explanation for the moment. Let us savour the rest of this late-night cab ride through London. I fear it may be among the last we shall ever share."

On that melancholy note, our conversation lapsed for several minutes, and I turned my attention to the passing streetlights, thrice blurred—first by the shifting fog, then by our rapid gallop, and, finally, by eyes brimming with sentiment. At length we entered the City, following the route Miss Adler and I had taken hours before. We passed into

Cannon Street and then found Upper Swandam Lane and, along it, the entrance to Fresno Street. The cab, moving slowly now, followed the deserted lane to the end, where stood the Aberdeen Shipping Company, its office giving out the only light among the darkened store fronts.

Our horse stopped, and we left the cab, Holmes instructing the driver to wait. Stepping up to the shipping office, I noticed a four-wheeler parked nearby, its driver also patiently biding his time.

"There they are, Watson," said Holmes, and I saw inside the illuminated building three individuals, two of whom were the agents Stannard and Pike. Both greeted us as we entered the company office.

"This is Mr. Charles Galloway, sir," said Langdale Pike, the languid man, who, in particular, served as my friend's source of society gossip that continually swirled about the metropolis. "He is the chief clerk. Mr. Galloway, may I present Mr. Sherlock Holmes and Dr. John Watson."

"Greetings, gentlemen," said the clerk, using one hand to stifle a yawn. "These are not our usual business hours, you understand, though I am prepared for the transaction."

"I do appreciate the cooperation," said Sherlock Holmes. "Your Mr. Harris explained the necessity of this to you?"

"He did, sir. Now, if you have the signed letter?"

"It is here," the detective replied, taking from his coat a folded sheet of cream-laid paper and offering it to Mr. Galloway.

The clerk unfolded the sheet and briefly read its contents. "Everything appears to be in order," he said, comparing it to another paper. "Now, there is but one other matter to attend to."

"And what is that?" said my friend.

"Have you proof of your identity, sir?" asked the clerk evenly. "Can I be certain you are who you claim to be?"

The detective gave the man an odd look, spent a moment in deep thought, and then said, "Mr. Galloway, you have been employed by Aberdeen Shipping for fewer than five years, having previously experienced the failure of a business you yourself owned. Your wife, who is significantly younger than you, is of German descent. Moreover, you have twin children, a boy and girl, one of whom is left-handed. I suspect it is the boy."

The clerk stared my friend straight in the eye for some time, his lips pursed. Then he declared, "In truth, sir, my wife is Dutch, but that's close enough for me. I reckon, after that performance, that you *must* be Sherlock Holmes. Here, allow me to bring out the parcel for you."

"You have obtained the information?" Holmes asked Pike as the clerk stepped to the back of the office.

"Yes, sir," said the agent. In his pale hand, he held out a packet, which Holmes took. "There's enough in those pages to spark a great deal of interest by the Yard in

Mr. Girthwood," Pike commented. "Though I cannot guarantee that they will suffice for a conviction."

"To delay him will be sufficient," said Holmes, handing me the large envelope. "When I have received what we've come for, please see Mr. Galloway safely back to his house."

"We shall," said Stannard.

The clerk returned with a wrapped parcel, slightly more than one foot in length. "It's a mite heavy," he said, setting it upon a counter. "Just sign for it here on this paper, Mr. Holmes, and it's yours."

The detective took a pen and signed his name across the bottom of the sheet.

"Thank you, sir," said Galloway. "Would you like to open her up, Mr. Holmes, just to be certain it's what you expect?"

"That will not be necessary," replied my friend. "The integrity of your firm is unquestioned." He then took the parcel in his arms and carried it toward the door.

"I bet the owner's got something valuable in there," Stannard whispered in my ear.

"We believe it to be," I replied, following Holmes out the door and into the street. The detective and I bade Pike, Stannard, and Mr. Galloway a good-night and entered our cab, the package sitting in the space between us.

"And so within this parcel is the Hapsburg falcon," I said.

"Certainly it is not my latest supply of shag," Holmes answered. He put one hand upon the bundle and gave it a firm pat then rapped the hansom roof with his knuckles. "Back to—"

"Baker Street," completed the cabby. "Aye, right away, sirs."

"What was the business with the cream paper?" I asked as the cab jerked to a start and then moved into Upper Swandam Lane.

"Aberdeen Shipping is a reliable firm, most scrupulous in its accounting and procedures. This parcel was sent from Paris by Miss Adler, with instructions that it be transferred only to her or her proven representatives. Written on the cream paper was a signed statement declaring me to be acting in Miss Adler's stead and authorizing me to take possession of the parcel."

"When did you obtain permission from her?"

"Oh, never," said Sherlock Holmes as the cab reached Cannon Street. "I simply wrote the note myself."

"What?"

"Yes, I employed the letter I had her write to Jasper Girthwood the other day as a model from which to copy both her script and signature." He smiled. "It was for just such a purpose that I had her write it in the first place, should such a ruse prove necessary."

"You anticipated such a need?"

Holmes looked languidly out into the darkness. "Sadly, yes, I did."

"Does she suspect that was your purpose?"

"I cannot say if the thought of such a tactic entered her mind on that earlier day, but I believe she now understands we will be returning with the statue, to her great disappointment."

Several minutes passed in silence. Then, patting the parcel myself, I said, "The woman lied about this as well then."

"Are you surprised, old fellow? Still, in the end, it is we who have the falcon."

"Yet we still do not have Robert Hope Maldon."

"No," replied Holmes, turning his attention to the passing streetlights as our hansom cut swiftly through the deepening fog. "No, we do not."

The last half of our return was, for me, but a blur, a memory muddled by lack of sleep. When, at length, we returned to Baker Street, I found I had to be assisted from the cab by our agent Hollins, who took the packet from my hands and guided me toward the door of 221. Mercer was there and informed us that all had been quiet during our absence and that Miss Adler had retired for the night.

"Well, Watson," said Holmes as we ascended the stair, he with the parcel cradled in his arms and I gripping the railing more tightly than usual. "Shall we at last have our look?"

"By all means," I replied with, I fear, a sleepy slurring of my words.

We entered the sitting room, still in our hats and waterproofs. Holmes carried the parcel across to his deal-topped chemistry table. Then, from one of his pockets, he produced a small knife and cut the twine from the paper, which he slowly unwrapped, eventually uncovering what lay within.

"Come here, Watson, and observe."

I shuffled over to the table and looked down into a nest of string, brown paper, and shredded newspaper. There, staring up at me, was a stocky ebony form I barely recognized as a falcon.

"We have it, Watson!"

"Indeed, we do," I must have said in a most uninterested manner, for at that moment, all I wished for was a soft, clean bed. Holmes said some few words in reply, words I cannot recall, and then he led me by the arm out to the landing and delivered me into the care of Mercer. The sight of my feet touching down on risers returns to me when I remember that night, as does the brilliance of a lamp at my bedside, followed by sudden darkness, the warmth of blankets, and peace.

CHAPTER FIFTEEN:

Kismet

It seemed only an instant later that I was awakened by Holmes. "Quick, Watson," he said, looming over me in the darkness. "The game may still be abed, but it will be afoot soon enough."

Shaking myself from drowsiness, I sat up. "It is early," were my first words.

"Yes, I suppose it is," replied my friend as he slowly retreated toward the door. "Certainly, it is not your usual rising time, but then we have a bit of unusual business to transact this morning. Would one of Mrs. Hudson's breakfasts induce you to stir?"

"I thought she was to remain in her quarters."

"She insists on providing sustenance before barricading her door," Holmes reminded me.

"I can ready myself in a quarter hour, if her ham and eggs are in the offing."

"Good. I shall see you down in the sitting room shortly then," he said, closing the door behind him.

Ten minutes later, I stepped into the sitting room, where Mrs. Hudson was delivering the meal to our table.

"Ah, I timed it to perfection," said Holmes. "Thank you, Mrs. Hudson. Come, Watson! We've not a moment to lose!"

I greeted our smiling-if-heavy-lidded landlady as she stepped past me on her way out and took my place at the table. "Is Miss Adler about yet?" I inquired.

"I convinced Mrs. Hudson to raise her, and I expect she will descend in a while. We all must be present when Jasper Girthwood appears at our door."

"The falcon is safe?" I asked, looking about as Holmes took a generous portion of eggs. "Have you hidden it?"

"Oh, it's sitting over by the window, behind your writing chair."

I looked in the indicated direction and saw the statue on the floor, noticing as well a dull, rusty object leaning against one leg of Holmes's chemistry table. "What in God's name is that?" I asked.

"What? You don't recognize my old portable basin?" Holmes replied. "I took it down from the lumber room last night. Many years have passed since it was in regular use, have they not?"

"For what purpose did you employ it?"

Holmes tilted his head back and forth as he speared a slice of ham. "Oh, I simply wished to while away the hours with some old experiments."

"Did you get any sleep at all?"

"None that I am aware of. Toast, please."

"Holmes?"

"Yes? Thank you, Watson."

"Holmes, for all the time this matter has taken, I feel we are no closer to finding Robert Hope Maldon than we were at the start."

"The resolution of all things is nigh, Watson. Trust to it."

"Speaking of resolution, are you still entertaining Mr. Stephenson's plea to return the shares without Lord Monsbury's knowledge?"

"You say the lad is truly penitent?"

"My heart tells me he is, Holmes."

"Hum. Well, we have performed such ruses before; no doubt we can offer another encore. 'Le coeur a ses raisons que la raison ne connaît point.'"[11]

Holmes checked the clock and then complained about the lack of a fresh newspaper to read. "As Briggs," he continued, "I have already sent a message to Girthwood at the Waymore Hotel telling him that I, as Holmes, am once again at 221. The message suggests he meet me, as his henchman, here and confront me, as myself, regarding you, Miss Adler, and the falcon. We should expect him, perhaps, within the hour."

At that moment, Irene Adler made her appearance for the first time that morning. She was attired in the white linen blouse and grey skirt that had once created such an airy, ethereal impression, but as she took a place at the table, her mood seemed that of stony depression.

"Eggs?" asked Sherlock Holmes, and our guest received them with a silent nod. "Watson? Do you wish more? No? Then allow me to finish the lot," he said, somewhat out of character, for though he enjoyed a fine meal, I knew him to eat sparingly. "Mr. Girthwood will arrive within the hour," he repeated for the benefit of the woman.

---

11   "The heart has its reasons that reason does not know." The quotation is from Blaise Pascal.

"And within a quarter hour after that, this case should, by my reckoning, be history. You may then begin, so to speak, your literary post-mortem, Watson."

Irene Adler stared at the table and ceased to show interest in the meal, other than her coffee. Seeking to ease her obvious discomfort, I sought to occupy her with conversation by first asking if she had obtained any sleep.

"I believe I did," were her only words, and I ceased my efforts, believing they would be embarrassing as well as useless.

At length, Mrs. Hudson came to clear the table. Holmes instead herded her to the sitting room door, where he whispered instructions to her. Our landlady swiftly vanished down the hall, and my friend strode to the bow window, which he unlatched but did not open. Staring down into Baker Street, Holmes smiled faintly for several minutes. Then he gave a start.

"None of our agents are in sight," the detective said. "That is good. Ah, our moment has arrived somewhat sooner than expected. The rope gently tightens; the noose quietly forms."

"Girthwood approaches?" I asked from the table.

"Yes," said Holmes. He turned round, rubbing his hands together. "Our last act."

I heard the house bell ring.

"Up from the table, if you will," Holmes asked of Miss Adler and myself. "Please, quickly take comfort round the hearth."

The bell rang again, and then I heard loud knocking upon the front door.

"I suppose I could have asked Oakes and the boys to return this morning," said Holmes in a wistful tone. "But they've earned their rest."

At length I heard the house door open. "Halloa!" came Girthwood's squealing voice. "Briggs, are you in here? Anyone? By gad, what a mess!"

"Up here!" shouted Holmes in the voice of Briggs. He sat down in his armchair beside Miss Adler, who had reluctantly taken to the sofa. I claimed the basket-chair.

"We're up here, cosy and all!" Holmes cried. "Come on, boss!"

The intruder's heavy ascent of the stair reverberated all the way to our sitting room. "This isn't like you, Briggs!" the man said in a huffing voice as he reached the landing. "The door was unlocked! Where are your men? Where is Holmes? I need to—"

Jasper Girthwood stopped as he entered through the open doorway. Glancing about the room, his eyes suddenly became wide with alarm. "Briggs?" he called, looking frantically among us. "They're untied and here! With Holmes! Unguarded! Briggs, you fool! Briggs, where are you?"

"Right here, boss," grunted Holmes in the criminal's voice.

Girthwood stared in shock at my friend.

"Briggs be here, sir."

"You," whispered the corpulent one.

"Me," replied my friend in his own voice.

167

Our visitor began to back out of the sitting room.

"If you wish to ever hold the Hapsburg falcon in your hands, Mr. Girthwood, I advise you to remain," declared Sherlock Holmes, rising to his feet and striding across the room toward the bow window.

Girthwood stopped and stared at the detective with malevolent suspicion. His flabby face seemed, in some improbable manner, to grow taut, while his spine almost appeared to arch above his massive bulk. "You've got it after all then, sir?"

"I do now," said Holmes. "After you submit to a search of your person for weapons, you may see it."

"Well, there's an offer that's straight and sure," replied Girthwood, regaining some composure. The man adjusted his coat and pulled himself back into the sitting room. "Mr. Holmes, I'll tell you right out I have no weapons. Must I suffer indignity piled atop injury?"

"Yes. Watson, see to it, please."

I rose from the table and searched the man—a hunt that produced brass knuckles, two knives, and an unloaded pistol.

"Perhaps," Girthwood said, "I should have said I had no weapons of consequence."

"Watch him closely, old fellow," Holmes told me as he reached down behind my writing chair and held up the statue, its form seeming even blacker against the morning light.

"The falcon," whispered Girthwood, momentarily enraptured by the vision of it. Slowly, as if in a trance, he stepped forward. The glint from its enamelled surface seemed mirrored in the large man's greedy eyes. He stroked his chin, and I thought I saw his tongue moisten his lips, as a gourmand's might when contemplating a sumptuous meal.

"Charles of Spain never saw it, gentlemen. Now I have. By gad!" exclaimed Girthwood, his dry voice wavering. "May I…may I now have the pleasure of holding it?"

"As you wish," said Sherlock Holmes, pushing open the unlatched window. "You'll have to catch it first, however." Casually, the detective tossed the bird out into Baker Street.

"Good Lord!" screamed Girthwood. "You're mad!"

"And you're without the falcon," replied Holmes as he closed the window. "Unless you hop to it, sir."

In an instant, Girthwood was out the sitting room door. The entire house seemed to shake as he charged down the stair. I bolted to the window and looked down into the street to behold the falcon moving off in the back of a wagon piled with straw. Suddenly, Jasper Girthwood's bouncing form emerged from the door of 221 in pursuit.

"Ha!" cried Holmes, who stood beside me. "He runs as a woman might."

"But what if he catches the wagon?" I asked.

"Where is my clay?" my friend said, turning from the window.

"Holmes?"

"The driver of the wagon is Stanley Hopkins," the detective said as he strode to the mantel. "Baker Street is lined with his fellows from Scotland Yard. Mr. Girthwood's part in our drama, I believe, is now played out. "

"But the statue!" I said.

"Sometimes a statue is merely a statue," said Holmes, filling his pipe. "Such is true in this instance—that and nothing more."

"But the jewels!"

"There are no jewels."

"The jewels have been removed? Even so, it is solid gold beneath the enamel—"

"The jewels never were there, Watson," said my friend, lighting his clay. "And whatever lies beneath the black enamel is certainly not gold."

In the corner of my eye, Irene Adler gave a start.

"How can you be certain?" I asked.

"Because I tested it, Doctor," said Holmes, tossing his vesta onto the coals. "I used my old portable basin there to float the statue in a pot borrowed from Mrs. Hudson's kitchen and then employed the well-worn principle of Archimedes to determine the statue's density. The value I obtained was not that of gold, though it was rather close to what one would expect of lead."

"That statue is a leaden forgery?" I said. "Then where is the real one?"

"If by that you mean the priceless statue supposedly created by the Order of St. John, then I must say I have no idea," replied Holmes. "Perhaps there never was such an object, the story Girthwood quoted being pure myth. Perhaps Konstantinides, the Parisian art dealer, had it made to pose as the real one. No matter, Watson. The falcon has played out its role along with Mr. Girthwood, which leaves but one more among our *dramatis personae* to deal with."

Holmes silently directed me back to the basket-chair, where I sat down.

"I am truly sorry about the statue," the detective said to Miss Adler as he stood by the armchair. "It is to be regretted that you suffered so much for something so worthless."

"There are always risks," the woman replied, her first words in several minutes. "No matter where one goes or what one does, there are risks."

"Yes," said Sherlock Holmes. "Life plants them everywhere, does it not?" He contemplated the ceiling briefly then removed the pipe from his mouth as he sat in the armchair. "You understand this is the final accounting," he declared. "The lies have kept peeling away, one after the other, Miss Adler, and time is short. In a moment, Scotland Yard will come through that doorway. We've time only for the core now, the truth and nothing else."

"You wish the satisfaction of the truth?"

"I believe I have the truth already, madam. My satisfaction, as you term it, would derive from hearing its admission in your own voice. That, indeed, is all that I have ever desired in all of this."

They stared wordlessly at each other, and then Miss Adler said, "Proceed."

"In the beginning, you were a reluctant ally of your husband and half brother in obtaining the falcon," said Holmes. "However, you soon determined to betray them both and take the statue for yourself alone. To accomplish that, you enlisted an ally of your own in the person of young Robert Hope Maldon. Whether you loved him or he you is no matter. What does matter is that you allowed him to learn the legend surrounding that avian *objet d'art* and then persuaded him to join with you in reaping its treasure, minus your husband and half brother."

Miss Adler thought to speak but did not.

"I should tell you," Holmes continued during her hesitation, "that I observed the message you had scratched upon the pillar-box."

"Ah," the woman said. "I could not be certain, but you never mentioned it. Yes, the impulse to betray Jasper and Godfrey was mine. I made the plans, not Robert, and he followed them. We travelled to Paris without informing the other two and there sought to steal the statue from Konstantinides's shop."

"The result of which was that you obtained the falcon and had it sent to Aberdeen Shipping in Fresno Street."

"Yes."

"From there, if you could elude your two betrayed partners and claim the statue, your fortune was assured," declared Holmes. "However, complications ensued."

"The shipment was delayed."

"That was not the complication I was referring to," said my friend. "I did not know of it until just now, and I thank you for that bit of truth. The delay added to your worry. The longer you had to wait in London, the more likely your husband and brother would find you."

"The complication was the separation then?" I asked on impulse, before abruptly putting my hand to my mouth. "My apologies, Holmes. In my anxiety, I interrupted."

My friend gently smiled. "Your exemplary conduct in this affair has more than won you a place in the discussion, Watson. And, though you do not realize it, your comment was most apt."

He turned again toward Irene Adler. "For the parting between you and Hope Maldon in Paris was, indeed, the complication I was referring to. Except, old fellow," he added, once more glancing in my direction. "It was not as the lady first told it."

Holmes then leaned back in his chair. "The man who rang up this house and spoke to Mrs. Hudson was not Robert Hope Maldon, though Miss Adler tried to convince us that it was." He stared at the woman.

"It was Godfrey," admitted Irene Adler.

"The card with the printed word 'Soon' that arrived here at 221 was not sent by Lord Monsbury's son."

"Godfrey sent it," the woman said.

"Robert Hope Maldon neither called by telephone nor sent a message, because he never returned to London. The person who called upon the office of Solicitor Lucius Crabbe—"

"Was I, in men's garb," confessed Irene Adler. "I came back from Paris with some of Robert's possessions and then obtained some few additional items from his rooms when I visited there briefly. It was then that I found Godfrey had apparently searched it, leaving the damaged photographs as a warning. I dressed as Robert and travelled to Crabbe's office simply to make an appearance, to make it seem as if Robert had, indeed, returned."

"But he did not?" I asked.

"No, he did not," said Holmes in a mournful voice. "At first, all I had was conjecture, but conjecture I found rather compelling. Always we just failed to catch up with the young man. He was seen at Solicitor Crabbe's office but appeared no more. He seemingly communicated by telephone once and never again. He sent a card with a word cut from a newspaper rather than writing the message, when I should think the evidence of his hand would reassure his presumed fiancée. Why? It was as if the foregoing had no purpose other than to support a belief in the young man's continued existence."

"A belief?" I said. "A belief in his existence?"

"Yes. For you see, Watson, the Honourable Robert Hope Maldon met his death before we ever took up this case."

I sat in the familiar basket-chair and yet felt as if I now inhabited a foreign world.

"Once in Paris," Irene Adler began quietly. "We surveyed the shop of Konstantinides and planned to steal the statue of the falcon. It was to be a burglary, and perhaps it would have worked, had it not been for Robert's complete inexperience and the fact that Konstantinides came back to his shop that evening, whether by chance or design I know not. No matter, he confronted us there. The two men fought. Robert struggled as best he could, but he had not led a rough life, and it was clear to me that he would lose the battle. As they were preoccupied with one another, I simply seized the statue and fled. As I went out the shop door, however, I turned and saw Konstantinides strike Robert with what would have had to have been a fatal blow upon the skull. I darted out before the shop owner noticed me. From there it was as I have previously said, and as you noted, with me sending to statue to London."

"For reasons of his own," Holmes added, "Konstantinides must have further mutilated the young man's body to disguise it as his own then set fire to his shop to further mask the identity of the victim. The motive is not obvious, but certain facts obtained by Shinwell Johnson in Paris lead me to that conclusion."

Irene Adler placed her head in her hands and said nothing. Holmes contemplated her for a moment before continuing.

"I thought it all rather odd from the very beginning," he said calmly. "Every photograph of Hope Maldon in his rooms that contained his adult image had been thrown to the floor, save for the one that included you. We knew two people had entered the flat, and so it seemed to me that the second had placed that photograph upon the table after the others had been scattered. You did not notice the pattern I have mentioned?" Holmes asked the woman.

"No," came the muffled voice of Irene Adler. "I am not as observant as you, obviously."

"You placed the photograph upon the table believing I might be called upon to investigate the young man's disappearance?"

"Yes. I thought it might intrigue you and motivate you to assist me should you enter the picture."

"I may be the more observant," commented Sherlock Holmes. "You, Miss Adler, are surely the more perceptive."

The woman did not answer.

"Our visit to the pillar-box, where the young man had read your message and responded, also aroused my suspicions, for you gave us the impression that it was Hope Maldon who had planned and directed the betrayal of Girthwood and your husband, yet, clearly, the actions at the pillar-box indicated the direct opposite."

The woman lifted her head from her cupped hands. "I did not know you had that knowledge, as I have said."

"The fact that you were alive immediately brought forth the possibility that your husband still breathed as well," Holmes said. "I remarked so to the doctor here. As Girthwood clearly could not have been the person who had initially broken into the rooms at Breton Mansions, there was obviously another player lurking in the wings, and Norton was a prime candidate for such a role. Moreover, when Girthwood first visited 221, I informed him that I had been engaged by a man to find Robert Hope Maldon, but I did not identify that man as his father, Lord Monsbury. Girthwood seemed to have a most antagonistic attitude toward this anonymous client, and I began to wonder who he assumed it was—Godfrey Norton? As I became doubtful of the evidence for Hope Maldon's presence, I also began to question the corresponding likelihood of Norton's absence."

"But, Holmes?" I said at last, while still in the midst of digesting these revelations. "Robert Hope Maldon hurled Norton to his death, did he not?"

My friend glanced at me with a kindly smile then let his expression become impassive as he turned back toward Miss Adler and simply waited, an expectant look in his eyes.

"I knew it was inevitable that Godfrey would come to Baker Street," the woman said, looking neither at Holmes nor me but rather staring into open space. "He had surmised I had come here, and from the telephone message—which was his—and the message on the card—also his—I knew that appearance would be, as indicated, soon. The kerchief in the window had been a well-used form of silent communication between us, indicating that he should attract my attention when he thought it safe.

"He came that night, tossing small pebbles against the pane. From my now-open window, I whispered for him to climb the tree and enter through the lumber room. He did so, and we talked there. Godfrey revealed to me that he had since broken with, and he suggested that I, in turn, discard my alliance with Robert—he, of course, had no knowledge that Robert was already dead.

"I was unwilling to comply with his suggestion," Miss Adler continued. "Godfrey began to threaten me. He began to lay hands upon me and—"

Holmes cleared his throat. "Please do not disappoint me, madam," he said.

Miss Adler looked at him steadily then gave him a wan smile. "Godfrey did threaten me, but I quickly acceded to his demands or at least pretended to do so. I gave him assurance I would return to him, and, satisfied with my pledge, he turned to climb out the window. It was as he stood in the frame, about to reach for a tree branch, that I pushed him sharply in the back. He fell onto the stone walk."

"And it was only after you had watched his form for a short while, sensing no motion, that you screamed in order to summon the two of us."

"Yes. Yes, Mr. Holmes. That is accurate."

I no longer felt myself upon an unfamiliar world but rather inhabiting a different universe altogether.

"People falling freely may, of course, twist and turn, but the position in which Dr. Watson and I found the body suggested that Norton's fall had involved no such motion. I have performed numerous trials, stretching back many years and including venues as novel as a lawn-tennis green," he said. The last remark evinced from Miss Adler a quick, bitter nod of the head. "From all appearances, it seemed to me that Godfrey Norton must have plummeted straight down from the lumber room window while facing toward the back yard.

"Had Robert Hope Maldon hurled him out that window during a struggle, I should have expected to find evidence of twisting motion, yet there was, effectively, none. Norton appeared to have fallen while facing the back yard, yet he certainly would not have turned his back on the young man during a fight. But he would, perhaps, have been willing to turn his back on you, madam, after your assurances had won his trust. Placing himself in that vulnerable pose, he paid the consequences."

"He paid the consequences for his past actions!" declared Miss Adler. "You've no understanding of the type of monster he was."

"I can surmise," said Sherlock Holmes. "As I can surmise the depth of your hatred for him. Why else would you have taken that glove of Robert Hope Maldon with you into the lumber room, unless you were praying for murderous opportunity even as you ascended the stair to the lumber room?"

Irene Adler, her eyes free of tears, nodded her head as I found myself slowly shaking my own.

"I commend your thoroughness in preparation," added the detective. "You even put your hand into the glove so as to warm it and make it appear as if only recently worn by Hope Maldon. Of course, as your own hands are somewhat large for a woman, that warmth extended all the way to the fingertips. Well done."

The woman turned away as her grey eyes began to fill. "Godfrey was a monster," she repeated. She covered her face and did not see the detective give silent agreement.

"Holmes," I said numbly. "What ensues next? The door below has just opened."

"We have touched one of Indra's jewels,"[12] Holmes replied in a hollow voice as we heard the tread of Stanley Hopkins upon the stair. "Let us see what reflections we behold."

"Greetings, Mr. Holmes," said the inspector as he entered the sitting room. "Dr. Watson. I believe"—Hopkins stopped as he watched Miss Adler uncover her eyes.

Miss Adler, in turn, stared impassively at Holmes. There was a moment of silence that seemed an eternity.

"Hopkins, this is Irene Adler," said Sherlock Holmes suddenly. "She is one of our many agents who played a role in this matter. Miss Adler, I present Inspector Stanley Hopkins of Scotland Yard."

The woman looked at Holmes and then toward the inspector, suppressing an expression of disbelief.

I simply gazed silently at my friend, who calmly smiled.

"Irene Adler?" Hopkins said. "Miss, I've just heard your name uttered more than once down in the street, from the man we just apprehended."

"No doubt," interjected Holmes. "But, Hopkins, here is a more important detail: Miss Adler has identified the man who slipped and fell to his death here the other night. He was her estranged husband, Godfrey Norton."

"And have you determined why he was climbing about the roofs of Baker Street, this one in particular?"

"We have no firm conclusion, but I believe he and Mr. Girthwood below were criminal associates. I have had my eye upon them for some time and enlisted Miss Adler, who, by coincidence, had family associations with both men."

"I see," replied Hopkins hesitantly. "But our Mr. Girthwood insists—"

"That Miss Adler was a partner of his as well? Yes," continued Holmes. "That was a pose I had her assume for the purposes of my investigation. The man will, no doubt, assert many tall tales in the next several hours. Rest assured," he added, without glancing at the woman. "I will vouch for Miss Adler."

---

12   Indra's jewels refer to a metaphor of Buddhist philosophy. Also called Indra's net or Indra's pearls, Indra's jewels symbolize the sense of infinitely repeating interconnections among all elements of the cosmos. It will be recalled that Holmes spent some time in India and Tibet following his duel with Professor Moriarty.

I stared at the bearskin rug, those words echoing in my mind.

"Well, that will satisfy me, I daresay," Hopkins declared. "Mr. Girthwood is being carted away as we speak."

"Inspector, I thank you. Another performance brilliantly executed!"

Silently, I agreed.

A policeman entered then, carrying the falcon itself. He handed it to Hopkins, who set it upon the dining table.

"Ugly thing," the inspector said, laying his hand upon its head. "What's the material, do you think?"

"The substance from which fantasies are spun," replied Holmes, contemplating the dark avian shape. Under his breath, I thought I heard my friend add, "*Le coeur a ses raisons...*"

With that, Hopkins bade us farewell and departed with the policeman. The house door to 221 had just shut when I rose and strode toward the open sitting room door. "I believe I shall go out for a time, Holmes," I said gruffly.

"Of course," my friend replied as I began my descent. Possessing an urge to fill my lungs with clear, fresh air, I donned hat and coat and stepped out into a sunny morning that seemed to hold an enticing hint of summer around a far corner. I set off to the south then strode along Oxford Street and did not stop until I was three quarters of the way to Holborn.

It was there I found a chop-house new to me and, once seated, ordered the most expensive offering possible from the menu. I savoured each succulent morsel and then took a cab to Northumberland Avenue for the catharsis of a Turkish bath. At last, somewhere in the middle of an afternoon that had no seeming prospect of ending, I returned to Baker Street and trod, as I knew I wished to for the remainder of my existence, the familiar seventeen steps to 221B. There I found Holmes as I felt he should eternally be, sprawled across the hearthrug in his dressing-gown, cutting out articles from newspapers, a glass of claret sitting nearby.

"Your guest has departed?" I asked without emotion.

"The one, yes." He looked up at me and smiled, clay pipe between his teeth. "I am, of course, obliged to travel to Lennox Square later today," he said. "To inform the Earl of Monsbury's household that Robert Hope Maldon is deceased, and I think it best to take that opportunity to make right Mr. Stephenson's predicament as well. Are you available to join me in those endeavours, Watson?"

Without uttering a word, I collected his unopened correspondence from a table-top and then strode to the mantel, upon which lay his old jack-knife, and, with a firm, overhand thrust of that blade, pinned the letters firmly to the wood.

I turned round and saw him staring up at me with an expression as close to stupefaction as I was ever to witness in his eyes, and after a moment, we both smiled the smiles of twenty-two years.

"I shall presume that to be a reply in the affirmative," said he.

As Holmes studiously returned to his clippings, I stood before the mantel to survey its diverse collection of curios: remains of the day's pipes, set out for the detective's reuse before breakfast tomorrow; foreign medals hung as if they were Christmas decorations; and the Hapsburg falcon itself, a new member of this odd little club.

Yet suddenly I realized that one object was now missing. I searched from one end of the mantelpiece to another but failed to uncover it.

"Holmes?" I said, turning toward him. "Where is the snuff-box? Has it been misplaced?"

"Misplaced?" said he, scrupulously setting down his papers and reaching for the claret. "No, Watson, I think not."

Appendix A:

On the Details of the Find

Each new announcement of yet another manuscript claiming to be a narrative from the pen of Dr. John H. Watson must inspire in many present-day Sherlockian readers a weary mix of anticipation and doubt. So many such works have appeared over the course of the past century and more, that based on sheer number—let alone style and factual errors—the vast majority must be relegated to the category of unabashed forgery. *The Hapsburg Falcon*, of course, cannot escape such jaundiced suspicion, and this addendum and two others are meant to place its supposed addition to the Holmesian record in perspective.

The preceding narrative was discovered in the form of a 276-page typed manuscript, the first twelve sheets of which are original typescript, with the remaining 264 being carbon-copy typescript. Numerous corrections in pencil have been made to most of these pages, almost all involving the substitution of British spellings for American ones. Accompanying these pages are seven sheets of foolscap containing a handwritten narrative roughly equivalent to the first five pages of the typed copy, with the phrase, "The Black Falcon of Malta," written at the top of the first of these sheets. These seven pages and the corresponding portion of typescript do not match precisely, there being slight differences in phrasing between the two. It should also be noted that the hand-written pages employ British spellings but do not appear to have been composed by the individual responsible for the penciled corrections to the typed manuscript.

These papers, all tied into a bundle with twine, were found in a trunk that was a fixture of the Greenwich Village apartment that my wife's brother moved into during the mid-1980s. The trunk's original owner is unknown, and according to one veteran building tenant, the trunk itself had sat locked in those rooms without a key since at least the early 1960s.

My brother-in-law simply covered it with a blanket for use as an improvised miniature sofa during the time he lived in that New York City flat, but one day his curiosity got the better of him, and he forced open the rusty lock. Within the trunk he found three vintage men's shirts in almost mint condition, a ream of blank typing paper, and five bath towels. Wrapped within one of those folded towels was the manuscript described above.

Nothing connected the trunk's contents to any particular person, and my brother-in-law quietly took possession of the items he had discovered. The shirts were bartered for credit at a vintage clothing store, the typing paper was eventually used for note sheets, and the towels—which did not inspire trust—were simply thrown away. My brother-in-law read and kept the manuscript as a curiosity, but he did nothing with it at the time.

In the early 1990s, my wife traveled from Portland to see her brother, who had since moved into a house in New Jersey. During that visit, he mentioned the manuscript to her, and, in turn, she—knowing my interest in Sherlock Holmes—told me of it. The news piqued my interest slightly, but as stated at the beginning of this addendum, Sherlockian pastiches are not hard to come across, and I did not follow up on an offer to have the manuscript sent to me. Instead, it sat on the East Coast for another several years. In 2008, however, my brother-in-law suffered a fit of spring-cleaning and decided to just mail the entire set of pages to me unannounced.

As I began to read the story, I was not surprised by the pastiche's ploy of reintroducing Irene Adler but was somewhat intrigued by the tale's mention of a black bird statue. The description of Jasper Girthwood also struck a chord. Then, two-thirds of the way through, I was startled by the description of the statue's history, given in Chapter 10. Having long been a devotee of Dashiell Hammett's novel *The Maltese Falcon* and John Huston's film adaptation of it, I realized at once that the story in my hands must relate Holmes's encounter with that legendary—and what I had heretofore taken to be fictional—artifact. Moreover, I simultaneously understood that the character in the manuscript named Jasper Girthwood could be none other than a young Casper Gutman, Sam Spade's antagonist in *The Maltese Falcon*.

The narrative presented within this volume is identical with the corrected, typed manuscript found by my brother-in-law, with some exceptions. Assuming that the seven handwritten pages represent the beginning of the original manuscript—and I am in awe at the thought that those of inky scrawls may, indeed, have come from the pen of Dr. John Watson himself—I have chosen to replace the word "hello" throughout by "halloa," which is the spelling employed in the handwritten portion. In addition, one pencil correction to a typewritten page changes "Hindoo" to the more modern "Hindu" spelling, while another converts "aether" to the contemporary "ether" variant. Since each former choice in turn adds a fleeting sense of period to the scene where both appear, I have opted for the antiquated spellings instead. Otherwise, the penciled revisions have been retained.

Moreover, as noted earlier, the original author's apparent working title for the novel was *The Black Falcon of Malta*. Seeking to emphasize the parallelism between this story and the Hammett novel, however, I have chosen to dub it *The Hapsburg Falcon* instead. Also, chapters in the typed manuscript bear numbers only; I have supplied titles for them. Finally, I have added a dozen footnotes to clarify certain references for the modern American reader.

I leave detailed speculation to the experts, but my suspicion is that the typescript represents a rewrite of a now mostly lost manuscript, the seven handwritten pages being the only portion of the original still extant. Without those missing handwritten pages—and there must have been over three hundred of them—one cannot be certain of the extent of any alterations or, if one prefers, fabrications. Nevertheless, the typescript—with revisions noted above—is offered for the public's consideration. Those versed in the Sherlockian canon far more deeply than I may judge it for themselves.

Appendix B:

Parallel Chronologies

The previous appendix to *The Hapsburg Falcon* gives a brief description of the manuscript and its provenance. In this second of three addenda to the novel, I wish to explore the internal chronologies of *The Hapsburg Falcon* and *The Maltese Falcon*, as well as the relationship between the two.

Offhand, one might believe that the events of *The Maltese Falcon* cannot be dated with the precision, if disputed accuracy, that one finds possible in the Holmesian canon. In fact, as shown by Glenn Todd in a note to an illustrated edition of the novel, published first by Arion Press and then reprinted by North Point, the events in the Hammett work must take place between Wednesday, December 5 and Monday, December 10 in the year 1928. The analysis leading to this conclusion is also discussed in Richard Layman's *The Maltese Falcon*, published by the Gale Group.

Those far more adept than I in the methods of Sherlockian hagiography may be able to better pinpoint the chronology of events in *The Hapsburg Falcon*, but my best guess is that the novel takes place in March 1903. Holmes is clearly nearing the end of his professional career, generally agreed to have concluded in that or the following year, with one important exception to be noted later. Queen Victoria is deceased, as obliquely noted by Holmes in his comments to Jasper Girthwood regarding the emerald tie-pin given him by that late monarch. This reference, by itself, places Holmes's encounter with Girthwood later than January 1901. In addition, Watson has, by now, moved from Baker Street into his Queen Anne Street residence, an event generally held to have occurred in the latter half of 1902. More specific evidence occurs toward the end of the novel, when Watson refers to having known Holmes for twenty-two years. Since the two are usually assumed to have met in 1881, that comment alone would appear to set the year as 1903.

There is, however, at least one piece of possibly contradictory evidence. Watson informs Irene Adler during a conversation that, after the hiatus of the late 1890s, a new story about Holmes was published "in the past year." This must be a reference to *The Hound of the Baskervilles*, which first appeared in serialization in *The Strand Magazine* in 1901. That year is not consistent with setting the falcon case in 1903, but it may be that Watson was referring to the first book publication of *The Hound of the Baskervilles*, which occurred in the spring of 1902.

The action in *The Hapsburg Falcon* appears to unfold over the course of six days, from the first arrival of Stanley Hopkins at 221 Baker Street to the final departure of Irene Adler. Watson indicates at the beginning that it is late spring, yet later in the narrative he refers to "winter's final frost." Although it may seem that Watson's highly personal sense of time may once again make precise dating of a story difficult or impossible, one remark by Holmes's landlady is worthy of note. On the second day of events, as she chastises Dr. Watson for allegedly mentioning the subject of rent to Miss Adler, Mrs. Hudson observes that the "quarter day" is in exactly one week. The quarter day, on which rents were traditionally due, fell on one of four religious holidays. The corresponding spring holiday is Lady Day, March 25.

From this, we may assume that Mrs. Hudson's comment was made on the eighteenth, so *The Hapsburg Falcon* runs from Tuesday, March 17 to Sunday, March 22 of 1903. Again, more diligent scholars may find corroboration or contradiction with other internal clues, but I do note that having the final day of the affair fall on a Sunday is consistent with a passing mention by Watson that on the concluding morning of the adventure, Holmes complained of no "fresh newspapers" to read—in Edwardian times, newspapers were not printed on Sunday.

While the internal chronologies of the two novels appear to be relatively tidy, serious problems arise when one tries to reconcile them with each other. In *The Maltese Falcon*, Casper Gutman (whom I believe to be the same person as Jasper Girthwood) informs Sam Spade that the Parisian art dealer who had the falcon, Charilaos Konstantinides, was murdered and the statue stolen sixteen years previously. This places the murder—which, according to *The Hapsburg Falcon*, was not that of Konstantinides—in 1912 rather than 1903.

Nine years is a bit of a discrepancy to explain, and reconciliation becomes purely speculative here. It is possible that Gutman did not wish to reveal the degree of his obsession to Spade—a quarter of a century in pursuit of the falcon—and so pretended his quest had been not as epic. Then too, it is not clear what happened to the man after the events recounted in *The Hapsburg Falcon*. Perhaps the damning material gathered by Langdale Pike was sufficient to put him in jail for a number of years—nine, perhaps? In that case, Gutman might not have wanted to account for them and so subtracted that period of time from his verbal record. In any event, the discrepancy between the two stories is a serious problem and suggests that one or both of the novels might actually be pure fiction.

One significant element that *The Hapsburg Falcon* does leave hanging is the fate of Konstantinides himself and, indeed, the question of whether the art dealer ever had the original statue intended for Charles V. In *The Maltese Falcon*, we are led to believe that he had the real statue but was murdered and that the Russian Kemidov eventually got hold of it. (A tantalizing reference appears at the end of *The Hapsburg Falcon*, where Holmes mentions a scandal surrounding a young Russian military attaché named Kemidoff. Could this be mere coincidence? I, for one, am inclined to believe it is not.)

In Watson's tale, on the other hand, it appears that Konstantinides had a quite ordinary falcon statue, which was then stolen by Irene Adler. In defending his establishment, however, the art dealer murdered Adler's accomplice and vanished, perhaps setting fire to his own shop in the process. But why? What motivated Konstantinides to flee and destroy his place of business? Could he have deliberately planted the fake statue, intending to vanish with the real one after destroying his shop to throw any pursuers off the scent?

Oddly enough, Watson's presumed narrative sidesteps these questions entirely. Clearly, more happened here than is offered to the reader. It is not unlikely that Watson deliberately obscured fact and chronology, and this apparent obfuscation may be a reason why Watson—if he, indeed, did write the present narrative—never offered it for publication. Yet another possibility is that the original, handwritten manuscript was never finished and the person who created the typescript added an incomplete fictional ending. Once more, I will let those more versed in the Holmes canon—and the Spade tradition—attempt to sort out these issues if they wish. Their resolution is certainly far beyond my capability.

Appendix C:

Sam Spade and Sherlock Holmes

In discussing the only detectives known to have crossed paths with the black falcon of Malta and the man known as Casper Gutman or Jasper Girthwood, we must be clear about one thing from the beginning. While the fact of Sherlock Holmes's existence as a real historical personage is generally accepted by most impartial observers, it may come as a surprise to some—as it did to me—to learn that Sam Spade, though slightly fictionalized by Dashiell Hammett, was, in truth, also a flesh-and-blood person, whom Hammett met while the latter was pursuing his own first career as a private investigator for the Pinkerton National Detective Agency.

Hammett had joined that firm in 1915, but three years later, during World War I, he was inducted into the army. While stationed in Maryland, he contracted the notorious Spanish influenza, and though that disease did not claim his life, it led to Hammett developing tuberculosis, which was responsible for his medical discharge from military service in 1919. All of twenty-five, the future writer then moved west and rejoined Pinkerton to work out of their offices in Washington State, Montana, and, finally, San Francisco. It was probably during that final stint that he met the man known to us as Sam Spade.

By the end of 1921, however, Hammett's worsening health led him to abandon Pinkerton and choose writing as a means of support for himself and his new wife and daughter. Later, during this second career, Hammett was inspired to use some of Spade's experiences, as well as his own, in writing short stories, many centering around an unnamed fictional detective known as the Continental Op. Two novels followed in the late 1920s, and *The Maltese Falcon* was first published serially in the magazine *Black*

Mask at the very end of that decade. In the early 1930s, three short stories with Spade as the main character appeared in the same publication.

In *The Maltese Falcon*, Spade, in an absent-minded way, identifies the handgun that killed his partner, Miles Archer, as a Webley-Fosbery thirty-eight automatic and comments to his friend, police detective Tom Polhaus, that he had seen them before. The Webley-Fosbery was of English origin, first manufactured just prior to World War I and never widely distributed, with only a few finding their way to American owners. Where might Spade have acquainted himself with this firearm to such an extent that he could immediately identify it and show relatively little interest in such an uncommon weapon?

Consider that justly famous episode in which Sherlock Holmes came out of a decade-long retirement to serve his country in 1914, the adventure known as "His Last Bow." This story is of interest on several grounds, including the fact that it is one of the few tales in the generally accepted Holmes canon seemingly not penned by John Watson. (This has, of course, led to a great deal of speculation concerning the identity of the real author, none of which is really relevant here.) In this story, Holmes disguises himself as an Irish American named Altamount and travels to the United States in order to be recruited by a German spy network headed by the infamous agent Von Bork. As Altamount, Holmes eventually winds up back in Britain, serving Von Bork along with several others, including a certain Jack James. James, like Altamount, is an Irish American, but his US citizenship does him no good when he is arrested by British authorities and incarcerated on the Isle of Portland—actually a peninsula in Dorset.

Who could Jack James have been? We should remember that in the later years of his career, Holmes employed numerous agents, many of whom appear in *The Hapsburg Falcon*. In fact, virtually all of those agents mentioned in the accepted Sherlockian canon, such as Langdale Pike and Shinwell Johnson, play a role in *The Hapsburg Falcon*, along with two who do not appear in Watson's stories: Hollins and Stannard. Given Holmes's resort to professional assistance in his later years, would it not seem likely that he would follow the same practice when dealing with perhaps the most important case of his career, an investigation of vital importance to the British government?

In my view, the answer is an emphatic yes, and that argues that Jack James could easily have been an agent and confidante of Holmes, set up to be recruited by the Germans in the United States as "Altamount" himself was. And by now the reader, no doubt, knows who I think Jack James really was: Sam Spade. We know that Spade was of Irish descent. We can also observe that the pattern of both names (Jack James and Sam Spade) is oddly similar: first and last names starting with the same letter and a short *a* followed by a long *a* vowel pattern between those names. In addition, consider two more agents whom Altamount mentions in "His Last Bow"—Hollis and Steiner. Those names are tantalizingly similar to the two agents in *The Hapsburg Falcon* referred to a moment ago—Hollins and Stannard.

All this would have put Spade in England before the outbreak of war, in circumstances where he might very well have become familiar with the Webley-Fosbery. Indeed, it is possible that he may have used such a weapon himself while masquerading alongside Sherlock Holmes as an informant for the Von Bork spy apparatus.

Is such a hypothesis consistent with the facts of Sam Spade's life? That's difficult to answer, since virtually no definitive biographical information on the American detective is extant. The Continental Op stories, for example, probably draw on some of Spade's experiences, but they are, no doubt, mixed in with episodes from Hammett's work as well, along with other elements that are complete fiction. One important fact, however, does appear in the short story "They Can Only Hang You Once." There we are told that Spade is thirty-eight years old. This tale was published in late 1932, so the events detailed there must have happened no later than that year. Moreover, reference is made in the story to the stock-market crash of October 1929, making that the earliest possible date for the events it chronicles. Thus, Spade was thirty-eight years old sometime between late 1929 and late 1932. This puts his birth year as somewhere in the interval of late 1890 to late 1895—roughly the same age or slightly older than his friend Dashiell Hammett. That, in turn, would mean that, while helping Holmes in August 1914 against Von Bork, Spade would have been in his late teens or early twenties.

I assert that as a young man, Sam Spade assisted Sherlock Holmes in his exploit against Von Bork. As Holmes's plot against the German agent drove to its conclusion, the great detective would likely have arranged for his own undercover men to be arrested by British authorities in order to guarantee their safety during the final act of this real-life spy drama. The British nationals Hollis and Steiner, if, indeed, they were Hollins and Stannard, would have been quietly released later, but James—or Spade, if you will—was an American citizen. Sherlock's brother, Mycroft, a quiet power behind the scenes in government circles, could have secretly arranged for the young man to be discreetly returned to America in the fall or winter of 1914, perhaps aboard a British war vessel—a feat made easier by the fact that the Isle of Portland, where James was incarcerated, housed not only a prison but also a naval base.

Holmes and Spade quite possibly stayed in touch with one another, though whether the American detective ever learned of the existence of the text I have titled *The Hapsburg Falcon* is, at this point, unknown. It is generally accepted, however, that Holmes and Watson were both still alive well into the 1920s, and perhaps after his brush with Gutman and the bird in 1928, Spade wrote about it to Holmes, who, no doubt, immediately recognized the statue and the man he had known as Jasper Girthwood. It is tempting to think that Spade received Watson's handwritten manuscript from Holmes or Watson and then passed it on to Dashiell Hammett, whose own revised version is the tale contained in this volume; however, no evidence, direct or circumstantial, points to such a heady scenario.

One final set of curious clues should be mentioned for the sake of completeness. Many times in *The Hapsburg Falcon*, dialogue and situations occur that are chillingly similar to moments in *The Maltese Falcon*. The sheer number of these matches makes it difficult to believe that both stories actually happened independently, just as they are narrated in their respective texts, but rather that one inspired the telling of the other. It would then be natural to assume that, since the events of the Holmes story predate those in the Sam Spade tale, *The Maltese Falcon* is perhaps fiction, in whole or in part, drawing some dramatic elements from Watson's original manuscript. The final such shared detail between the two stories, however, creates a problem with that hypothesis. It occurs near the conclusion of *The Hapsburg Falcon*, when Holmes remarks that the statue is made of "the substance from which fantasies are spun." In content, this comment is remarkably close to the line uttered by Humphrey Bogart as Spade in John Huston's 1941 film version of *The Maltese Falcon*: "The stuff that dreams are made of."

This coincidence, among others, might suggest that Hammett at least saw Watson's presumed earlier manuscript, even if he didn't actually rewrite it, and used details from it to flesh out his retelling (or fabrication) of Spade's encounter with the falcon. The line mentioned in the previous paragraph, however, appears only in the Huston screenplay; it is not present in Hammett's original novel. This leaves the door open to another, far more disappointing possibility: perhaps it is *The Hapsburg Falcon* that is merely fiction, and its author planted the "fantasies" remark, along with other elements drawn from *The Maltese Falcon*, in hopes of enhancing the suggestion of a Spade-Holmes connection, all without realizing that Bogart's line is from the 1941 film, not the 1929 novel.

So is *The Hapsburg Falcon* an altered but essentially true narrative by Dr. John H. Watson or pure hoax? I suspect that, as with much in the realm of Sherlockiana—both the apocrypha and the sacred canon itself—we shall always feel the burden of constant doubt while trying to lift ourselves on the wings of eternal hope.

Made in the USA
Lexington, KY
14 May 2014